—L.K. SCOTT—

NIGHTMARE EVE

Oasis Creative

Published by **OASIS Creative** ®
July 2012
2nd Edition October 2014

Nightmare Eve
Paperback ISBN-10: 1478364718
Paperback ISBN-13: 978-1478364719
Copyright © 2012 by Logan K. Scott. All Rights Reserved

This book is a work of fiction.

Cover design copyright © 2012 by Oasis Creative

OASIS Creative ®
March 2012

© 2012 L.K. Scott

All rights reserved. No part of this book may be reproduced or transmitted in any form or by any electronic or mechanical means, including photocopying, recording or by any information storage and retrieval system, without the written permission of the Publisher, except where permitted by law.

—

This book is a work of fiction. Names, characters, places and incidents are either the product of the author's imagination or are used fictitiously. Any resemblance to actual events, locales or persons, living or deceased, is entirely coincidental.

Novels by L.K. Scott

—

Massacre'ade Party
Nightmare Eve
She Tried the Window

L.K. SCOTT

Nightmare

Eve

Chapter 1

Evelyn Harris gagged on the salty water. Her body, weak against the stormy currents, collapsed on shore. Through blurred vision her eyes scoured the beach for her fiancé. She was alone and when she called out to him, her cries were choked back by the water that purged from her gaping mouth. Her body trembled and she fell again.

In the downpour, each icy raindrop beat like fists against her tired body. She swallowed hard, her heart hammered within her chest. She stood, but only for a moment when her muscles failed and she collapsed again. From the sand, she raised her eyes. Against the black veil of night, she saw the overturned rowboat bobbing up and down in the churning waters. It was no match for the thrashing waves and finally sank beneath the violent waters.

Nightmare Eve

Was that her crying? She wasn't sure. She couldn't hear over the roaring in her ears.

David! Where's David? Her fiancé and his daughter hadn't made it back to shore.

She inched closer to the water by digging her fingers into the sand and pulling her body forward. It was a miracle Evelyn had survived. She wasn't a strong swimmer like David, but she couldn't leave him behind, just like he wouldn't leave his daughter.

With the shores desolate of tourists, David's only rested with Evelyn and her pathetic swimming skills. If she tried to swim, she'd surely drown, but she had to take that chance anyway. She loved David and without him, life wasn't worth living anyway. Evelyn clawed her way to the water's edge, but only until her limbs gave out and her hands fell limply at the water's edge. Against her will, her head hit the sand and her eyes closed. The ringing in her ears grew as the world faded to black.

Chapter 2

One Year Later . . .

Evelyn jolted awake. In the haze of sleep, she barely recognized her surroundings. She was no longer reliving the tragedy at the coast from last year, but safe in her room, tucked protectively under the covers like a child hiding from the monsters in the closet.

    The monsters now were no longer hidden in closets anymore or lurking under her bed. They haunted her dreams, where she was forced to watch the rental boat rock side-to-side at the mercy of the storm until it succumbed to the ocean waves along with David and Ivy. She was convinced their bodies would never be recovered and to fight the nightmares would be in vain. What could she do, stay awake forever? Impossible. Even awake, she felt the ominous presence of David, certain that he once stood over her bed, his face inches from hers. Evelyn wiped the sweat off her forehead with the back of her hand, she could still feel his breath on her skin.

Evelyn felt around the sweat-laden sheets until her hand found her cell phone. Her fingers brushed against the screen and the hostile light burned her eyes. She squeezed them shut and waited for the sting to subside before gently casting a quick glimpse at the time on the display.

Two o'clock.

She glanced around the room, austere yet fashionable, with a queen bed that once slept both David and Evelyn, a wooden dresser handmade from a local craftsman, a pair of beveled glass nightstands, a simple turquoise lounge chair angled to face the window that overlooked the second story view of the parking lot and the white apartment complex across from her and beyond, a glowing orange cityscape in a rainy haze. She didn't care for unnecessary furnishings like silk plants, the eighty-year-old banyan bonsai tree on a stone bench was real, purchased from an elderly gentleman in Ueda, Japan during one of her excursions. A couple photographs of her and her brother were mounted to the wall, opposite of a colorful painting she picked up at a market in Morocco.

Her bedroom door was still closed. Whatever presence she had felt was now very faint, but not entirely gone.

In the glow of the light she caught a glimpse of her face illuminated in the picture frame on her bedside table. Her ashy blonde hair was matted to her forehead and stringy down to her shoulders. Her pale skin, usually smooth and creamy like porcelain was splotchy and dark eye bags gave her a much older, exhausted appearance. In the picture, David smiled back.

The photo was taken at the pier on their very first date. Well, it was hardly a date. They were supposed to go walk along the beach to a nice steak house just a block from the pier and then see a movie downtown, but his eleven-year-old daughter, Ivy Rose had been constantly texting and calling throughout

Nightmare Eve

the evening, interrupting every intimate moment. It was all quite very annoying.

Evelyn didn't have any children of her own though she had often imagined what it would've been like to be a mother and raise a daughter. David, who had Ivy Rose from his first wife, had demonstrated uncanny fatherly instincts and dedication. To her, David was the perfect husband and a great father to their future child. Ivy, however, was in such constant need of David's attention that they inevitably rushed through their date, taking the entrées home in boxes and skipped the movie entirely. Neediness was such an unattractive trait in people, but a year after David's death, she was feeling particularly needy herself.

They stopped at the pier first for a picture, which now that she looked back on, was a terrible idea because neither one of them cared for the water. He had spent most of his life in service for the United States Navy and had sailed nearly every ocean. Evelyn on the other hand simply never lived near any ocean, lake or even a poolside. Aquatic life didn't suit her. Still, it was the best photo of them together, on of the only in fact, and it was nice to always have him at her bedside. As long as the photograph was at her bedside, David's handsome smile would be the last thing she saw before falling asleep and the first thing she saw in the morning.

Evelyn looked away from the photograph and brought the light of the cell phone to the empty bed space where David used to sleep. It had been a year since he drowned—a year since he'd slept in bed with her—a year that she had the bed all to her own, but she still couldn't bear the thought of crossing to his side. In his place was his body pillow. She kept it in his place and snuggled against it when she slept. Some nights, if she imagined, she could still smell his intoxicating musky fragrance on the pillow.

Her eyes weighed heavy with sleep deprivation, but she couldn't bring herself to stay in bed any longer. Sluggishly, she pulled off the covers and reached for the lamp. With her cell phone still in hand, she crossed the room, entered the hallway, moving with light steps so as not to wake her live-in personal assistant, Anna Morgan. Then Evelyn descended the stairs of her two-story townhouse and entered the kitchen. Some warm tea would soothe her frazzled nerves. She had picked up a strong variety on her last trip to India over a year ago, but wasn't sure if it was still any good.

The air in the kitchen was chilly, especially since the sticky sweat cooled on her body. As the kettle warmed on the stove, Evelyn entered the living room to her desk that faced out the front window to the patio, and just beyond, the city sidewalks.

Scattered across her desk was the usual stack of assignments neatly organized: edited travel articles on the left, puke drafts on the right, in and out-going mail boxes, and notecards scrawled with the names and addresses of business contacts, tourist destinations, translators, and underneath, several issues of travel magazines where her articles had been published. She had quite a few deadlines coming up over the next few weeks, but she didn't mind. It was a sufficient distraction from her worries.

She sat in the chair and as soon as she opened the laptop, a familiar Vera Lynn broke the silence.

. . . we'll meet again, some sunny day. . .

Evelyn's fingers shot outward and crunched the space bar. The music silenced. She froze. She hadn't been listening to music when she closed the laptop last night. She *never* wrote with background music—too distracting—and even if she were listening to music, it sure as hell wouldn't have been that song. She hadn't heard it since that tragic night on the coast. It was supposed to be "their" song.

In the saloon-like restaurant at the resort where they were staying, an old jukebox in the corner accepted Evelyn's quarters. It was supposed to be a nice touch, reminiscent of the night they first met that ended in their first kiss.

The hiss of the teakettle arrested her attention and she sprung from her. In the kitchen, she poured the steaming water into a mug, her assistant Anna Morgan stepped into the kitchen. Her eyes were red and puffy with sleep. Anna was a petite girl, plain but pretty with naturally black hair and a sharp intellect. She wore a pale pink bathrobe with fluffy slippers and thin, white socks. Her eyes, wrought with concern, met Evelyn's.

"Are you alright, Miss Harris?" Her tone was soft and mousy, just like everything else about her. She was much shorter and much thinner than Evelyn, and hardly ever looked anyone in the eye. She was good at her job: excellent fact-checker, grammar and spelling editor, plus having her around made the townhouse feel a bit less dreary. There was no silence like the torturous and haunting silence of a deceased lover. Anna, as quiet as she was, did her best to make Evelyn feel not so lonely.

"Anna, you don't need to call me Miss Harris." Evelyn's nose squinted. She hated hearing it, even when it came from Evelyn's own mouth. "You may be my assistant, but that's not all you are. You *live* with me, Anna. You are the closest thing I have to a family now. My home is your home, so let's just forget the formalities and call me Evelyn. Or just Eve."

Anna smiled gratefully to her. "You still have a brother."

"Hardly. The last I heard from him he was living in a farming town somewhere in Colorado, but that was years ago. He could be anywhere with children and a wife by now. Or husband for all I know. Anyway, I was just making some tea. Would you like a cup?"

"That would be very nice." Anna's worried expression still clung to her face. "Are you alright? I heard music."

Evelyn reached for a second mug. "Did you use my laptop last night?"

Anna's face twisted with confusion. "No, of course not. I would never touch it without your permission first."

"You weren't listening to music?"

"No. Well—"

In the first ten seconds of asking the question, Anna looked befuddled, "—I mean, I was listening to music, but not on your laptop. I went to my room just a few minutes after ten to write in my journal and listen with my headphones. What did you hear?"

"I'm sure it was nothing." Evelyn shifted uncomfortably. Anna, usually meek, continued to stand in the center of the doorway—Evelyn's only escape from her inquisition. Evelyn already knew where Anna Morgan was headed.

"So how far did you get?" Anna asked. Her head bowed low, her voice growing dominant.

"I don't know what you mean." Evelyn faced away from her assistant and picked up her mug of tea.

"Did you make it to shore this time?" Anna Morgan was persistent.

Evelyn was uncomfortable, but her poise was stoic. "I made it to shore this time," she admitted. Evelyn sighed into her mug. "It seems like every time I have that nightmare, I'm closer to shore." Evelyn's expression hardened with worry.

"What is it, Eve?"

Her voice was soft and ripe with worry. "It's just I have this feeling that something is unfinished."

Anna looked at her boss concerned.

"I'm not crazy," Evelyn snapped. "I know David's gone, but it feels like he's still here. Sometimes at night I can still feel him."

Anna's expression softened when she moved closer to brush her hand down Evelyn's arm in a supportive, friendly gesture. "Of course he is. He's everywhere, all around you, looking over you in a better place."

"No." Evelyn shook her head, her ashy blonde hair tumbling over her shoulders, her body rigid and she pulled away from her assistant. "That's not what I mean."

"Then what is bothering you, Evelyn? You hardly eat, you barely sleep and when you do you have these nightmares over and over again. I'm worried."

"I think David is still here. I think he is with us, watching me—and he's angry."

For a moment that lasted a little too long, Evelyn lowered her head, her hair like a curtain protecting her face from Anna's concerned expression. She couldn't imagine what Anna was thinking about her right now. Probably calling her crazy, and maybe she was right.

"Maybe you should take some time off," Anna suggested. "We can reschedule the hotel reviews for Corpus Christi and San Antonio for another month. You could use some time to catch up on sleep."

"No!" She snapped causing her assistant to jump. "I don't *want* to go back to sleep. Work is the only thing keeping me occupied. Without it, I'd surely go mad."

Anna's eyes drifted to the floor, her voice returning to the timid tones that Evelyn had grown used to. "Sorry." she murmured barely above a whisper.

"I'll clean up here, Anna, thank you."

Anna turned from her and exited the kitchen.

Evelyn raised the mug to her lips and breathed the steam deep. Beneath the soothing light flavors of Chamomile was a hint of saltwater.

Leaving the kettle to cool, she took her mug into the living room to her desk, which faced the street-view window. The laptop screen glowed light a calming nightlight. She sat at the chair in front of the screen and selected her latest articles.

Evelyn Harris stared at the rough draft, then to her mug. Should she postpone her article deadlines? Tell her freelancing colleagues she needed a vacation? What would she say? That she had the Plague?

She took a deep breath and stared at the screen. It was her company, *her* articles. If she wanted to take the time off...

The lights flickered.

In the screen's reflection, she saw the silhouette of David. She jerked hard away from the computer, his expression hovering inches over her shoulder, his face pale with purple bloated lips and his black eyes wide and accusing. Then he was gone.

The jolt of fear came and went like a bolt of lightning, replaced by heartache. She missed him like red roses the roses in her garden miss the summer sun. She loved him, she *still* loved him—why was he doing this to her? Haunting her?

She slammed the laptop shut and immediately regretted it when darkness succumbed the room. She froze, her eyes darting madly around the black room, though she saw nothing. Her breaths were rapid and beads of sweat formed on her forehead and dampened the neck of her nightshirt.

Though her eyes were wide and almost unblinking, her trembling hand reached into the void, searching until it found the back of the couch. She forced herself to breath and concentrate on the contours of the room ignoring the feeling of another's presence in the room.

Her hand continued to slide across the velvety cloth until it sloped downward toward the space between her and the end table. She took another forced breath, but couldn't stop her imagination from picturing David hovering an inch from her face, his skin bloated and saturated from ocean water, his purple wormy lips mumbling something so rapid and sinister that it was inaudible. Though her eyes were wide open they still hadn't adjusted to the darkness and Evelyn squeezed them shut tight, mentally forcing the haunting images out of her head. No matter how hard she concentrated on maneuvering across the room and up the stairs, the feeling of someone watching her, following half a footstep behind, was paralyzing.

It wasn't until she reached the midway point up the stairs where she became eye level with the carpet on the upstairs floor. A beacon of light shined brightly from the cracks beneath Anna Morgan's door. From upstairs, her eyes adjusted to the thin, but sparse light that illuminate the hall to the bathroom. Immediately her paranoia was tamed and her heart rate slowed.

Evelyn Harris was always a down-to-earth, rational woman. Even as a young girl she had had a tight grasp on her imagination and was more rational than the other children she'd known growing up. She felt ashamed now for getting so worked up. She just needed to get a good's nights rest and focus on work. David was gone and it was downright crazy to believe he was back. Even crazier to believe he was trying to contact her. The dead don't exist. Ghosts don't haunt people. People haunt people.

Feeling embarrassed and glad there were no witnesses to her mental lapse of rationality, she entered the upstairs bathroom on the left and turned on the light before shedding her nightclothes soaked with sweat. She kept her back facing the mirror so that she didn't have to see herself. She didn't have to stare into her reflection to know how terrible she looked. She could just feel it: tired, dark eyes, her skin pale and loose from a lack of sleep and a negligent diet. And then sweat from her night terrors. So much sweat.

Realizing that she had forgotten her tea downstairs, she shifted the tap at until cold water flowed into the sink and she stuck her face under, slurping greedily at the chilling, refreshing water. Then as she used the toilet, steam rose from the shower and she dabbed her still damp forehead with toilette paper. The steamy water beckoned her into the shower.

She stood beneath the shower head, guiding her hands around her pale, slender body, the water beating against her back and saturating her hair. She shut her eyes tight and dipped her head beneath the stream, inhaling the humid warmth and exhaling the stress away. There was no such thing as ghosts. It was her imagination. And even if there were such thing as ghosts, she didn't do anything to deserve being haunted by David. Her only crime was loving him too much. The only rational explanation was that she was experiencing survivor's guilt. She just needed to breathe and let it go. She forced herself to concentrate on the water, the comforting massage of the showerhead pelting her skin and washing the stress away.

She missed David. She missed him so much. If there was only a way she could see him again. To talk to him. To apologize. To feel his arms slip around her body and pull her tight in a reassuring embrace. She urged to feel his hands voyage across the mounds and valleys of her alabaster flesh, exploring the tundra of her waist and the tight narrows between her thighs. He wrapped around her like atmosphere and she breathed him deep until the sensation became all too real and her eyes shot open and she could still feel him pressed against her.

Not real, not real. It couldn't be. Her arms pricked with fear.

"David?"

She searched the shower, glancing behind her, in front of her and then behind her again. Despite the heat, she gave a chill. The only arms wrapped around her now were her own and she felt vulnerable.

She reached for her towel without stepping out of the shower and hid her breasts beneath her arms until the towel was protectively wrapped around her body.

The hallway creaked as she tiptoed from the bathroom past Anna's bedroom and hid in her own room. As usual, but grateful, she stared at the photograph of her and David on her bed stand, wishing he was here beside her until her eyes collapsed into a heavy, despairing sleep.

Nightmare Eve

In her dreams, she recognized the crumbling sodden buildings, the thick brambling shrubs, and the strong, masculine figure that ran from her through the woods. He stayed just out of reach, but when she fell behind, he waited. He wasn't running from her, he was leading her. Leading her to a place called Amherst-By-The-Sea.

Chapter 3

"Wait! Where are you going?"

His silhouette, barely visible through the murky fog, drifted in muted silence over black filigrees of tangled branches. Above, the abysmal sky speckled with diamond starlight. Evelyn raced through the night, headless of the snarling underbrush. Twice she stumbled on wicked tendrils that reached through the fine grain mist like skeletal fingers reaching from rich, sodden earth. She tried to run but stopped at the cold sight of her lover—abandoning her in the hellish forest.

"Wait for me!" The stale breeze swallowed her faint voice.

Nightmare Eve

She struggled against the branches clawing at her, her movements rigid with despair. Salt cracked her lips. Collapsing waves taunted her sense of direction and she peered into the ocean below. The sounds of her voice and the mad ebb and flow of churning waters were stolen by the stagnant night. There were no echoes in this living nightmare. Evelyn Harris may have gone to sleep in her own bedroom, but this place she woke to was real. It was a special town that she could only visit when she was asleep, but it was no dream. This town, a machinery of nightmares, was as real as her pain and David was the operator. This void was a giant vacuum sucking away at the sounds of the forest, the only static in her ears. This forest was unlike any other. The woods were silent as death. She ran through the brambles that scratched and broke at her legs and the echo seemed endless, but David's remained silent. Not a bird chirped nor a single cricket. The shore was void of life. Somewhere beyond the brambles and shadowy conifers was her fiancé devoured by the unnatural darkness. So moribund. So surreal that he, and the island, was untouchable, just beyond her reach.

Taunting her.

Consumed with hopelessness she stumbled down the woodsy path, the sting of branches whipping at her delicate skin. Evelyn stopped dead and gasped at the crumbling boardwalk stretching across the black waters, crowned by the condemned city made of wood. The impossible boardwalk extended over furious waves without the support of wooden beams or trestles suspended by unnatural forces. Rising above the marine layer, much taller than any other structure was a deteriorated Ferris wheel, the merry baskets with hideous wire cages, lined with razors, stained crimson with blood and rust. Beyond the decaying amusement ride, the ominous contours of a derelict lighthouse peaked just above the fog. There was no horizon. Only blackness. Evelyn stepped onto the boardwalk and felt wetness on her cheek. The first sign of rain.

A storm was coming.

Each board creaked under Evelyn's tentative steps. Between the gaps, the earth descended into the seething waters. Feeling vertiginous, she forced her gaze to the sinister angles of the bent street lamps, their light bulbs smashed. Filigrees of Spanish moss hung from the posts in long, silvery swaths. The sour stench of decay and mold invaded her nose as she approached the city. A convenient store with crumbling walls buckled under the weight of its sagging rooftop. A break in the support beams allowed scattered starlight to filter through casting the room in a pale unearthly glow. Evelyn stopped when the board beneath her croaked and, proceeding with caution, placed the offending weight of her heel on the next board before continuing forward.

What was this place? What was Amherst?

The few raindrops that sprinkled from the cloudless night had grown into a light drizzle, dampening her clothes and bringing a chill to her skin. Her airy blouse offered little protection against the elements and she shivered either from the approaching storm or from nervous fear. If the storm intensified she'd be forced to seek shelter in one of the abandoned shops. Her only real concern though, was for David and their daughter Ivy.

They were still out there. A high-pitched squeak like a creaky gate brought her eyes to a weather-scrubbed sign hanging by metal hooks. The faded grin of a cartoon smiley face glowered back at her. Watching her.

Mocking her with its over-enthusiastic smile.

Below the sign was a toyshop, dark and empty, just like the others. A toy coal train was carefully placed on display. The train, pristine and new, stood out among it's disintegrating environment. Its metal shell sparkled under the starlight as if she were meant to find it.

Another chill swept through her bones. Her hands fell away from the window, turned from the children's store.

Behind her, a lighthearted giggle echoed from the shadows.

Ivy? Was she somewhere inside?

Evelyn turned around again, but the windows remained dark. Shadows remained still. Raindrops splashed against the glass then trickled down, collecting in a small puddle on the frame. The happy-face sign swayed in the growing winds.

She looked closer and noticed the toy train was now resting on its side on the opposite end of the track.

Uneasiness crept through her. She watched the street for signs of movement, afraid to look away from whatever lurked beyond the display. Overwhelmed with uncertainty, she pressed her hands against the glass and leaned close. A veil of darkness prevented her from seeing beyond her own reflection.

She pulled back, her hands at her sides. She scolded herself for allowing her imagination to get the best of her. She strolled forward, a brilliant streak of lightning in the horizon. The incipient squall approached the horizon, rain pelted her and strong gusts rumbled over the boardwalk. Somewhere in the vast wooden city, a building collapsed followed by a gigantic splash from the water. The only sound she'd heard since she arrived. Her gaze remained locked at the end of the boardwalk just few feet ahead.

Nowhere else to go.

She scanned the road back, contemplating her next move: follow the perimeter of the boardwalk, or retrace her steps back to the mountain.

If she chose to retrace her steps, she'd have to pass by the toyshop again; the thought terrified her.

Evelyn sighed. She remained mired with indecision until she sensed movement. A dark figure staggered through the dense haze. He appeared entirely in black—face, skin and clothes—null of light. Just a black silhouette.

Evelyn let out a sibilant gasp as the figure closed the distance between them—his rigid arms extended reminded

Evelyn of a zombie. He shuffled forward in silence until she could make out his glossy eyes. She felt invisible when he moved past her. She clutched her hands to her chest and wide-eyed, she watched him teeter on the edge.

The swells below raged upwards. He held his arms out reaching, stretching into the storm.

And he took a step. A wide step—into the churning waters. Evelyn stifled a gasp, watched as he disappeared beneath the surface of the maelstrom.

A sibilant gasp escaped her lips. She thought of David terrified for him and their little girl. Could he have fallen too?

No, she couldn't think about that. She had to keep searching. That's what he would do for her.

She faced the small, seaside village. More shadows emerged.

The shadow people came from the alleys of sodden businesses and dilapidated homes. More shambled down from the streets in a sea of shadowy people. She wanted to run, to hide, but there were too many. She was surrounded. As they approached, Evelyn's heart raced and her muscles tensed. And still, they kept coming in an inexorable march. With nowhere else to go, she lingered on the edge. The shadowy figure closest to her—a woman with the same, black, empty stare, crumpled limp like a ragdoll into the water. The swarm of faceless people shambled past and marched into the writhing depths. She frantically spun, lost and dizzy among them. Silent, unmoving lips that whispered: *1200*.

She burst forward, shoved her way through the crowd. Her shoes thumped loud against the boards and didn't stop until she saw the road sign. Words appeared scratched as if someone had carved it from pocket a knife: *people will die.*

And beneath in bold letters: *Welcome to Amherst.*

From somewhere far and high above the tree-lined mountain peaks, velvet with ferns and pines, above the marine layer, where the air and starry skies were crystal clear, echoed the gentle hum of an ancient gong.

1200 people will die.

Chapter 4

The clock on the nightstand flashed 12:00.

Evelyn Harris wanted to believe she'd just had a nightmare, the images were just too real. The saltwater cracked her lips. Her bed sheets clung to her damp skin, smelling of sweat and marsh water. Noon. It wasn't like her to sleep so late. She peeled the sheets away and rose to her feet. She didn't intend on spending another second in bed. The air in her bedroom was chilly, but refreshing against her exposed skin.

After a quick, nervous shower, where she scrubbed vigorously and fidgeted with the water's temperature, she proceeded downstairs and found Anna staring out the window.

She was somber. "It's raining."

Evelyn didn't say anything as she moved behind Anna to the kitchen. The teakettle was precisely as she left it. She refilled it with water, placed it on the burner and reentered the living room.

"Anna, I need you to do some research for me. I need you to find out all you can about this place called Amherst."

Anna turned away from the window. Her plain face appeared as solemn as the weather. Her head bowed low and behind the curtain of straight, fine dark brown hair, her usually olive skin appeared ghostly pale in the grim blue daylight.

"Amherst, Evelyn?"

"Did I stutter?" She spoke quietly, barely above a whisper, and she meant to sound more impatient, but her words came out tired and uncertain.

"It's just—why do you want to know about Amherst?"

Evelyn breathed. "You've heard of this place before?"

Anna nodded.

"Please. Tell me, Anna." There was a hint of quiet desperation in her tone.

Anna avoided Evelyn's hard stare. "I didn't know it was even a real place."

"What do you mean?"

Anna hesitated. "When my great aunt Myumi passed away, Amherst was all uncle Ambrose talked about."

Evelyn listened quietly.

"I don't remember what happened, I was too young at the time. But I remember visiting uncle Ambrose as a child in Japan often. The doctors couldn't find anything physically wrong with him, but he was depressed and he slept more and more every day. At first it was just a few hours a night, but almost two weeks later, he was sleeping fifteen and twenty hours each day. When he woke, he talked about this town he'd discovered. He had a job there and a lovely wife who was expecting a child. The stories all seemed very normal, like they were real to him, but they couldn't have possibly been. He seemed so much happier there. He was under constant supervision and never left his bed."

She opened her mouth to say something but hesitated again and withdrew.

"Anna, what happened?"

Anna took a moment to stare out the window. Rain drizzled against the glass and formed a puddle on the outside windowsill. A red rose from the Black Magic rose bush outside the window bobbed against the pelting rain. The skies and her expression grew darker.

"One day he fell asleep and he didn't wake up. He was alive still—he had normal functioning brain activity, as if he were still living day-to-day. And then one night, when a nurse went to check on him, he was gone."

"You mean he died?"

"I don't know."

Evelyn looked at her with disbelief. How could she *not* know if he was alive or dead? It would seem rather obvious. But she hid the irritation from her voice. "How do you mean?"

"The doors and windows were locked. There was no possible way he could've gone anywhere, but he was gone. The sheets were crumpled as if someone had still been sleeping there and in his place was this dark, tar-like substance."

Evelyn shook her head. Not possible. She was a rational woman and nothing about Anna's story could possibly be real. It had to be nothing more than the product of a child with an over-active imagination grieving for a relative's death and feeling isolated, forced to live in another country opposite end of the globe. After all, children are sensitive creatures too.

"Evelyn?"

"Yes, Anna?"

"Where did you hear about this place, Amherst?"

"I read about it." Evelyn lied. She avoided Anna's intense, coal-black eyes. "While doing research."

Nightmare Eve

Anna's gaze lifted from Evelyn and landed on the floor. In the midst of the heavy silence, Evelyn could practically feel the palpable doubt Anna felt towards her.

"I'm sorry to hear about your aunt and uncle," she said.

—

Evelyn woke up to the gentle patter of rain against the townhouse. The navy skies and rolling black clouds offered no hints to the time or day. She groggily pulled herself from her bed. She wasn't looking forward to researching or writing this morning—or afternoon?—and hoped that Anna had returned with a bit more information. Perhaps even a precise geographic location.

She slid into a thin cashmere sweater, a rich champagne color and a pair of comfortable faded jeans, and headed into the hall. The hall was dark and silent. From the balcony she looked to the front door where Anna normally kept her shoes. They were gone. As she reached the bottom of the staircase, she heard the static of the television set. Curiously, and slightly uncomfortable, she approached the flatscreen with caution, reached for the control and gently pressed the *power* button. Without removing her eyes from the black screen, she gently edged back and placed the control on the coffee table instead. Anna hardly ever watched television. She'd rather go to bed with a historical or fantasy novel than stay up late for some sitcoms or Netflix. Then again, Evelyn remembered, Anna had gone to bed before her. Perhaps a documentary had caught her attention and she forgot to shut it off before she left. No, that was preposterous. That seemed too absent minded for Anna who was, in fact, scary intelligent.

She looked around the living room. Her simple, yet modern, "L" shaped couch and loveseat created a "U" around the circumference of the living room separated by a square glass coffee table with black iron supports. The furniture faced the flatscreen, mounted on the wall above a narrow tower of Blu-rays. In each of the corners were various luscious ferns and ficuses. Devil's ivy and Moonflowers entwined around the bookshelves and the hum of the refrigerator echoed from the kitchen. Everything seemed as usual, but there was something different still. The air seemed to feel heavier, suffocating the natural sounds right from the room and the baleful presence that had woken her felt stronger—watchful from the sinister shadows. Was that movement from the corner of her eye? Did the silhouette of a figure just pass by the window?

Oh! Where was Anna? The sky had become a rainy tufts blue, the storm showed no signs of letting up, and Anna still hadn't returned!

Calm down, she told herself. It was just her imagination. Storms always made her uneasy. The churning of angry grey clouds and the puddles of deepening water. . .

A glass of wine would settle her nerves. Then she'd bunker down in her room until Anna returned.

In her desk, she always kept a spare bottle and retrieved a glass from the kitchen, trying not to look in her peripheral vision in fear that she might see something staring back. Then she returned to her desk.

Contemplating on dialing Anna, Evelyn stared first at the cell phone resting on her desk, then to the envelope beside it. Her name was neatly printed on it. She hadn't noticed it before. In fact she was sure that it hadn't been there a moment earlier.

She took a deep breath and glared at it.

No. It hadn't been there. There was someone in her house.

Evelyn lunged for the phone. Her first instinct was to dial Anna, but as she swiped the screen, the phone rang with the haunting lyrics of Vera Lynn's *We'll Meet Again*.

Evelyn jumped back, toppling over her glass. It didn't break, but it rolled across the desk, spraying the dark red wine, looking black in the dim room, and puddled like thin blood from the desk as rained along the carpet.

Nightmare Eve

She clenched the cell phone in her fist and backed slowly away from the desk, staring at the blank screen. No name, no number. Her fingers shook as she answered the call.

Before she could even say 'hello' the voice at the other end—the pre-reordered voice of a male solicitor—was already speaking, sounding far away and muffled by heavy static.

"Relax and take it easy at the Cliffside Inn. The Cliffside offers luxurious accommodations with beautiful ocean views. Kick back and enjoy the social atmosphere of Pan's Art Gallery or wine and dine with your loved ones at Paradise Pantry Bistro. After a meal take a look at the beautiful Pacific Ocean from the top of Ghost Head Lighthouse."

Evelyn let the phone fall from her ear. It hit the back of the couch and then landed on the cushion.

Overwhelmed and frightened, Evelyn shoved herself away from the couch, turned, and collided with a dark figure. Evelyn screamed and raised her hands to shield herself from the attacker.

"Evelyn, what's wrong? Why are all the lights off?"

Evelyn opened her eyes and lowered her arms. Anna stood short of Evelyn, her thin arms toting grocery bags. "Are you alright?"

Evelyn stammered. Anna's eyes scoured the spilled wine and then back to Evelyn's terrified expression. "Are you hurt?"

"No." was all she managed to say.

Anna promptly brought the groceries in the kitchen, filling the house with light and chasing the shadows away as she went. She returned a second later with a cloth and proceeded to mop up the mess.

"I didn't mean to scare you." Anna said, "Didn't you hear me come in? What happened?"

The truth was Evelyn wasn't sure what had happened.

"I could hear you cry out from the porch. I was worried. You've been having so many nightmares lately."

It couldn't have been a nightmare. It was too real.

"You work so much, to exhaustion sometimes. Perhaps you had a glass of wine and fell asleep at your computer." Anna proceeded to remove the wine bottle, but Evelyn snatched it back.

"No!" Evelyn snapped.

Anna stared at her in surprise.

Evelyn sighed and took a moment to insert a modicum of reassurance to her voice. "It's just the storm, Anna. It startled me."

"I could make you some tea."

"I'm going to need something stronger than that." Evelyn took the wine bottle from Anna's hands.

Anna frowned.

"I'm nearly done with the last travel article. When it's finished, I'll take it easy for the rest of the week, I promise."

Anna retained her solemn countenance. She dubiously complied by handing the overturned wine glass back to Evelyn.

—

Evelyn Harris sat down the fresh glass of Merlot next to the nearly-empty bottle on the nightstand. The reflection of David's image rippled in the dark glass bottle. She slid her feet into her bed still aware that she had, in fact, slept all but five hours in the day yet she couldn't resist the heaviness weighing in her eyes. It seemed like even though she slept, the nightmares kept her body in such a tense state that when she woke she felt as if she hadn't slept at all. Hopefully tonight the heavy red wine would ease her into a restful slumber.

As she sipped from her glass, she picked up a copy of *Sunset* and flipped through the pages until she came across one of the articles she had written several months ago about the West Coast's top 10 beach towns. There were towns that were best for honeymooners and others boasted themselves as getaways for thrill-seekers and adventurers. Then of course there were the historical towns and communities where the landscape was reserved for sanctuaries and bird watching. She'd been rather unhappy with the article for it's generic content and lack of precise details—restaurants to dine in, off-the-beaten-path sights—but *Sunset* seemed quite pleased as it offered a great opportunity for the photographers to show off their dazzling photographs. She'd done more research than necessary for such a fluff piece. It was during her research that she came across the small beach town—that was if you could call it that inhabited with nothing more than a couple log cabin, a clubhouse, a single gas station, Laundromat and two restaurants—that appeared idyllic for a woodsy get away for her, David and Ivy. Evelyn figured that if she knew the West Coast well enough to discover such a remote community, then how come she had never heard of Amherst? Why wasn't it on the map?

After a few minutes of frustrated contemplation, Evelyn dozed into an uncomfortable, restless sleep.

She didn't dream of anything particular that night. A few hazy images of murky waters and then David's emotionless face appeared and dissipated, followed by her laptop as she diligently wrote articles. She saw a thicket of brush and clouds among various shapes and undecipherable texts and images. She slept comfortably and peacefully.

Just before dawn, still fast asleep, she rolled onto her side and felt the warmth of David's body as she pressed herself against him. His arm slipped around her waist while he ran his fingers through her hair and she shivered.

"David, it's cold." she uttered only half asleep.

"Come closer," he whispered.

She felt an icy chill brush her ear as he spoke.

"*Closer.*" This time he spoke in a long, breathy hiss.

Her eyes shot wide open. His arms slipped away from her body. She whirled around to see she was alone again, but his words still hung in the room. Her heart thundered in her chest. She flung herself from the bed, bumping the nightstand where she saw the envelope, the one that she had left downstairs on her desk, now resting only inches from her. There were only three things she could be sure of now: the nightmares were real, David desperately needed her help, and something evil waited for her in the town of Amherst.

Chapter 5

Dawn came later than usual. The skies were still sickly gray and the first sprinkle of rain tapped against the windows when Evelyn rushed downstairs, carrying the envelope with her.

Always the early-riser, Anna sat on the couch downstairs with her morning tea, steam rising from the fresh mug and her face buried in a historical fiction novel. Anna's eyes grew wide with surprise when Evelyn came barreling down the stairs, waving the envelope at her.

"Did you do this?" Evelyn's voice was quiet, shaky and accusatory.

"Do what?" Anna stammered. "What's wrong?" She seemed to sink deeper into the cushions, her expression genuine.

"Did you bring this letter to my room after I fell asleep?"

"I don't know what you're talking about. I haven't seen any letter."

"This one, Anna!" She shoved the letter closer.

"I don't know what that is. I haven't seen it before."

"I left it on the desk last night."

Anna stammered, her bewildered eyes darted thoughtfully around the room. "No, I didn't touch anything."

Evelyn threw her arms up exasperated.

"What's in the letter?" Anna asked.

Evelyn ran her hands over her tired face. She sucked in a deep breath as distant thunder resonated in the distance.

"What is it?" Anna asked again.

Without answering, Evelyn rushed back upstairs to her room, slammed the door closed, threw herself on the bed, and ripped open the envelope.

Inside was a tri-folded glossy brochure with the header of a woodsy ocean-side resort town, the shore lined with sandy beaches, clear waters, a harbor populated with bobbing catamarans and sailboats and a boardwalk that ran the length of maritime shops and clothing boutiques.

Welcome to Amherst-By-The-Sea!

Welcome to one of America's most livable communities. People have lived on this stretch of the coast for at least ten thousand years. We're happy to have you too. Take some time out of your busy schedule and enjoy a nice restful vacation with us. Amherst offers rows of picturesque old houses, luxurious boutiques, quaint restaurants, a gorgeous mountain landscape, and a beautiful ocean view from one of our fine hotels for an ever-changing beauty. From sunrise to sunset Amherst will move you and fill you with the peace you deserve. Your time will be pleasant with memories that will last forever! You may never want to leave!

Nightmare Eve

Evelyn raised her eyes from the pamphlet to the picture of her and David on the nightstand. His eyes burned into her.

"David, what are you trying to tell me?" She looked hard at him as if waiting for a response. The mysterious brochure in her hand was all the response she needed. "I'll find you," she declared. "I promise."

In one minute she had stripped out from her nightclothes and let the water warm in the shower. She had at first wanted to skip the shower, but unsure of the exact location of her final destination, she reconsidered. Who knows how long it would be before she got to shower again? By twelve minutes she was out of the bathroom and dressed in a comfortable pair of charcoal-colored dress slacks, a beige cashmere sweater, black boots that served a tri-purpose of comfort, durability and a bit of style. She figured, after studying the town's images in the brochure, trying to deduce the precise location by geographical characteristics, Evelyn would be doing her share of walking and probing through the town. In her professional experience as a travel writer people were more likely to engage in conversation and reveal information when she dressed in casual business attire rather than jeans and a t-shirt. In forty-five minutes, she had overstuffed her suitcase with clothes and toiletries for all weather conditions. And by eight-thirty in the morning, she was toting her luggage down the stairs.

Anna watched her curiously as Evelyn descended to the living room. She eyed the luggage suspiciously.

Evelyn hoisted her suitcase to the front door and ignored Anna's expression as she went into the kitchen and removed several bottles of Fiji water from the refrigerator.

When Evelyn entered the living room again, Anna was standing over the suitcase with the brochure in her hand.

"There aren't any directions." Anna said matter-of-factly. She clenched the brochure as she hovered in the front doorway. "This isn't a good idea."

"I have to."

"You're just under a lot of stress right now. You need to rest. You need sleep."

"I don't have a choice." Evelyn said quickly. She pushed passed Anna and shuffled through her travel files at the desk and withdrew any map, brochure and guide that could hint at Amherst's location.

"You don't even know where you're going."

"There are only so many towns on the coast, Anna. All I have to do is follow the shore heading north. I'll find it, even if I end up in British Columbia."

Anna was such a sweet, sensitive girl. Very quiet, her voice always sad and never confrontational. So it surprised her when the young assistant blurted: "David is dead."

Evelyn opened her mouth to say something but no words came out.

Anna spoke smoothly. "He's gone, but there's still so much of him right here. A bed that you shared, all these photographs on the walls and at your desk, the articles you wrote on vacations with him. This is where his spirit, his memory, is. It doesn't make any sense to drive to a town that neither of you been to—a town that may not even exist."

Evelyn sighed. Her eyes filled with determination were locked on Anna's. "They never found his body."

Anna's face twisted with confusion.

"If there is a chance he is alive, I have to know. I *have* to find him."

Anna lowered her eyes. She held out the brochure. "It just doesn't feel right."

Evelyn took the brochure from her assistant and reached for the door. As it swung open, she was met with cloudy morning twilight, black clouds churning against an ominous blue sky. A chilling breeze cut through her sweater and icy rain dotted her face. However bad the weather may be here, it would be much worse on the coast.

Nightmare Eve

A feeling of uneasiness crept into her stomach. As she stared into the cold, acrid, drizzling morning and the dark horizon, she thought of her bed and how warm and cozy the sheets were, how she liked to sink deep down surrounded by thick pillows with a cup of hot tea—especially on rainy mornings. Of all the good things her bed was, safe was not one of them. Not anymore. Not since she started dreaming of Amherst and David. He was haunting her. She needed him. Time to face the cold.

Evelyn stepped into the rain, the door closing behind her.

Chapter 6

Evelyn Harris had been driving in the car for nearly ten hours straight, only stopping for restroom breaks and drive-thru for food. The storm broke only a few hours after she left, allowing cheerful rays to bounce and refract in the sun showers. Traffic thinned the further north she drove and warm steam rose from the still damp roads. She noted the last palm tree before a long stretch of straight and narrow and lonely highway, past sharp cliffs, rocky islands populated with seals, historical lighthouses until a gradual incline took her into the thick woods of Northern California.

  Evelyn always drove too fast, especially now there was an emergency, but the winding roads and the setting August sun and the soupy fog had slowed her grueling progress. She didn't particularly enjoy the nighttime either. Nothing ever looked quite the same after dark and the silvery swaths of Spanish moss took on a forbidden appearance. Even the acrid air, carrying the pungent scents of saltwater and forest decay, seemed stronger. In the distance, beyond the cliffs and jagged islands, water stretched and roared endlessly to the west, black and heaving. In the daytime, and when the weather was more agreeable, the scenery would be more relaxing, like a beautiful northern getaway, but not tonight. Tonight she looked upon the edge of the world.

The roads curved sharply around boulders and steep ridges that plummeted down further than Evelyn cared to see and the patchy fog kept her nerves on edge, having to break suddenly and then accelerate when it cleared.

It wasn't until the steep road hit the apex of the mountains before it's descent into a dark, woodsy canyon when she noticed a second pair of headlights swerving through the night behind her. The first car she'd seen since dusk and it was barreling around the sharp corners of shoulder-less roads that sank from the constant battery of ocean winds and soggy earth. Another treacherous curve and Evelyn was forced to slow, continuing through another thick blanket of patchy fog. A nervous glance at the headlights rapidly approaching and Evelyn cursed under her breath. The maniac veered into the other lane before dodging back. The Cliffside loomed dangerously close but then extended for a narrow stretch. The white SUV swerved into the other lane. As she sped past Evelyn she caught a glimpse of the driver. A young woman, chatting vehemently away on her cell phone, seemingly unaware of the hazardous road conditions.

"Crazy bitch." Evelyn muttered as her car zoomed forward. A half-mile ahead the road gradually curved to the left. She let out a soft cry when she saw the SUV continue to shoot forward, speeding toward the embankment and a wall of massive sequoias. It was as if the woman hadn't even attempted to turn. Not even brake.

Nightmare Eve

Evelyn slammed her own brake pedal to the floor as her compact car slid forward, her eyes wide and locked on the SUV. Her car slowed, tires skidding on the asphalt, but did not stop in time before colliding with the high bumper of the SUV. Evelyn slammed forward, her seatbelt locking her in place. She felt the pressure of the seatbelt jab hard against her waist, tightening across her torso and left breast. The wind knocked out of her, she choked. By the time she caught her breath and removed her seatbelt, she could already feel the tender soft spots on her flesh, the making of a bruise.

She tumbled out of her car. Smoke rose from beneath her hood and joined the drifting mist. The air was cold and filled with the spicy decay of pine and salt water. The trees towered higher than any she'd seen, raising like spears from the squishy earth. She coughed again and adjusted her sweater, grateful for the extra layers. She'd be fine. Her car wasn't so lucky. A large dent had formed on her bumper.

"Hey!" she shouted to the driver of the SUV. She took a wary step forward, braced herself against the hood. "Hey, are you alright?" When she didn't answer, Evelyn felt her chest tighten. Great. That's all she needed right now. To be stranded in the middle of the night, in the middle of the woods in bumfuck nowhere with a dead body on her hands.

Evelyn balled her fists. She wasn't a violent person, but if that woman wasn't already unconscious or dead, she'd want to make her that way. Whether it was the fear snaking it's way from the bowls of her organs or impatience with the negligent driver, anger flushed through her. Using her right hand she reached out and opened the driver's side door. The seat empty, the driver had vanished leaving the keys still in the ignition.

How was that possible? She'd watched the driver maneuver around the sharp corners and hadn't taken her eyes off since. If the driver had left her vehicle, Evelyn surely would've noticed.

Nightmare Eve

She took a step backwards away from the vehicle and then turned, suddenly aware of her isolation. On either side of the misty, damp road, abundant woods, thick and taller than she'd ever seen, stretched into the midnight sky. The hills surrounding were thick with trees sloping up jagged peaks that seemed to puncture the ethereal moonlight. Tough foliage, twists of raw roots, and massive dew-covered ferns populated the black forest floor. Evelyn stood alone and vulnerable in the hostile night, a sitting lamb for rapacious wolves.

She had no choice but to walk. Ahead, a lonely road descended into pale mist and abysmal night. Just beyond, deep in the coastal valley and tucked behind razor-peaked mountains, red fire light glowed into the marine layer, beckoning her in.

As she drew nearer, the steady rhythm of a deep drum could be heard. A gong's gentle clang echoed off the mountains. Through the breaking trees, a widening pathway of decaying pine needles passed below a wooden archway. Above, the sign read:

WECLOME TO AMHERST

Chapter 7

The discovery of the mysterious resort town brought about anxiety and fear to Evelyn. So much that she'd momentarily forgotten about her broken down car and the vanished SUV driver. The town beyond the forest was only a mere resemblance of the images in the brochure once again reminding her that everything appeared more sinister at night.

Most unusually was the lack of streetlights. Even though the crest of the hillside from where she stood obscured part of the town, she saw that it was in a complete blackout. If it weren't for the ominous red glow at the south end of town, where the abrupt cliffs rose two hundred feet above the churning waters, the town would've been completely blanketed by night. The pale moonlight lit up the rooftops and reflected against the empty windows of shops and houses. Tendrils of fog

Nightmare Eve

snaked through the vacant streets. Ahead of her, movement arrested her attention.

"David?" she whispered uncertainly.

He glided through the fog, swaying at each of the path's switchbacks. She followed. He stayed at the edge of visibility as she jogged cautiously, avoiding the tough black roots that tangled over the path. At the final switchback he was gone. She paused, looked through the woods and to the edge of town and back up the trail. The entrance was gone too, the path overgrown with thick brambles and berry shrubs. No. The path had to be there. It couldn't have vanished. In the fog, beneath a clear night and the shadows of the canopy of trees, she didn't feel so sure. If the trail had vanished, it still wouldn't be the most unsettling thing to happen to her this evening. No matter how hard she tried, she couldn't rationalize the vanishing driver. And then she thought: what if her assistant, Anna Morgan was right about this town? She was genuinely afraid when Evelyn had mentioned Amherst to her.

She pushed aside her fear. Whatever hell this place was, she could not—no, *would not*—turn back. David and Ivy were both out there and she was the only one who could rescue them. If this place was as nightmarish as Anna made it sound, then she couldn't just leave them there.

Evelyn lost sight of the red-robed people and their flickering torches when the cedar-lined trail dipped low into the humid valley until she came to a cul-de-sac at the end of a narrow alley.

To her left, behind the cracked window of the general store, darkness was it's only customer. Condensation collected in the vacant display. She moved warily though the alley, each step cautious and easy as if she were walking on the thin ice of a frozen pond. As she crept deeper, the ocean breeze, blocked by the row of dilapidated buildings, lessened. Only the tattered delicate plastic sheets gently wafted in what remained of the breeze, now stale and reeking of mold. They hung on wires stretched between the buildings while others covered broken out windows. The sheets gave an unearthly glow when the pale moon broke through the clouds, the alley tunneling into darkness. They fluttered like ghosts when she passed through them.

A noise at the other end of the alley startled her. A soft cry escaped her lips. Her eyes scanned the darkness ahead, coming in and out of her view obscured by the drifting plastic.

The noise occurred again, closer this time, sounding as if something heavy was being dragged across concrete, moving towards her.

She stopped when the thing in the darkness took a step closer. It emerged from the curtain of night, larger than any human she'd ever known, at least eight feet, with arms and legs as round and solid as boulders. Evelyn wasn't sure if it was just the moonlight, but its vascular arms with purple and red veins throbbed under thick grey skin, the pale color of death. He wore tattered black leather clothes, slick with blood and rainwater. Each heavy step the ground shook. He moved slowly under his own incredible weight. The plastic sheets slipped over his face as he moved closer. She caught a glimpse of something behind him. A blade, Evelyn realized. The hooked knife, half as big as the behemoth, scraped along the pavement. He clutched the weapon, chained to his hands and pushed forward until he slipped through the final sheet where Evelyn could see the dark burlap sack chained around his head.

Evelyn let out a shuddered cry and took a step back. Her heel caught the side of some disregarded boxes and she toppled into the pile of rags. The stack of boxes collapsed around her. The monster continued to advance. Snorting, his veins pulsed with aggression.

The monster loomed over her. With surprising speed he grabbed for her, her scream cut short and abrupt.

Suddenly she was somewhere else. She was no longer in the alley with that *thing*. She was laying on her back somewhere

Nightmare Eve

looking up at a dome, brass-looking ceiling, in a wide and round room with no walls, just brass support beams allowing the strong ocean breeze to blow through. Several people knelt around her, their faces hidden beneath the black shadows of their hooded crimson robes. She tried to sit up, but quickly found herself restrained to the floor. She balled her fists and shook to loosen and free herself, but she was fastened securely. That's when she noticed her hands. They weren't her own soft, pale and delicate hands, but the strong, brutish, hairy and calloused hands of a healthy man who'd spent his life in hard labor. This wasn't her memory, Evelyn realized. She was seeing through someone else. This was someone else's memory.

But she could still feel the restraints.

And the fear was real.

And when the others who knelt beside her pulled out seven inch hollow needles, like sharpened straws, she tried to choke out a scream in a voice that wasn't her own, but in a man's voice that sounded as if he'd had a lifetime of cheap whiskey and cigars. They raised the needles high, each one clutching a single one in their fists. At the sound of a gong, Evelyn screamed as they brought the needles down, puncturing her flesh and ripping deep into her muscles.

—

Evelyn Harris woke up in a bed that did not belong to her. The fragrant pine and saltwater air told her she was still in Amherst, but where? And how long had she been unconscious? The moan came from her, but it sounded separate and far away from her. She tried to lift her head off the unfamiliar, sandalwood scented pillow. The pain caused her to cry out. She opened her eyes and saw the strange bedroom. An instant of panic flared. She fought to keep down the nausea.

Baby blue diaphanous curtains allowed diluted rays of soft light through the window, casting the room in a dull grey-blue color. She separated the drapes and scanned the landscape. The sun hovered over the grassy hillside where a single leafless oak bristled in a gentle breeze. Was the sun rising or setting? She couldn't tell. Her eyes darted around the spacious, plainly decorated room. Well-worn wood floors, a simple square nightstand with a generic light and a single over-stuffed rocking chair adorned the room. Other than the bed and a petite side-table, those were the only furnishings. One peculiar oddity stood out right away: in the corner across the room sat a ragged, worn-out porcelain doll with a large left eye and hollow right eye, coifed in a dark kimono. Were they watching her? She wanted to touch the old toy, but its creamy pale skin had deteriorated to pale yellow and appeared fragile enough to crumble at the slightest touch.

The final door was the bathroom. All the basic necessities were there, toilet, sink and shower plus some fancy sea green and lavender-colored soaps below a neatly folded towel draped over a rack. She braced herself against both edges of the sink and stared into her morose reflection. Her hair, frizzed from humid weather and her chocolaty eyes where still puffy and groggy from sleep. She studied her lightly freckled pale skin and sharp angular curves of her jaw line to her slender cheeks. Then, to the narrow bridge of her nose, self-conscious about its size. It fit her face well enough, but proportionately, she found it too big compared to the rest of her features like her thin, pale lips; strong brows and almost non-existent eyelashes. She wasn't a very pretty woman, but she wasn't a train wreck either. She was jealous of David's features; especially his eyes that were green and sparkled like sea water and lips, plump and cherry-colored. He was the most handsome and sweetest man she'd ever known and loved him more than words could describe. From the pit of her stomach, she knew that he was alive. He had to be. They never found Ivy or David's body. It's possible that they drifted to shore during the earliest parts of the storm and were happened upon by patrols or even tourists enjoying the change of weather. Some people liked storms and rainy days. Evelyn was not one of them. And then maybe they

Nightmare Eve

were rushed to a hospital. Evelyn couldn't imagine one being close so transport would've been likely. Days in recovery, probably. Or what if either one of them—or both—had amnesia, or was in a coma for months and that's why she hadn't heard back from him. Maybe he was dreaming about her and their love was strong enough to reach into her thoughts as she slept. From her traveling experiences, she remembered that some cultures believed they could project their thoughts to loved ones in times of despair and great love. And she did love David. More than life itself.

She leaned over the sink and splashed water on her face. She used her fingers to comb away the frizz and then toweled off. Finding nothing else of use in the bathroom, she returned to the bedroom in search of any clue that might elucidate her on her mysterious arrival. Perhaps whomever brought her here had reported her car. Or at least a note. She searched the desk, the nightstand, and under the bed and still found no note. Evelyn huffed, inconvenienced. She was most certainly grateful for whoever had brought her here and given her a nice bed to sleep in rather than leaving her bleeding in the ditch, but still a note would've been appreciated. She rose to her feet and spotted an unusual painting mounted above her bed. She hadn't seen it before because the table lamp had obscured her view. But now that she stood at the center of the room, the unusual painting was impossible to miss. There were two characters depicted, neither had a face, blended over in smooth flesh tones. The woman lie on the floor with her arms reaching out while the man hovered over her as if ready to hoist her to her feet, like prince charming rescuing a damsel in distress. Other than the lack of eyes, Evelyn felt warmed by the image. With a wistful smile she thought of David and Ivy.

When she approached the second door, she noticed the faint aroma of fish and garlic drafting from somewhere close. It lingered only for a moment, and Evelyn wondered who would be preparing salmon. She pressed her hands against the door and pushed just enough to peer down the hall.

An elderly man with a slight hunch wearing high-watered, brass-colored slacks and a baby blue shirt shuffled down the hall, past her bedroom and to another door at the farthest end. His face was unfamiliar and doubted that she'd met him before. He was a withered old man with a round face and lanky arms barely able to walk on his own. He didn't notice Evelyn watching him from the gap but she could clearly see the red ring around his eyes and she knew that he'd been crying. From the dampness of his cheeks, he'd been sobbing heavily only moments before. When he stood outside the door, he reached out, turned the knob, and disappeared inside the dark room.

When her phone's shrill ring ripped through the silence, her train of thought derailed. Her cell phone! How stupid of her to forget! She'd been so wrapped up in the bizarre occurrences happening around her that she had forgotten she'd stuffed her phone into her pocket at the last rest stop before colliding with the vanishing driver in the SUV. She let her adrenaline rush subside before crossing the room and yanking the phone off the receiver.

"Hello?"

Loud static.

Evelyn withdrew the phone from her ear. She stared into the earpiece; the static grew louder. She hoped it was David dialing her from his cell phone, checking in on her. She could imagine cell service was weak this high in the mountains. She hung up the phone, a grim expression on her face. A nervous tingling stirred in her stomach and she couldn't flush the sense of urgency sneaking up her nerves.

She moved across the room and once again, pulled open the door. The hallway was empty now and the scent of baked salmon grew stronger. Evelyn was positive someone was downstairs cooking dinner, someone who could fill her in on what she'd forgotten. As she neared the stairs she heard the soft clatter of pots and pans followed by heavy steps and a woman muttering. The floorboards creaked under her weight as she edged down the hallway and stopped to admire the simple yellow and blue wildflower bouquet resting on a decorative wooden table. The unusual ornate carvings etched on the surface were unlike any pattern she'd seen. It appeared to be created by an Asian artisan. The symbols appeared to be in Chinese, but she couldn't be sure. Art was merely a hobby and she by no means considered herself savvy.

The entire foyer was visible from the top of the stairs. She was in a cabin-like home. A cherry-oak door led to the outside in the foyer at the bottom of the stairs. A crimson tapestry was spread across the wooden floors between the front door and what appeared to be a podium at the bottom of the stairs. Beside it, another wooden table with a guestbook penned with names and addresses.

A bed and breakfast, Evelyn realized.

Deciding to inspect the guestbook first, she slinked down the stairway keeping her steps light. She didn't want to be caught snooping without knowing exactly what she was doing here. How could she explain herself without a memory? She tiptoed around a wicker chair adorned with various paperbacks and several hardcover novels. Beside it was a stack of magazines. She paused when a newspaper caught her attention. A passenger train had derailed at the county border. The train derailed and plummeted into a ravine killing everyone on board except for a single survivor: Mrs. Maria Lupez, who'd boarded the 4:50 from San Diego with her family.

The horrific image of the mangled crash was spread across the front page and Evelyn thought it was a miracle that anyone could've survived. The train cars were tossed off the track like a child's toy reminding Evelyn of the toy train she'd seen during her most recent vision or premonition or whatever the hell it was. The coincidences were uncanny. She also remembered the strange shadow people mumbling 1200—the number of people killed in the train wreck. And after she awoke, her flashing digital clock. People will die. Did it mean people would die at 12:00am? Or would 1,200 people die? It felt too real to mean nothing.

The story below the disaster featured an image of Mrs. Rosecrans, a middle-aged woman with red hair in a conservative flip-do style like Evelyn had seen in 1950's films. She looked like a professional type coiffed in a crisp white blouse buttoned to the top of the collar and a charcoal-colored wool skirt. Her plain face, bright with a cheery disposition and alabaster skin with caramel-brown eyes stared at Evelyn from the page. The article described the location and condition of her body, discovered in the early morning by hikers on a trail near Westminster University. She'd been severed completely in half and forensics revealed that whatever had caused her death, had done so in a single clean swipe.

Only someone with immense, monstrous power could be capable of something so heinous.

She scanned the rest of the local paper for more information but it seemed arbitrary enough; a dance recital at Westminster Theatre. A new exhibit at the local art gallery. . . Nothing that perked Evelyn's interest for the moment. She shut the paper and read the header in the corner. The date did her no good, considering she didn't know how old the paper was. For all she knew, the paper could've been laying there for days, weeks or even months. But there was one thing Evelyn could be sure about. The paper was from here, the town of Amherst. And after what she'd seen before she tumbled into the ravine, she believed Anna was telling the truth after all.

There was something seriously wrong with Amherst. Something monstrous and evil inhabited this town, hidden from every map and outside societies.

More rustling from the kitchen distracted Evelyn from the paper. She peeked through guestbook labeled *Shady Nook*

Lodge and perused through the unfamiliar signatures of the past guests—only Evelyn's name was missing. She flipped through previous pages to the front of the book. David and Ivy's weren't among the other guests either.

Outside the front door window, the sun dipped low behind the mountains, distorting the oak tree's shadow and stretching it past a granite boulder and down the grassy hillside. The pastel sky dusted with fluffy clouds and a slight breeze swirled the grass, stirring up dust and leaves before subsiding. She pulled away from the window and inadvertently glanced at the love seat between the door and the corner ficus. From her viewpoint, the dark leather wallet protruding from between the cushions was easily noticeable against the off-white upholstery. It was a masculine-looking wallet made from unique leather. Assuming some desperate man was in disarray without it, especially while on vacation at a bed and breakfast, she retrieved the object from the cushions. As soon as her fingers brushed against the hide an image flashed in her mind:

A juggernaut of a man with immense vascularity restrained by handcuffs and Hessian burlap sack over his head snorted with the vengeance of a charging bull—the same monster that had attacked her in the alley! The disembodied, bereaving voices echoed through the stone chamber.

The image faded.

Evelyn choked out a shallow breath.

What kind of memory was that?

She realized her hand was aching and saw the wallet squeezed tightly in her grasp. She loosened her grip on the cryptic wallet and placed it in the pocket of her cargo pants without inspecting the contents. She felt weird for taking it, like removing flowers from someone else's gravesite. She hoped to get rid of it as soon as possible. She couldn't put her finger on it, but something about the object just felt *wrong*.

A woman's voice rose from behind, startling Evelyn. "Excuse me? Where do you think you're going?"

Chapter 8

Evelyn faced the plump woman. She lingered in the kitchen archway with a warm smile on her rouged face. She stood nearly as tall as Evelyn, but a hundred pounds heavier—festively plump and cheerful. Her faded auburn hair was tied back into a fringed bun and her freckled cheeks, dusted with white flour. She wiped the bits of food clinging to her hands on her floral-print apron over a frilly yellow blouse boxy slacks. Her circus-wide smile and eager demeanor made Evelyn feel scrutinized by a strict nanny.

"You look as if you haven't eaten in days, practically emaciated! Come now, I insist you join us for dinner. I won't take 'no' for an answer."

Nightmare Eve

Her voice was loud and demanded attention. To Evelyn, it sounded more like a threat than a request.

"I'm looking for my fiancé. His name is David. He has a little girl, nine years old. Her name is Ivy."

Something in her expression changed. Her smile stiffened.

"I'm sure he'll turn up. Our community isn't very big. Have a seat at the table and we'll help you figure everything out. You've been on quite a trip. All this traveling must be exhausting. Too much time on the road can make anyone's brain feel liked mashed potatoes. Nothing a hearty meal and a warm atmosphere won't fix. Now, please, dinner is nearly ready."

She lingered in the doorway with forced patience. Nothing about her seemed friendly or welcoming. Evelyn felt trapped. Without options, Evelyn obeyed the boisterous woman. She sat down and stared at the food. She wasn't hungry, but the idea of a warm place with company—who might elucidate her—seemed better than wandering in an unfamiliar town. With her luck, she'd freeze to death or get eaten by a bear. Nights in the mountains were cold. Evelyn figured no matter how uncomfortable the spongy woman made her feel, her best shot of finding her fiancé and their daughter was to endure this awkward dinner.

She looked around the elegant dinner table and greeted the other faces across the lavish décor of autumn leaves and candelabras. Beside Evelyn, a teenage girl with the same round face and auburn hair as the innkeeper, poked at her food. The girl offered Evelyn a frigid smile, similar to her mother's. It was clear the young girl was forced into proper dinner etiquette. Her head lowered, she sat in reticence, unblemished by adulthood and brimming with the secret life of newfound responsibilities. A troubled time for any teenager. Her eyes dropped back to her plate, severing connection between them.

Nightmare Eve

The other man at the table was at least ten or fifteen years older than Evelyn. His face, both stern and friendly with rich genuine eyes, still carried a youthful glint. He smiled. Evelyn nodded, observed his unusual clothing—dark grays and blacks; a thin floor-length black coat with draped, billowy sleeves and a black vest. The outfit would've blended well with the steam-punk trends in Chicago, Los Angeles or other worldly cities but was surprising to see in a small town like Amherst. He was well mannered and polite, and sat himself only after Evelyn had. The gesture was polite; however, unnecessary.

The dining table was festively decorated. Evelyn was impressed by the centerpiece featuring a bouquet of autumn flowers and maple leaves in various shades: brown, yellow and crimson with spiced orange blossoms, draping willows and black oak twigs in a ceramic Chinese vase.

Before any of them had the chance to speak, the innkeeper returned to the room presenting a covered silver tray. Evelyn got a strong whiff of a spicy citrus and cinnamon fragrance rising from the cooked salmon just before the innkeeper removed the platter lid. The flavorful side dishes—baked sweet potatoes and a fresh pear salad topped with caramelized almonds and dressed in spinach leaves straight from the garden—was one of the most detailed meals Evelyn had ever seen. Or at least she could remember. And even still, the nervous flutter in her belly suppressed her appetite. How could she enjoy such generous meals while David and Ivy were still out there?

"I picked the ingredients from the woods and in my garden. There's nothing else like homemade loganberry crumble." She placed the aromatic desert in front of Evelyn. "And the salmon came right out of the harbor. I like to get everything local. It's better for the economy and much healthier than buying those expensive ingredients in chain stores, packed with poisonous preservatives." She turned to Evelyn with a dish in her hand. She noticed a small imprint in her skin where a

Nightmare Eve

ring used to be. "Amherst is a very close community so you won't see any chain stores. Not here. For that stuff you need to drive to the city. But why do that when the best of everything is right here?" She snatched Evelyn's plate and globed on several scoops of sweet potatoes. More food than Evelyn could possibly eat—not even on a good day. She stared reluctantly. Her stomach cringed. Without David, she had no appetite. Instead, she felt sick with worry.

"It smells wonderful," Evelyn forced an unconvincing smile. The innkeeper returned with another smile, equally fake.

They sat in unnerved silence. The young girl held the butter knife as her hand trembled, clicking on the plate. Her mother stared with bug eyes at Evelyn from the other end. The strange man beside her slurped the pear salad. Among strangers, Evelyn sat with dread.

"The salad is exquisite." He dabbed his lips with the autumn cloth napkin. "You've outdone yourself again, Ms. Smith."

The plump innkeeper, Ms. Smith, gushed with appreciation and spoke with exuberance. "Dinner parties are such a fine way of culinary exploration as well as getting to know the neighbors. I know how uncomfortable it can be to break bread with strangers but I've hosted many dinner parties before so I figured it might as well me who'd break the ice. Has anyone tried the salmon yet? I hope I didn't overcook it like last time."

Evelyn stared at the uneaten whole salmon on her plate, invading the potatoes. Its eyes stared at her as if pleading for help. She looked away. Evelyn was too anxious to eat and her mind drifted to the empty seats where David and Ivy should've been.

"Oh gosh!" Ms. Smith burst with excitement, dropped the napkin to her lap. "Where are my manners? I haven't introduced you to the others! This is my daughter, Charity"— pointed to the young girl—"she's sixteen years old and has been a great help keeping this place running. It's really wonderful to have the extra set of hands, especially during tourist season when it gets so busy."

Evelyn forced a polite smile and a gentle nod.

"And this honorable gentleman is one of the finest men in town. Doctor Jack Dullahan. He works at one of the medical clinics downtown but his responsibilities don't end there. He's also on the city's board. The details are complicated but he works with the council to make sure every expectation of the citizens are taken care of. He's very good at it and makes it appear almost effortless, but we really know otherwise. It's a difficult job to keep this town running smoothly."

Dr. Dullahan nodded modestly. "It's mostly just pushing papers. Not much happens in this community and we all stay pretty healthy, but we like it that way. It's quiet and nestled between the mountains and the ocean, separating us from the larger cities in the area. In fact, all major roads bypass us. A lot of people in the county don't even realize we're right next door. We're completely isolated."

That didn't make Evelyn feel any better.

"It helps preserve its charm, don't you think?" Ms. Smith asked.

Hopefully Ms. Smith wasn't expecting an honest answer from Evelyn. This place was a bitch to find and even then she only found it by accident. This place scared the fuck out of her.

"I have a daughter too," Evelyn said to Ms. Smith. "She's not really mine, but I love her as if she was. She's actually my fiancé's adopted daughter but we raised her since she was an infant. Her name is Ivy Rose. She'll be turning nine this year." As Evelyn glanced at her plate for a second bite of sweet potatoes, she noticed the man, Dr. Jack Dullahan shoot Ms. Smith an angry look. Ms. Smith pretended not to notice.

"Well, welcome to Amherst-By-The-Sea," Dr. Jack Dullahan said with forced cheer. Even though Evelyn had only just met the doctor, she could see he was irritated with something. He continued to glance at Ms. Smith in annoyance while she continued the introductions.

"This is Evelyn Harris," said Ms. Smith to Jack. "She's visiting Amherst with her soon-to-be husband and daughter."

"Congratulations!" Jack said to Evelyn. "Have you set a date, yet?"

Evelyn shifted uncomfortably. "No, it's not like that." How could she explain to them that she'd come to Amherst to search for her thought-to-be dead husband and daughter? They would surely institutionalize her or blame it on a concussion after they fished her out of the ravine.

Ms. Smith and Dr. Jack Dullahan eyed her curiously.

"It's complicated." was all Evelyn said.

"Of course it is dear," Ms. Smith replied. "Love, actually, is quite complicated."

"Complicated matters are always worth the rewards." added Dr. Dullahan.

Their words were kind, but something stirred in their eyes. Disapproval maybe? They were troubled by something Evelyn had said, but they weren't willing to show it.

"That's wonderful." Ms. Smith said as she passed the doctor a refresh of his wine.

"Have you decided on a location for your wedding?" the doctor asked persistently. He picked up his glass and took a sip of a smooth merlot.

Evelyn's jaw clenched wishing for them to change the subject. The more questions they asked, the more she had to lie. She was never a very good liar. She hated to do it, but in these circumstances it was probably for the best, though the more questions they asked, the more she had to lie and the more she lied, the more suspicious they became of her.

They continued to stare at her, waiting for her to respond. The pause lasted too long as Evelyn remembered the night David proposed to her.

Nightmare Eve

  Before she met David, she never considered herself as the type of woman to become seriously involved. She didn't care for one night stands either. Her career as a travel writer had dominated most of her time. She traveled around the world so much that she didn't have time to be in a relationship and she never trusted a man to stay faithful to her and only her while she went overseas for sometimes two and three months at a time. She didn't believe in luck, nor did she believe that anyone could have a single soul mate. If luck did exist, she found it in business, but not in love.

  Even as an only child adopted into a medium-wealth family she found little connection with them or anyone else in life. With her parents always away for work Evelyn learned at a very young age to be self-reliant and work with strong, independent ethics. She studied very hard in school, lacking the distractions from social life, as it was difficult for her to relate to her peers. No one had ever asked her to a dance and she never went to prom or overnight campouts with her classmates. She spent the rest of her high school life blending in as an invisible girl and less than a week after graduation, she kissed her home-life goodbye and enrolled in the University of San Diego's journalism program. She didn't lose her virginity until the end of her first year of college when she met a man who'd accidentally spilled chocolate milk in her lap.

  He was a geeky man and Evelyn wasn't sure what surprised her more—the fact that someone spilled a beverage on her lap; or that a grown man was drinking chocolate milk from the carton. It was a brief relationship where she found his boyish charms, a collection of comic books and video games, cute. She'd never had a childhood crush before and though she was now an adult, she had imagined that this would've been as close as it got. Fortunately or unfortunately, that's exactly what he was: a boy. Not long after she lost her virginity to him—two months to be precise—they had broken up. He stopped taking her calls and only once after they had slept together, did she see

Nightmare Eve

him again, avoiding her during lunch in the cafeteria where they had first met.

Five years she remained celibate—but not by choice. She excelled at her academics and, along with her thirst for knowledge and ambition grew along with her shortened temper. She had a talent for finances, problem solving and her comprehensive understanding of world geography had given her the advantage to later become a travel journalist. Within a few years of smart investments and freelance journalism, her income had generated into substantial wages; but where she succeeded in business, she failed in love. She was too plain and introverted, driven by success and still lacked a social life.

One similar characteristic between her previous relationship with Trino and her fiancé David was the intensity of passion. Trino, with cunning wit and charming boyhood demeanor, was big in the social scene: a party always to be attended, a show to see and invitations that overwhelmed Evelyn. She was a stranger to people and her social awkwardness caused many fights, both insignificant and extreme. They were polar opposites and after just a few short months, their relationship met a bitter end.

As her relationship with Trino ended, her freelancing business boomed and forced her to hire extra help and expanded into foreign and domestic travel. On the night of a colleague's birthday, she was introduced to a Navy man, David Morel, a cook on base. She was immediately drawn to him, falling for his comedic personality and incredibly good looks. He was more than a head and a half taller than her, solid and strong with tattoos down both arms and across his shoulder blades. When he laughed his deep cerulean eyes shimmered like stars. No matter how hard she denied it, the feelings were inexorable. It was love at first sight. She had managed to suppress the emotions for a mere two weeks as lingering thoughts of David invaded their way through her daily routine. Love would never find her. She was determined to keep it that way no matter how often she dreamed of him. Two weeks later, Evelyn and David were on their first date. Dinner on the pier. She'd been nervous and stuttered most of the evening. Once she spilled her cocktail across the tablecloth and again a shrimp from the appetizer, smothered in sauce, slipped from her fingers, slid down her blouse in a splattered stain and landed in her lap. There were better moments too; they laughed and exchanged intimate details about their personal lives that neither of them would've normally shared on a first date. By the end of that evening, Evelyn felt like he'd known her for an entire lifetime.

David was the one and their relationship was barreling forward like an out-of-control freight train.

They were together for only three months when he asked her to move in. On their first night she told him how the most romantic, wonderful place in the whole world wasn't watching the sun set at the beach or a candle lit dinner in a fancy restaurant, but lying in bed burrowed deep in his arms. Then one night after making love, she rested her head on his shoulder and ran her fingers through the thick mat of dark blond hairs blanketing from his chest to stomach, still glistening with aphrodisiacal sweat, she asked him why his heart was still beating so hard.

He told her he'd never felt this way about anyone and how badly he needed to spend every moment with her and praised how well she'd connected with his daughter, Ivy. That's when he proposed.

Evelyn gave Dr. Dullahan a short, but honest reply to which he responded: "A very pleasant story."

Ms. Smith sighed. "Love is the most powerful force on Earth. It brings out the best and worst in people. It's unpredictable and can raise you above the clouds or devastate you until reality shatters and nothing seems real anymore." She paused and then added, "Well it's no wonder you've been so exhausted. Working as hard as you do, planning a wedding and maintaining your family. It's not an easy job, believe me. I was once there too." She gestured to her daughter, Charity Smith, who poked at the fish with her fork. "When you got here to Shady Nook you were drenched from head to toe and covered in mud. What on Earth were you doing sleeping in the creek bed anyway?"

Evelyn struggled to remember. Creek bed? She didn't know anything about that. What about the alley? Was it just a hallucination? Some sort of bad dream? She'd been rather frantic when she was moving down the paths. And it had been raining so she couldn't be sure she had seen anything. It just seemed so real. Too real. Why was Ms. Smith and Dr. Dullahan lying to her?

"Thumped your head pretty good." Ms. Smith said. "Luckily our good doctor was headed home early from one of his evening strolls."

"The weather was poor," said Dr. Dullahan. "If it had been a clearer night, I probably would've taken the back paths home instead."

"Left you to the wolves, he might've." Ms. Smith chirped. "There was mud all over your nice clothes."

Dr. Dullahan plucked a bit of salad into his mouth. "Looked like you slipped and fell right off the path. Got a nasty bump on your head too, but it could've been much worse."

She reached up and touched the swollen spot on the side of her head. Sure enough, it was tender. Evelyn winced. Maybe what they were saying was true. Maybe she did slip into the ravine and clonk her head on a rock.

"My clothes?"

"They're dried and hung in your closet dear. The nightgown you're wearing was donated from a lovely young girl who owns a little clothing boutique downtown. She often drops by, a very close friend and frequent guest of the Shady Nook Lodge."

Evelyn shivered at the thought of a stranger bathing her and dressing her unconscious body.

"One of the nurses," Ms. Smith continued, "who works for Jack here changed and cleansed you and looked after you for the night."

"The night?" How long have I been here?" Evelyn's chest tightened. The clock was ticking. If Amherst was as dangerous as Anna Morgan claimed, then she couldn't waste a single moment dawdling.

"No one can be quite certain as to how long you were laying in the ditch for, but the doctor brought you here last night just before dusk, you were cleaned and placed in your bed by midnight and you were out all day until just now."

Evelyn opened her mouth to speak, but the doctor known as Jack Dullahan, dressed in a sort of old-fashioned evening attire, possibly Victorian clothes fitted faultlessly to his tall, athletic figure, had waved his hand indicating no worries. "I can assure you Miss Harris"—Evelyn frowned at the title—"that you suffered no concussion and there shouldn't be any permanent damage. At the very most, some slight memory loss. All I can recommend is for the next few days you take it easy."

Ms. Smith nodded in agreement, her smile forced, eyes grim. "You might as well make yourself at home. You'll be staying with us for quite awhile."

As if on cue, the conversation was cut abruptly short by a sudden gust of wind that rattled the windows of the Shady Nook Lodge.

"A storm is coming." Charity whispered. Her eyes rose to the swaying chandelier above. Everyone became silent. Ms. Smith's face tightened. Dr. Dullahan swallowed stiffly. His forehead appeared damp.

"If you're not from the coast," Ms. Smith spoke in quiet unease. "you'll learn the squalls are sudden and violent." She lowered her fork to the plate and calmly dabbed her hands with the autumn-colored napkin. Jack Dullahan remained still, a concerned expression passing through his countenance before releasing a deep sigh.

"Dinner was wonderful as usual, Ms. Smith," he said as he rose to his feet. "I'm absolutely stuffed. I couldn't possibly eat another bite. You must save me a slice of that loganberry crumble for when I return."

"Don't be absurd, doctor." She shot him a warning glare, her voice in forced politeness. She glanced at Evelyn then locked gaze again with Dr. Dullahan as she rose to her feet.

Out of politeness, Evelyn stood too.

"There's still awhile before the storm hits and you're just down the trail. Not very far at all." She urged him to stay, but her nervous hands fiddled with the napkin, her eyes browsed him with uncertainty. She was clearly frightened.

"I really must be going," Dr. Dullahan insisted with more urgency this time.

Charity stood with them, her voice shrill, but sibilant, with panic. "It's nearly eight-thirty!" She leaned closer to him and hissed, her eyes drifting from her mother to Evelyn, "You can't be out after curfew!"

"Curfew?" Evelyn asked.

She was met with bewildered expressions as if they'd forgotten she was in the room.

Charity stepped back from the table and made her way towards them. Her eyes were directed at Evelyn. "There's a killer out there. People will die if they stay out past curfew."

"Don't be foolish, Charity." Ms. Smith snapped at her. "That's just a rumor to keep little girls like you from staying out past their bedtimes." Charity's face crimpled into a frown, her head bowed. "Just nonsense to sell some papers, really." Ms. Smith reassured Evelyn. As she spoke, she ushered Dr. Dullahan to the door. Charity followed with Evelyn close behind. Ms. Smith continued to speak warily. "The idea of a killer in this town is absurd. Amherst is a very small and peaceful town tucked away in the woods. We rarely get visitors and people will do pretty much anything to bring in more outside business. Amherst is one of the best kept secrets. A treasurable and pure community. I, personally, enjoy the isolation away from the corrupt influences of larger cities. The last thing this town needs is a Starbucks or a Wal-Mart to deteriorate its charm. Anyway, I'm afraid it's getting late and nearly bedtime for me as well. I'm not the young mischief I used to be. Why don't you both run along and Miss Harris"—Evelyn winced again—"you'll find your room fully stocked with everything you need. Should you require something more, let me know." Ms. Smith guided the three of them through the kitchen and into the foyer where Charity maneuvered past them and ascended the stairs.

Evelyn said goodnight to the doctor and thanked the hostess for dinner and then followed Charity upstairs. She paused in front of the old man's door but after hearing only silence from his bedroom, she entered her own.

Chapter 9

It must've been no earlier than eight forty-five, but no later than nine when Evelyn Harris opened the closet door and stared at her fresh cashmere sweater and cargo pants, pausing reflectively. From the diaphanous baby-blue curtains, had she cared to look out, she could've seen the storm churning over the hillside from which the Shady Nook rested at the end of a forest-lined pathway.

    She could've seen a number of rooftops in the valley below, among the structures towering high above its rocky shores and neighboring beaches, surmounted by a pale, gleaming lighthouse. The atmosphere was bleak without Ivy Rose playing her fairytale games with her dolls scattered across the floor. Evelyn looked at the recently drawn bed. For every second David was gone, her heart felt as if it would burst. Her eyes landed on the phone at the bedside table and considered whether she should try his cell phone. It was a ridiculous idea though. His cell phone had met its watery grave the night they all drowned. How easy she wished it would be, to simply pick up the room phone and dial him. But if she did, if she had the courage to dial his former number, who would answer? As she reached for the handle, movement outside the window caught her. She stepped up to the glass and far below she saw the attractive dark-skinned woman darting past the lodge.

Evelyn remained elusive in the shadows as she watched the young woman in her late twenties approach the sharp curve in the path and press her back against a rocky mound jutting from the hillside. She glanced down the path to see whom she was following so furtively. The doctor rushed past the grassy hill, battling against the winds. Lightning illuminated the sky and exposed the horror twisted across his face. His worrisome eyes rose to the blackening sky.

It was nearing the end of twilight now and the sky at the horizon was cast in dark blue while blackness consumed the atmosphere directly above. Enough light still filtered over the hillside for Evelyn to watch as Jack Dullahan brought his left hand up to the collar of his lengthy wool coat while his other held his cap to his head. He fought against the gusty winds as he shuffled onward, weaving around the winding corners. Evelyn and the strange girl continued to watch until he was nearly out of range. She managed to lean a little further into the glass before her breath fogged the surface, obscuring her view entirely. When she wiped the condensation away, both Jack and the mysterious woman had disappeared beyond sight and a light rain speckled the window.

Nightmare Eve

She strolled back across the room just as the last remnants of twilight turned to darkness. She reached for the lamp next to her bed and flicked on the light. Dark angular shadows fell upon the room. The shadow of the child's rocking chair stretched across the floor and partway up the pale wall while the pale ambient light glowed from the porcelain doll's skin. The light from the alarm clock blared and blinked red. The time needed to be reset. Without her cell phone she couldn't be sure of the exact time, but nevertheless she couldn't afford to sleep in. Not when Ivy and David's life depended on her. Charity's room was located directly across from hers. It would be easy for Evelyn to ask the young girl for the time and while she was there she could inquire about the wallet she'd discovered. She didn't trust Ms. Smith to tell her the truth by the way she stole glances and seemed to speak in code with the doctor. Charity, unlike her mother, was very open to the secrecies brewing in Amherst. What was this curfew and what about this killer? And whose wallet did this belong to?

Evelyn removed the leather wallet from her room and studied the texture again. It was brown like molasses with an almost greenish hue and lines, like cracks zig-zagging on all sides—not because it was old, in fact it looked rather fresh, but because of the unique properties of the material.

What kind of animal? Too thin to be cow or deer.

She opened it up, revealing the contents. No identifying marks, signatures or even a driver's license. Evelyn tilted the wallet so that the light caught the edges. Strange. Not even a brand name. Even if it were custom, the creator would've added his signature somewhere. Truly unique. She separated the deepest flap. There was no money or credit cards inside, only a business card tucked in one of the pockets. It was a pale pink card with bold gray and baby blue lettering from a store in Amherst named Pan's Art

Gallery. Decorative artistic swirls and landscapes embossed the card. She pulled it from the slit and placed it in a separate pocket from the wallet and then pulled open the door and crossed the hall, knocking on Charity's door. When she didn't answer, Evelyn pressed her palms against the door and pushed gently. The door silently opened barely wide enough to see Charity shut her bedroom window, overlooking a similar view as her own. Evelyn wondered if the young girl had seen the doctor and the woman too. Charity then spun around and abruptly stopped, startled by Evelyn who peered through the crack in the door.

"I'm sorry, I knocked, I didn't mean to—."

"I heard you," came her quick reply. She blocked the doorway. Evelyn was taller than the young girl and saw past her shoulder to the window. Uneasiness crept through her.

"I'd do the same if I were you." Charity warned after following her gaze. The way Charity stared at her, stoic and emotionless, made Evelyn feel as if she walked in on a punch line without hearing the rest of the joke, but more cryptic.

Evelyn stuttered while she fumbled through her pocket, feeling the wallet in her sweating palms. She held it out for Charity to see. "I found this."

Her eyes narrowed. "Is that—? I don't want that!" Her eyes went wide. "Get that away from me! Get rid of it, get rid of it, *now!*"

Evelyn took a step back, confused. It was just a wallet. The only damage it could possibly do is ruin good taste. It was a rather hideous accessory but nothing to be frightened about.

"Just go back to your room, lock your doors and windows and keep the blinds shut until morning. Stay quiet and just get rid of that thing." She spat out that last word and slammed the door shut.

"Wait! I didn't get the—" the door slammed in her face. "—time." Evelyn finished. She returned to her bedroom wondering what could be so damned important about this wallet.

Chapter 10

Dr. Jack Dullahan's legs couldn't carry him like they used to. His joints ached and he was losing the race against nightfall. The sleepy cove was grateful for the summer months when nights were short and the safety of daylight was stretched well into the hot, well-lit evenings. The evergreens towered high into the sky, damming what little remained of sunlight. Down here, it was already night. He briefly contemplated returning to the Smith's residence and asking Ms. Smith to put him up for the duration of curfew but he'd already traveled too far into the woods to turn back now. There was no way could make it back before Amherst succumbed to the hungry nightmare that swallowed the town more and more each night. Once night fell, it was like an eternity of darkness.

He'd never been afraid of the dark, not even as a young child who looked forward to playing flashlight tag with the other neighborhood kids in the vacant lots of urban neighborhoods. The homes, nothing more than mere skeletons set in foundation was like laser tag to him. His strapping young body was much stronger then. He had great endurance and could leap across partially constructed banisters with adroit covert skills to dodge the beams coming from his friends. He was younger then, with dense bones and fresh blood that kept his muscular endurance vigorous, his flocculent penis tumid, and strength like a wild prairie steed. Over time, despite being a medical professional, he stopped taking his own health advice and despite his encouraging words to patients. He stopped working out at the gym and his rare treats of junk food and chocolate malts became a more frequent occurrence with age. Soda instead of water and whole milk weakened his muscle and skeletal density and at this point in his life, living a bachelor life in a small town, he figured, what's the point? Most of his patients with health concerns felt the need to be in better shape for aesthetic purposes. Some wanted to set a good example for their kids and to live long enough to see their grandkids grow up. Dr. Jack Dullahan had no immediate family or a spouse to look attractive for and eventually, after so much of his life had passed, he became ever more aware that love would never find him. Options for a relationship here in Amherst were impossible and once somebody decided to stay, there was no escape.

He heard the echo of a passenger train on the edge of town, it's high-pitched whistle jolting him from his sprint. It was too late. There hadn't been a train in Amherst for what seemed like a hundred years until that woman showed up.

Nightmare Eve

With her came her nightmares, her burden and guilt. Whatever the story was, was her ordeal, but strangely enough, by coincidence or not, the train whistle occurred precisely at curfew and everyone—including Jack Dullahan—was in danger after curfew. His only benefactor against the curfew—the sun, had sank. The whistle like a buzzer going off at the end of his college exams perhaps eighty, maybe ninety years ago, shuddered the town. The siren was a deadline and he had met the end. By now every door in Amherst was locked and the shades were drawn. Familes huddled closely in their homes. Their windows closed, locked, the curtains drawn and the gaily laughter of the day ended in somber silence as the darkness flexed around them. The nightmares had come.

He turned at the sounds of heavy footsteps. His breath stuck in his throat.

It was close. Somewhere along the same forest trail. He stifled a breath and listened further. A soft clang of something metal—a long curved blade dragged across the forest floor. Coming this way.

Even closer now. In front of him? Behind? Jack spun around. He looked down the pathway. Bluish ambient light filtered from a mist-filled peat bog drifted through moss-covered trees. In front of him, the path led to complete darkness.

His lungs ached for air, but he resisted. He stood frozen in absolute silence like a frightened deer. No crickets chirped. No nightbirds squawked for they were in the presence of a predator. Only this predator was more evil, more unnatural, born in the depths of someone's personal hell. Like that poor woman who manifested that train, some guilt-laden citizen of Amherst brought this brutal monster. And then the storms came when that woman, Miss Harris, arrived. Soaked in rainwater and splattered in mud. What evils lurked in her mind? What nightmares haunted her and what did she bring with her inside this storm?

A branch snapped under heavy foot.

He remained silent, his body quaking in fear. Blood maddening loud in his ears.

Silence in the forest.

His lungs couldn't hold any longer. He sucked in a deep gasp, alerting his stalker who let out a cavernous snarl—stampeding through the woods, crashing through trees and exploding the earth as he charged like a crash of rhinos.

Dr. Jack Dullahan's scream was ripped to silence.

Chapter 11

Evelyn was sitting on the edge of her bed when she heard the unearthly snarl. Her startled hands dropped the wallet. She jumped to her feet as it landed on the quilt and stared at the window. She'd locked the window and drew the blinds just as Charity instructed.

Although their interaction was minimal she felt the child was more forward and honest than the other dinner guests. Perhaps she felt the closeness to her because she reminded Evelyn so much of Ivy Rose. Quiet, but honest.

Evelyn drifted across the room, careful to avoid any creaks and groans in the floorboards that might alert the other guests, including Ms. Smith, of Evelyn's furtive investigations. Outside the window the afternoon haze had fell to night offering her a sharp picturesque view beyond the grassy hillside.

Nightmare Eve

A gaping moon in a full starry night sky reflected off the calm sparkling waters of the Pacific Ocean. Along the bay, dense pine trees blanketed the valley and climbed the sharp ridges stretching into the cloudless sky. It was one of those most beautiful and frightening views Evelyn had ever seen. Somewhere, lost in those mountains, was her fiancé and daughter—along with whatever creature had made that bone-chilling sound. Too big to be a wolf. A bear maybe? Do bears even howl like that? She pressed against the chilled glass with her delicate fingertips. Her breath collected on the window fogging her view and she lowered her head until her forehead rest against the glass. The cold, smooth surface was soothing against her head. She stared at the floor in a lover's helpless despair.

We'll be together, don't know where, don't know when...
The radio!
Evelyn's eyes shot to the radio on her nightstand. The clock still flashed 12:00 like an emergency light.

Her heart raced while she crept across the room, so as not to disturb the other guests. Somehow, the radio had turned on. The classic tune was distorted as if it were being played directly off a warped record, speeding up then slowing down again. Unable to find the off switch, she reached for the plug behind the end table and yanked hard, nearly toppling over the lamp in the process.

Her heart continued to thump in her chest as tears stung her eyes. She needed David *now*. Without him her world has become a living nightmare.

Se toppled over the bed and clutched the pillow against her breasts and stared into the moonlit night, tears streaming down her cheeks. Wherever David was tonight, she hoped he knew how much she loved and missed him.

We'll be together, don't know where, don't know when...
No. Impossible. Her breath choked in her throat.

Nightmare Eve

Evelyn checked the power outlet. The cable was still unplugged, resting in a tangled heap behind the nightstand. She stared at the clock still flashing 12:00 and again the warped tune repeated. She remained on the bed mired in fear and clutched the pillow tighter. She forced a deep breath hoping to catch the scent of vanilla-mint that she fell so deeply in love with. Uncontrollable tears streamed down her face while she rocked herself back and forth. The malformed melody repeated. She clutched the side of her head, mumbling loudly to drown out the music until she finally couldn't take it. She swung the pillow hard at the radio, smashing it against the wall with a loud crash and pounced toward the door with the grace and silence of a clumsy deer, but when she reached the door, she paused.

Something was not right. Something in her room was different, had changed in some way. Enough to send trickles of unease like thousands of hairy spider legs dancing across her skin. Her eyes darted around the room, first to the window where the moonlight cast long, bright shadows along the wood floors. Weren't the curtains closed before?

Then her eyes fell on the bed, scanned the unusual painting just above, of a man holding a woman in his arms, and then to the bathroom door, closed as she'd left it. But no, there was something different. She was sure of it. She could *feel* it.

The doll. It was the tattered doll in the child's rocking chair, it's eyes glinting in the ethereal light. She met the toy in a staring match that seemed all too lifelike. That's when she realized what was wrong.

When she'd gone to bed that evening after supper, the doll was facing the bed. But now it was pivoted so that it faced the doorway, its eyes staring in the exact position where Evelyn stood.

It was watching her.

...We'll meet again, don't know where, don't know when... The music repeated.

Nightmare Eve

When it finally processed, she swung open the door and found the hallway empty. As she rushed toward the stairs she glanced over her right shoulder and saw she'd left the bedroom door wide open. She didn't care. She'd be gone before anybody would notice. She returned her gaze to the stairway and let out a surprised cry when she saw it had been obliterated to splinters and, just before she fell into the abyss below, reached for the last rung on the banister, hugging it for dear life.

A crumbling floorboard broke off and fell silently into the blackness below.

She crawled to the floor, her chest rapidly rising and falling with heavy breath. If she hadn't caught herself on the banister... She stared into the bottomless pit.

Was this just another dream, no different than the others before? She held her breath. Everything will be alright once I wake up. Everything will be normal, she reassured herself.

Her reassurance was unavailing though. Everything about this nightmare world was the same, except sodden with dilapidated walls and dangers lurking in the shadows. She'd have to be more careful. No more panicking, no more running off without thinking first.

She cocked her head to the side so she could peer down the hallway from where she came. There were 6 doors, including Evelyn's which remained open. There was another door on the same side as her room and one at the very end with three on the left. Strange, she was sure there were only two before. One room, the one directly across from hers was Charity's bedroom. One was the old man's bedroom, a bathroom, but what was behind door number three? Obviously the stairs weren't going to be her way out. Not without jumping to her death.

She released the banister and edged away from the ledge and walked carefully down the hallway to the mysterious new door.

Locked. Disappointed, she was ready to turn away when muffled voices on the other side stopped her. She listened carefully. Although the conversation was too muffled to distinguish precise words, their harsh tones were irate and Evelyn struggled to listen.

The woman in the room hissed presumably at a man who could hardly get a word in edge-wise. After a break in her rude and downright mean comments he spoke timid and hurt.

"You're just drunk."

The woman said nothing more, but Evelyn, unable to make out any more of her slurred insults, backed away from the door.

She reached in systematic fashion for each door, checking the door handle to see which ones were locked and which could offer an escape from this hellish world. Each door was locked and so Evelyn, defeated, was forced to return to her severely austere and depressing bedroom.

Even before she entered her room she could hear the classical melody of the radio drifting into the hall. In dubious motions she strode into her room and just beyond the doorway spotted a slip of paper barely visible between the radio and the lamp. It seemed entirely possible considering the circumstances that in her hysterics she overlooked such a small detail. A perfect example of why she shouldn't panic. She couldn't risk overlooking anything. Not when the lives of her and her loved ones were in danger.

She strode across the room and saw it was a photograph of her and David on their very first date. It was the same photograph she kept by her bedside back home. Not remembering packing it, let alone standing it on the bedside table, she was grateful to have it regardless of how it got here. With her back toward the radio, she placed the photograph on the pillow beside her and stared at the image until she cried herself to sleep.

Chapter 12

The following morning, Evelyn woke to dreary skies that cast the room in the same gloomy atmosphere as when she woke the night before. Last night's rainstorm had subsided and the air was calm once again. She lay in bed with drowsiness still tugging at her eyelids, urging her for more sleep, but she forced herself to study the cracks in the ceiling for several minutes until her eyes fell to the empty pillow beside her. The photograph was gone. She forced herself into a sitting position, the smooth floorboards cold against her bare feet. She slumped forward and buried her head in her hands, rubbing the sleeplessness away while forcing back more tears. Her body, wrought with fatigue, resisted as she rose to her feet. She just wanted to sleep forever, to sleep through this nightmare until David came back.

She glanced at the clock, still flashing 12:00. The plug still removed from the wall. Battery powered, maybe. Why didn't she think of that the night before? It was like she was stuck in a time warp and even though the sun continued to rise and set, time never moved forward.

Evelyn craned her neck upwards to the painting of the young man hovering over the woman who reached out with open arms. Although the painting hadn't physically changed, Evelyn now viewed it with sinister perspective. Their faceless heads angled toward each other. The woman sprawled on the floor wasn't reaching out as if being rescued by her prince charming; she was shielding herself from him. He loomed over her aggressively in a preparation of striking.

The artist's name, Nora Brooke, was scrawled in the bottom right corner.

Evelyn rose from the bed and allowed her unsteady legs to carry her into the bathroom where she quickly showered and toweled dry. She avoided her reflection in the mirror as she pressed the mirror's rim. The mirror swung out revealing a medicine cabinet. Inside was a sterile toothbrush sealed in a plastic wrapper, a travel size tube of toothpaste, and a mini deodorant stick. They all seemed ordinary toiletries, but the one that stood out was a bottle prescribed to her.

Evelyn stared at her name beneath the prescription number. She had never seen this bottle in her entire life! She removed it from the shelf and, hearing the pills tumbling around inside, she could safely assume that the bottle was nearly full. She continued rolling it in her fingers until she saw the prescription Doxepin prescribed by none other than Dr. Jack Dullahan from dinner the previous night.

Not only had she never met Dr. Dullahan before, but she'd never even heard of Doxepin. It was as if the people at Shady Nook Lodge were playing some sort of cruel joke on her.

Nightmare Eve

Evelyn thought hard and careful. Maybe it was some kind of antibiotic given to her to help feint infection from her head wound or a painkiller or even a sleep aid to help her rest at night during her recovery. With nearly a full bottle though, she hadn't taken many, if any. And if she had, she certainly hadn't taken any while she was conscious.

There had to be more answers. These nightmares, the memory of the monstrous-sized man, dressed like some nightmarish chain-bound executioner, the people in the robes who pinned her down with needles—they were all linked somehow.

She jerked her head up. A new prescription filled by Dr. Dullahan. She'd been right all along. He knew more than he was telling and she was determined to get some answers by going straight to the source. She rushed back into the bedroom and changed into her only remaining set of clothes—beige colored cargo pants and her white cashmere sweater. She rushed for the hallway but stopped when she heard Charity in the bathroom vomiting.

"Why didn't you tell me Jack was coming to dinner?" She heaved into the toilette again.

"Why did it matter, pumpkin?" Ms. Smith spoke calmly. "Would you've preferred someone else?"

Charity responded by heaving again.

Seeing as they'd be preoccupied for awhile, Evelyn used the distraction to rush down the stairs where she took a moment in the foyer to check the paper resting on the Sheraton sideboard near the entrance. It was the same paper that had been resting since her first night at the Shady Nook Lodge.

With growing frustration, she spun from the foyer and reached the front door when, through the opaque, beveled windows, saw a large crowd gathering at the base of the hillside—fenced off by yellow crime scene tape. Just as she reached for the doorknob Ms. Smith called out to her from the top of the stairs.

Nonchalantly, Evelyn turned and saw Ms. Smith sickly pale and grim faced.

"Breakfast will be late today," Ms. Smith informed. Her voice was scratchy and weak. "I'm not feeling well, but there are several plates of scones in the kitchen and the tea kettle is still hot if you'd like."

Evelyn politely said, "Thank you."

"Also, I took the liberty of washing your muddy clothes, but they still need a bit more time to dry which shouldn't take too long. I'll have them sent to your room as soon as they're ready."

Evelyn nodded. "Thank you," she said again. "What's going on outside?"

"Dr. Dullahan was murdered last night." Charity's sickly voice rose from the hallway.

Ms. Smith gave a sharp look over her shoulder to her daughter who had exited the bathroom and was now weakly making her way to her bedroom.

"The stupid old man tripped over his own feet last night on his way home. The fool cracked his noggin on a rock. He was so smart in life, but always fumbling over himself. A tragedy nonetheless, but still he should've known better than to take off in such a rush, especially so late at night." As Ms. Smith spoke, she had to take deep breaths between every couple words. She spoke slowly barely above a hushed whisper while clutching her stomach and wiping sweat from her pale cheeks. "These woods are dangerous after dark. Can't even see the ground beneath you, you can't."

Evelyn nodded with heightened suspicion. "I hope you and your daughter feel better soon."

Ms. Smith nodded.

Evelyn reached for the doorknob and swung open the door. The fresh, pine and ocean-scented air hit her face but before she could step out the door, Ms. Smith called out to her one more time.

"If you plan on going out, don't wander too far. And don't be out late."

Something in her sickly voice sounded cold and threatening like a strict mother warning a disobedient child. "This town is small, and very safe, but still the curfew is the law around here."

"I understand," Evelyn reassured.

Ms. Smith nodded before disappearing into Charity's room.

Evelyn felt relieved once she stepped onto the porch like a prisoner being released for the first time. She sucked in a deep breath unable to enjoy the spicy fragrance of wet pine needles and grass beneath a salty maritime breeze. The humid air wasn't as cold as she expected from the gray clouds rolling overhead, but she knew she'd be cold in anything lighter than what she was already wearing.

She followed the path, occasionally kicking up dirt and a bit of mud and pinecones. A copse of trees thinned out over the grassy hillside, the very same crowned by a single oak, and down below was a gathering of people swiveling for a better view of the forensics team scurrying beyond the yellow tape.

With as much discretion as she could muster, Evelyn approached the crowd from behind as they stirred, exchanging murmurs amongst themselves. Evelyn pretended not to notice the suspicious stares locked on her as she watched the medical crew hoist the stretcher carrying Dr. Dullahan's body concealed under a bloodied white sheet.

Dr. Dullahan who had prescribed her the Doxepin, the man who could give her some answers, was dead.

She felt terrible for the doctor and helpless for herself. Now what could she do? Someone else had to know something. She'd have to take an indirect approach, careful to stay as discreet as possible without divulging too much information. Especially in this town where already the citizens seemed aberrant.

She considered her options. Charity was an outspoken and honest girl. Of everyone she'd met so far, Charity seemed the most trustworthy, but getting her away from her overbearing mother would prove difficult. And still, Charity, as a child, probably didn't have all the information she needed.

Ms. Smith seemed highly knowledgeable and from her strange behavior last night, Evelyn was sure she knew more than she was sharing. Ms. Smith would be a tough one to crack. Her tongue was locked tighter than a Roman statue and something about her, possibly her forceful attitude, made Evelyn believe that she could become quite dangerous if pushed too far.

And then there was the nurse. An unnamed woman Dr. Dullahan and Ms. Smith had mentioned over dinner—a nurse who had watched over her and bathed her until she regained consciousness. She'd be difficult to track down without knowing her name and she doubted Ms. Smith would give it to her outright.

Lastly, there was the wallet in her pocket. As far as Evelyn could recall, there were only two men staying at the Shady Nook Lodge last night—the old man who shuffled into his room and the doctor, which opened up a slim possibility that the wallet she found belonged to one of them. If by chance the wallet had belonged to Dr. Dullahan then maybe the business card on the inside—Pan's Art Gallery, could give her a bit more information about the doctor, and possibly the nurse who had cared for her. He had to be close with someone. Close enough to share with them about the Doxepin.

As she contemplated her options, a man in a sheriff's uniform stopped short of the townspeople just beyond the yellow tape and, in a reassuring tone, instructed for everyone to continue about their daily business. Grim faced, they shuffled around for a few minutes, bumping shoulders as they dispersed. Most everyone headed in the town's direction on foot, which meant Amherst couldn't be far. Evelyn remembered barely

Nightmare Eve

seeing the rooftops in the valley from her bedroom window at the lodge and from what she saw, Amherst couldn't have been very big. She waited for the crowd to thin until only a few remaining stragglers drifted down the path. Evelyn followed them, hoping they would lead her to Amherst.

She felt a pair of eyes following down the path. When she looked up, she was right. A young blonde girl, a teenager, possibly seventeen or eighteen with fine, waist-length hair, a plain pale face and vibrant sea-green eyes glared accusingly at Evelyn. Her lugubrious boyfriend, with his arms wrapped tight around her, eyed her with a similarly bitter expression before turning his gaze back to his girlfriend. Evelyn shook her head all while wondering what their problem was. She, in her determined ways had begun to March toward the hillside path, giving them a head start, but was abruptly prompted to stop by an interjecting sheriff.

"Don't mind them," the sheriff said politely. "The townspeople can be a little superstitious at times, and we don't see many tourists."

He was a head taller than her and he spoke with authority and kindness. A fair dusting of brown hair bristled his smooth tanned face. He was handsome under his sheriff's hat and he stood tall and confident, but with the polite servitude of a butler. "It's okay. I'm sure they're just grieving. Is Dr. Dullahan really dead?"

The sheriff frowned. "I'm sorry. Did you know the doctor well?"

"I only met him last night, but in that brief time he seemed polite."

"Right. He mentioned the other day that he had dinner plans up at the Shady Nook. You must be Evelyn Harris, am I right?"

"Guilty." Evelyn replied.

The sheriff chuckled. "You caused me quite a bit of trouble down at the station. Had to file a report after Dullahan called the station about you. Told me he found a girl passed out in the ditch somewhere. No one around here knew you so we'd been calling you Jane Doe until we searched the wallet in your purse. Was surprised, who travels as far as you without carrying any cash?"

"Wait, what? You went through my purse?" Evelyn's face twisted in bewilderment.

"We had to find something out about you in order to file the reports and to notify your emergency contacts—which you didn't have in any medical records. The name that you had previously used, David Morel, was disconnected. A quick Internet search told us you are a travel writer. Are you writing a piece on Amherst?"

Evelyn opened her mouth to speak, but no words came out. She stuttered, fumbling to form a believable lie. "Actually, I am."

She expected the sheriff's eyes to light up and his mouth to form a delighted smile as it often did when she shared with others she was a travel writer. Local shop owners especially were usually excited, offering her business cards, discounts and samples of products, free meals and hotel rooms. Evelyn waited for the excitement to light up his face, but he remained stoic, maybe even concerned.

"I'm Sheriff Rhett. I take it you'll be staying at the Shady Nook Lodge a bit longer?"

Evelyn nodded. "Just a little while.

"Ms. Smith's such a proper, sweet woman. She's been bragging about you these last couple days. Said you were just the most adorable little thing, but I think I can tell you might be trouble for me." His grin revealed a set of sparkling white teeth, a smile that seemed too perfect, as if it had been practiced in the mirror for days, if not months, and much too forced to be natural.

"So what exactly happened?" Evelyn asked, deflecting his coquettish advancements.

Sheriff Rhett glanced over his shoulder. A group of professional-looking men and women with clear evidence bags and clipboards, jotted notes as they investigated.

"That's what we're trying to figure out."

Evelyn saw from where she stood, that the doctor didn't have much farther before he would've arrived at his home. Between the thick trees, above the dense ferns, tall grasses and shrubs, only the top floor and triangular shaped rooftop of Dr. Dullahan's log home could be seen. She could see the top railing of an ocean-facing balcony, but her view below that was obscured by a rather scraggly and thorny looking shrub. Wild raspberries maybe?

"It looks as if the path goes right up to his home," said Evelyn. "Why would he wander away from it?"

"There are some theories."

"Care to share?" she asked.

He shook his head. "Ah, I don't think that's quite wise, at least not until we are certain, until then, all I can say is that it appears to be an accident." He flipped through his notes. "How was dinner last night?"

"Dinner was fine. Ms. Smith made some fish and a salad. They were very talkative."

"Was Dr. Dullahan acting strangely? Demonstrating any odd behavior?"

She wanted to tell him that they all seemed very odd. "Well, I only just met them," Evelyn replied instead.

"Right," said the sheriff. "I mean, did there seem to be anything suspicious, like maybe he was afraid of something, maybe he was tense or perhaps feeling sick?"

Evelyn thought for a moment. "There was one thing I thought was strange."

"What is it? Tell me. The littlest piece of information could be crucial."

Evelyn took a deep breath and spoke with thoughtful consideration of her words. "They all seemed to be having a nice time. Charity was pretty quiet. Night was approaching and Ms. Smith tried to convince him to stay so he didn't have to walk home after curfew. He only lived down the road. Anyway, he finally got around leaving around eight or so."

"Eight, are you sure?"

"Not really." Evelyn strained to remember. There were no clocks on the walls and she didn't even remember seeing a microwave in her kitchen let alone the time. The clock on her nightstand—stuck flashing 12:00—was no help either.

"You had asked if he was sick. Why?"

Sheriff Rhett's shoulders barely raised then fell. "Just considering all options."

"I could hear Charity in the bathroom. Her mother didn't look very well either. I don't see what that has to do with the doctor straying from the path."

Sheriff Rhett looked at her. "Wherever he headed it must've been important enough to risk going out after dark."

"Was something chasing him?"

Sheriff Rhett tilted his head quizzically, "Chasing him, why would you think that?"

Evelyn reluctantly explained: "I heard there was a murderer in Amherst. Is that why everyone is acting so strange? When Dr. Dullahan left, everyone looked concerned."

"Just a local superstition," he said. Evelyn knew a fake smile when she saw one. His eyes were hard, jaw tight. He was more annoyed than he was letting on. "This was just an unfortunate accident."

Evelyn studied the numerous professionals moving about the crime scene and the white sheet with an abundance of blood. More blood than there should be for someone who fell on a small rock.

"If you hear of anything else, please let me know. You can find me at the police station near the center of town."

Evelyn cocked her head to the side. "I most certainly will."

Nightmare Eve

"Enjoy your stay in Amherst." The sheriff reached out as if he intended to shake her hand, but his eyes drifted. "It's a nice place, but sometimes, I wonder. Why anyone would choose to vacation here is beyond me." His eyes locked on hers. "Good day, Miss Harris."

Evelyn grit her teeth and watched him duck low beneath the crime scene tape.

By the time Evelyn had departed the crime scene at the grassy hill and arrived at the start of the trail leading to the town, the air had warmed slightly. Evelyn, still embraced the complacent comfort of her sweater, trotted up the slight grade to the apex where the Pacific breeze whipped at her hair and filled her nose with the organic aroma of salt and moss.

She followed the pathway around several switchbacks to the edge of the suburbs where the picturesque village of Amherst appeared, nestled between sharp woody mountains and a quiet harbor. The charming fairytale-like village with tall yellow and blue wildflowers adorning the switchbacks was much longer and narrower than she'd expected. Numerous piers stretched into the placid ocean waters and rows of shops and cottages with manicured lawns lined with Victorian red and white climbing roses arched over boutique terraces.

"It's pretty, isn't it?" The voice from behind startled her. She turned and recognized the weeping man—the same man Evelyn had sheen shambling into his room in the upstairs hallway of the Shady Nook Lodge.

"I suppose." she replied. It was a nice view; she loved the wildflowers, but she didn't care for the ocean.

He sat properly upright, his chin held in dignified superiority. "Who are you? Why do you come to Amherst?"

"My name is Evelyn Harris," she responded. "I'm trying to find my fiancé."

"Lots of people come to Amherst in search of answers. They don't always like what they find. What did you say happened your fiancé?"

Evelyn remembered the night of the accident. The night David and his daughter presumably drowned, their bodies never discovered.

"He died."

He looked at her curiously. "And you think he's here?"

"They never found his body. If there a chance he might be alive then I have to find him."

Mr. Morgan's frown deepened. He rose from the bench. "I lost someone I loved too. Every day I bear the guilt and despair for my mistakes. It's difficult to accept the things we can't change. We all come to this place in search of something we've lost: forgotten memories, a missing loved one or even a second chance. The search for truth is on a dangerous road. Sometimes it's best to let sleeping corpses lie. If you keep digging for the truth, be prepared to unearth the answers. Be prepared to fight."

He turned away, ready to shuffle toward the town, but Evelyn stopped him. "Wait, what's your name?

He looked at her with tired eyes as the marine layer began to drift in. "My name is Leonard Morgan."

It couldn't be—could it?

Evelyn felt as if the air would rush out of her lungs. It wasn't until her teeth clicked together that she took a breath.

Mr. Morgan looked at her and said, "I'm sorry to hear about your fiancé. He turned and walked away.

A rumble came from the clouds above. Time to get moving.

Evelyn shuffled along the wildflower path. Pine needles cracked beneath every step and, with every step, the sequoias grew taller and wider and the ground-hugging mist brewed thicker. She looked up. The dark grey and black clouds churned like black oil in water. The storm would arrive soon and the nightmare would begin.

Time to keep moving. Find David. Find Ivy. She reached in her pocket and pulled out the strange wallet and

Nightmare Eve

removed the business card for Pan's Art Gallery. That would be the first place she needed to look for answers. Someone there could point her to anyone who worked closely with Dr. Dullahan—the nurse who looked after Evelyn hopefully. She gathered from the address on the back of the card that Pan's Gallery was located somewhere downtown.

She continued down the gentle grade and settle curves of the switchbacks, passing endless rows of tall grasses and fragrant yellow and purple wildflowers. The breeze on this side of the hill was stronger than at Shady Nook, which was sheltered by the dense forest and jutting mountain peaks. The hiking path was a pleasant walk and gave Evelyn a few minutes to sort through her whirling thoughts.

She looked out across the village rooftops and scanned the mountains encompassing the harbor. Evelyn wondered if David and Ivy could see the sky and if they were looking at it now. She wondered if they were scared or hurt and hoped that wherever they were, they knew she loved them. She'd never give up. Her face grew hard with determination.

Evelyn ducked her head beneath a low branch and stepped to the edge of a cul-de-sac located at the corner of town. The cul-de-sac, surrounded by weeds and boulders, was located in the underdeveloped outskirts of Amherst where the city limits ended and the grassy savannah met the forest. Just a few yards beyond the cul-de-sac, towards the city, the voices of three men rose from the side of a convenient store. Evelyn spotted the men standing in a triangle not far from the dumpsters, two dressed in similar navy denim jeans. The other in a simple white t-shirt stained with mud, blue cargo shorts and street shoes. He carried a soccer ball against his hip where the handle of a knife was visible in his waistband. The man standing to the left had black tribal tattoos up his thick forearms and wore a black V-neck shirt. The third one approached the other two while thoroughly wiping his hands into a rag. He wore his shirt open, his grungy jeans had holes torn in them and his brown hair looked as if he'd just woken up. When she moved closer, Evelyn could see his lip was split. He rubbed the back of his hand across his jaw. None of them looked older than twenty-two.

The one in the board shorts looked even younger, though the wrinkles in his pinched eyes and sunken-in cheeks suggested he was the victim of rapid aging due to drug abuse.

The man with the tribal tattoos pointed to the split-lipped man's chest. "You got blood on you still."

He looked down and saw the thin speckles across his bare chest and shirt. He wiped the rag down his skin, which smeared the blood down to his stomach rather than soaking it up. He tossed the rag to his buddy in shorts. "Whatever. That asshole deserved what he got. Eddy, give me your flask."

The one with tattoos, presumably Eddy, reached into his back pocket and removed a silver flask. "How 'bout you get your own?"

"Don't be an asshole, man. Come on."

"We got a few hours before curfew, what do you wanna do?" The one with the soccer ball wore a grin too big for his face and teeth too big for his mouth. The intensity in his eyes brought a chill down Evelyn's spine. There was a little too much whiteness around his iris's, which made him look sadistic "Got any ideas, Johnny?"

The one with the split lip, Johnny, was first to spot Evelyn emerging from the alley. "You boys do what you want, I got my eyes on other things."

The other two followed his gaze. Upon seeing Evelyn, the one carrying the soccer ball let out an eccentric nervous giggle. Johnny's lips were drawn into a tight sneer, his eyes narrowed to slits.

"Where are you off to in such a rush?" He asked. He looked back to the trail from where Evelyn had come from. "Hasn't anyone told you that the woods aren't safe for little girls?"

Nightmare Eve

"I heard something kind of like that," Evelyn replied. She glanced between them. The one holding the soccer ball pulled a length of hair behind his ears. Eddy's head was bowed forward, but his dark eyes were locked hungrily on her like a gothic vampire ready to feast. When Johnny moved closer, she saw a man's body lying behind the dumpster stained with dirt and blood.

"Is he dead?" Evelyn's heartbeat quickened.

Johnny didn't bother looking behind him. "Relax, lady. I didn't kill nobody."

Evelyn tore her eyes away from the body and landed on Johnny. "He'll be fine."

"Sure will," said the one carrying the soccer ball. "He'll come back just like last time! There's nowhere else to go!" he let out a strain of giggles.

"Shut up, Corey," snapped Eddy.

"You didn't do this?"

"Like I said, I didn't kill nobody. At least not around here. And not lately either."

"You guys aren't friends with that Executioner thing are you?"

Johnny smiled and shook his head. The two behind him exchanged glances. "Executioner thing? I don't know what you're talking about. Why would I want to hang out with anyone called the Executioner?" He was silent for a moment. "There are a lot of strange things going on. Something is out there killing people and none of us want to stick around to find out what."

"Do you know anything about Jack Dullahan's murder?" Evelyn asked.

John's face grew hard, offended.

"Now why would I know anything about that? You don't even know me and you're already calling me a killer?"

From over Johnny's left shoulder, Corey giggled again. "That's what happens when you stay out past curfew!" he said.

89

"We all do bad things sometimes," said Johnny, "but tomorrow is a new dawn. A chance to make up for things."

"Just relax and enjoy yourself," said Eddy as they crowded her.

"Look, I don't know what happened here, but whatever it is, I think you should get out of here."

"Yeah, you're probably right," Johnnie responded.

They took a step closer, except Corey who remained behind them, standing still but ducking and swiveling his head around as if dodging a bee. "Did you hear that? It's coming! You guys, it's time to go!" Corey took another step back.

"It's alright, Ed," said Johnny as he pulled his friend away. "She won't be going anywhere." They turned and ran around the corner leaving Evelyn standing alone by the dumpster. She looked down and noticed the man's body had disappeared.

She whirled around. Was it getting darker, or was it just her imagination?

Several blocks away, the stores were shrouded in thick fog, obscuring her view of stoplights, street signs and even the sun. Not a single vehicle cruised down the streets and each shop looked into the fog with darkened windows like black eyes.

Where is everybody?

Wide streets were free of traffic. The rows of brick and wooden buildings appeared like wood and cement tombs, bright colors sponged away by the grey clouds overhead that threatened to rain. Only a few cars in angled parking spaces occupied the streets and from here Evelyn could barely make out the pier in the haze.

Not a soul in sight.

Maybe the music she heard was coming from a city event, like a fair or festival and most of the town had been attending. Or perhaps it was Sunday afternoon and, like many small towns she'd traveled to, the shops stayed closed all day.

Nightmare Eve

She strolled forward, each footstep echoed through the desolate community, as she strained to hear if the music was coming closer or moving further. She listened again. It sounded like a violin not far from here.

She moved past a cozy diner with tables and chairs on the terrace. The rustic wooden sign in the dosor read OPEN, but peering through the dark window, she saw only vacant dust-covered tables and a shadowy kitchen with every mixing bowl and dish in its proper place. She backed away from the window and stared at the other unoccupied shops lining the streets in every direction. This place was like a ghost town.

Despite the tepid air, a chill moved through her. There was definitely something *seriously wrong* with Amherst and the people who lived here.

She reached in her pocket and removed the business card for Pan's Art Gallery and re-read the address. The shop was located on the corner of Market and Poplar.

She looked up to read the signs at the nearest intersection. The fog had grown thicker so she cautiously, quietly stepped into the center of the street and slowly approached until the street signs emerged from the darkness. Her footsteps seemed lonely in the desolation.

She stood at the corner of Ivy and Rose.

Evelyn frowned. This was impossible.

"What is going on in this town?" she said to herself. "Am I crazy?" It was as if this town was mocking her. Rubbing it in her stupid face that she'd lost her family. Irritated, she made her way across the street to an empty floral shop on the edge of Ivy, clueless of the direction she should be headed. She figured Amherst was only a couple miles wide. One direction would dead end at the ocean; the other, a dead end at the mountain. Options were limited. They had to be here somewhere. Amherst was only so big.

She found Market Street at the next intersection. The fog grew thicker each minute the sun dipped lower in the sky.

Nightmare Eve

By now she'd gotten too turned around, traveled too far to get back before dark. Tonight, she'd break curfew.

Be ready to fight, Mr. Morgan's words repeated in her mind. *Don't go out after dark. . . Don't break curfew . . . This town is full of terrible demons. . . Be ready to fight.*

Be ready to fight.

She looked up and down the length of Market Street. To the left—four or five city blocks before the buildings thinned out and the road narrowed to a small mountain path. The other direction headed deeper into the desolate town where the air was dark with the first signs of night and thick with fog. Moisture had already begun to collect against the empty and cracked shop windows. It was that direction she was quite sure she'd find the art gallery. There was a Laundromat beside the sporting goods store and across the street was a bakery with the CLOSED sign facing the street. A bar, lit by neon lights, with a jukebox playing and a *Bud Light* sign flashed in the windows. It looked open but the inside appeared empty—deserted like the rest of the town.

A small grocery stand with fresh produce lined the sidewalks before she reached another vacant intersection. She stood at the crosswalk feeling ridiculous while waiting for the green light to turn red. If she were in Los Angeles or San Diego again, she'd cross regardless of the sign if there weren't any traffic. The next intersection was Market and Poplar. She was headed in the right direction.

She rushed past a movie theater with some classic black and white movie she didn't recognize playing, then past a pawnshop with black plastic covering the windows before spotting the sidewalk sign for Pan's Art Gallery. Above the sidewalk A-frame sign, red geraniums hung from a flower basket. Lucky that the sign read OPEN she figured it must not quite be Sunday.

With her breath held, she pressed her body against the door and pushed her way inside.

Chapter 13

Evelyn lit up with elation to see a young woman standing behind the desk whose eyes shot up from her magazine. Judging by the frightened expression on the young girl's face, Evelyn had startled her. It took a second for her to realize the woman in the gallery was the same young woman who had been spying on Dr. Jack Dullahan the night he was murdered. She was even more beautiful up close with long black hair and mocha skin with strikingly pale eyes, high cheekbones and a pointed chin that made her look like an exotic sexy snake.

"Can I help you?" she stammered, still shocked by the way Evelyn had burst into her store. Her voice was delicate as her skin, but shaken.

"I think so," said Evelyn. "I found a business card for the art gallery. I do a bit of painting myself and thought I'd come check it out." She forced a sweet smile, but her voice lacked confidence.

The young female clerk hesitated to move out from behind the counter, but did so with caution, taking reluctant steps to an array of paintings adorning the front wall.

"Nearly all of the artwork in here, including the pottery and sculptures, was created by the students at our local university."

"University?" Evelyn raised a curious brow.

The other woman's eyes narrowed, a sly smile spreading across her face. Her teeth were perfect, pearly white. "You must be new around here," she said. "We don't get very many outsiders. My name is Carly Williams. I spend most of my time working here in the studio, but during the week, I am—or was—a housemaid for a local resident."

"Was?" Evelyn asked.

Carly Williams nodded. Her black hair fell over her face. She used a delicate finger to pull a strand away from her eyes. "A hiker found him dead this morning."

"Dr. Dullahan?"

Carly Williams looked up at her. "Yes, how did you know?"

"Tragic news travels fast." Evelyn responded.

"Such a terrible accident. As if this town hasn't experienced enough tragedy already." Carly shook the sadness from her head and forced a perky countenance while offering Evelyn a polite handshake.

"I'm Evelyn Harris."

As they engaged in arbitrary conversation, Carly described the background of several paintings and portraits. They strolled down each of the aisles and Evelyn was surprised to see how much larger the gallery was from the inside with a loft in the back and an extended ceiling.

"So what brings you to this neck of the woods?"

"I'm just here on vacation with my fiancé and his daughter. I seemed to have gotten separated from them."

Carly's eyes grew wide, her mouth opened in surprise. "So you're the one Dullahan got the call about the other night. How's your head doing?"

"My head?" Evelyn raised her right hand to her still tender skull.

"He said you had a wicked bump, but I wasn't there so I didn't really see anything first hand. Are you feeling okay?" Carly gave Evelyn the strangest look, as if she was expecting Evelyn to faint, fly off the handle or something worse. It was how Evelyn imagined a therapist would examine a mental patient for the very first time, noting every personality tick, every subtle movement for signs of instability or physical danger.

"I'm still a little groggy, I think." Evelyn lied. "I still don't remember much. I don't even know what time or day it is right now."

Carly nodded. "Don't worry," her voice was reassuring. "Everything will come back to you eventually." Then she raised her right arm and pointed to the counter. At first Evelyn wasn't sure what Carly was doing. She stared at the potted pink tulips before realizing that Carly was actually gesturing to the digital clock on the cash register.

12:00

A stifled gasp erupted from Evelyn's throat.

Carly took a long step back from Evelyn, her eyes wide and hands outstretched as if to shield herself from Evelyn. "Are you alright?"

"Twelve." Evelyn breathed. "Twelve *again?*" Or was it twelve *still?*

Carly nodded slow and uncertain. "Yes, it's twelve. It's been an awfully long day for everyone with that horrible scene on the hillside. By sunrise the whole town was in a buzz. It seems like so much later, doesn't it?"

"Right," Evelyn said, shaking her head. "I guess I just lost track of time."

She swiped her hand across her face, applying light pressure and squeezed her eyes tight, but only for a second.

Only noon? She didn't believe it. Not for one second. The sun was clearly going down and Evelyn had been up for hours. No way possible it was still noon. It was as if day and night continued to change, but the time always remained the same. None of it seemed possible.

"I don't suppose you've seen my fiancé or our daughter, have you?" Evelyn asked in breathy despair.

Carly shook her head, shrugged and apologized. "No, I'm sorry. I haven't seen anyone other than you since this morning. It's quieter than usual today. It's dead. Even for Amherst." She paused and must've seen the concern growing across Evelyn's dropping face. "Don't worry," she added with forced optimism. "I'm sure they're fine wherever they are."

But Evelyn wasn't so sure. Where was David? Did he even care that she was lost without him?

They stopped at a row of similar paintings mounted on the wall. The same artist created each painting approximately two feet wide and three and a half feet tall, making them easily noticeable. The painter used hard, quick brush strokes using deep colors and hard lighting.

The first was a group of people huddled underneath a dead oak tree, similar to the one on the grassy hill. A single woman in a cloak was barely beyond the crowd.

In the second painting, the same woman was painted on the corner of the canvas just beyond the shore. The rest were all variations in a similar color scheme and technique.

"These are some of my favorites," Carly motioned to each of them. "They were a series done by an art major at the University. The artist was very much in love with the young woman. Notice how he positioned her so that her back is facing us and always just to the side of the canvas."

"She's always just out of reach," Evelyn said softly.

Nightmare Eve

"So romantic and so tragic to love someone with someone so close and still unobtainable."

Evelyn studied the woman in the painting who stood cloaked and hooded with chocolaty brown wisps of hair tousled over her face and the violent brush strokes of thick dark color that made the water and the sky appear murky and grim. Evelyn could practically see the wind moving her hair and tugging at the tattered cloak and the ocean humidity against her face. The cold air rouged Evelyn's cheek as she felt herself falling deeper into the painting until the roar of the ocean overwhelmed her ears.

"Whoa." Evelyn tore her eyes away.

Carly gave her an unusual stare. "I'll give you a few minutes to look around. If you need anything else, don't hesitate to ask."

Evelyn nodded and thanked her. She turned away from the young woman and sauntered along the rows of paintings and line drawings. Charcoal and line drawings were framed and mounted among watercolors and ceramic pots on columns. Evelyn enjoyed browsing art, but she didn't know much about art history or techniques. She could hardly define the difference between an expressionist and impressionist piece of work, or the hard noir shadows of an old lighthouse over thrashing waters.

Wait. A lighthouse over water. Evelyn stepped closer. *The Lighthouse* painted in oil by Nora Brooke.

Evelyn had seen that lighthouse before. It'd been in her nightmare just before she woke up at the Shady Nook Lodge. The piece next to Nora's painting was an original piece donated by Nora's father, Dr. Theodore Brooke—a chemistry professor at the same university. It was a mask of some sort, unlike anything she'd ever seen. It stared with gaping malformed eyes and a wide mouth that stretched ear to ear in a ghoulish scowl and the texture was the same as the wallet. With her right hand she reached forward and gently caressed the rough edges of the mask.

The world melted away and Evelyn was somewhere else, lost in another vision, or memory that never belonged to her.

A gargantuan man shackled inside a metal cell wore a burlap sack over his face. The rocking of the boat caused his head to swing side to side. Chains scraped against the wood floor.

On deck, men were shouting. The boat tilted to the side and sea water gushed through the cracks. The prisoner grunted awake. He grabbed at the chains. A crash from above rained more seawater, this time with splintered wood. The boat shifted suddenly and the boards began to loosen and crack. The chains snapped, and the prisoner, heavy and slow, rose to his feat and snarled through the cell around him. Grabbing the bars in the front corner where the boards beneath were the weakest, the prisoner waited for the boat to tilt again and with inhuman strength, broke through the cell walls and expelled a ferocious growl.

Evelyn was back in front of the display again. Her heart pounded in her chest. She removed her hand from the leathery face. Another hallucination, or some kind of vision, just like the one she had when she touched the wallet. Were they connected? Evelyn read the card beneath the artifact.

THE MASK OF FLESH

Evelyn shivered. Behind her, Carly had returned to the desk. Evelyn pretended to inspect the paintings, letting her eyes wander through the swirls of color without really seeing the details. When Carly was out of view, Evelyn snatched the Mask of Flesh from its mount and slipped it beneath her sweater.

The mask felt like thinly sliced beef jerkey against her bare stomach. She cringed and made her way to the door. Carly nodded a farewell and watched with curiosity as Evelyn exited out the front door.

Nightmare Eve

Gloomy skies sprinkled with flecks of rain, dotting the uninhabited streets and collecting on the empty shop windows. A slight breeze rose from shore. The temperature had dropped enough that even the minuscule chill invaded her sweater. She adjusted the downy cashmere turtleneck and to the other end of the block before removing the mask hidden in her sweater. It was approximately the size of a small tea plate, capable of fitting in one of the larger pockets of her cargo pants. It was lighter in her hands than she thought it would be, but she was sure the leather was the exact same as the wallet.

She placed the mask carefully in an empty pocket of her cargo pants and checked herself for the other items: a prescription for Doxepin from Dr. Jack Dullahan and the wallet.

Evelyn's pace diminished as she reached the center of the crosswalk. She stood listening to the silent community hearing only the sounds of the shore breeze and the rustle of pines. Where the hell is everybody?

The only lights on the block came from the window of Jay's Bar between the movie theater and the Laundromat. She half-jogged the remaining length of the crosswalk and noted missing person flyers posted on the bulletin board posted just outside the shop. Nearly a dozen faces stared back, many of them children, men and women and a few elderly. Evelyn checked the dates and saw that each of them had gone missing just over the last couple weeks. How was it possible that so many people have gone missing in such a small town? People were missing and the ones that weren't were probably too afraid to leave their homes.

Another flyer displayed a photo of a young businesswoman, her hair wrapped in a conservative bun and a smile that reminded her of a realtor's mug shot. Evelyn leaned in closer to read the description indicating that she'd last been seen driving a white SUV toward Amherst. Evelyn knew that description. The white SUV that had veered dangerously close to the edge of the ravine and collided with the embankment had been one of the last things Evelyn had seen before stumbling down the hiking trail into Amherst.

Evelyn backed away from the bulletin board. Jay's bar was right next door and she could certainly use a drink to relax and a moment in a warm place to regroup.

The front door had been propped open using a small flowerpot. Soft, warm lights dimmed lower than ambient outside twilight. Several booths in the back curved around the far wall to the elevated stage where two lonely microphones stood and a karaoke flat screen, mounted to the wall, glitched with static. Just off the stage against the side wall, behind two pool tables and next to a dartboard, a jukebox emitted soft 80's rock.

She stood at the vacant bar and called out. When no one answered, she hoisted herself on a stool and waited. She caught a glimpse of her reflection in the mirror mounted behind a row of vodka bottles. No makeup, her cheeks were rouged from the cold. Her listless damp blonde hair tumbled over shoulders and her eyes turned dark and grey from sleeplessness. Her eyes retreated from her reflection and dared not to look again. At least she was showered and her clothes were fresh from the morning, however it did little to assuage her from her life-threatening worries.

She brushed a strand of hair behind her ear and lowered her eyes to the empty rocks glass stacked at the other end of the bar next to an almost full bottle of whiskey. They sat at the corner as if the bartender had suddenly abandoned the pour to take care of a different matter. Evelyn ran her fingers along the edge of the counter until she stood next to the bottle. The bartender hadn't yet returned so she grabbed the bottle and poured herself a modest pour and then rose to the pool table. Several scattered balls lingered near the pockets with a cluster near one end. A pool cue lay carelessly on the floor. The last players had abandoned their game. She whiled away the moments swilling the drink and then used the pool cue to sink a

Nightmare Eve

solid purple. Then a green stripe. When she moved around the table, her eye on a solid blue, she heard faint voices drifting from the back hallway. They were quiet enough, which explained why she hadn't heard them sooner, and as she moved closer, their voices grew familiar: the same bickering couple she'd overheard fighting at the Shady Nook Lodge.

Across from the restrooms, the voices rose from behind closed doors. At the end of the hall, beyond the glass exit door, the parking lot appeared vacant and the evening marine layer approached. The voices drifted through the first door on the left. She pressed her body against it and listened.

"I'm sorry," the woman sobbed, her words slurred. "Could you forgive me?"

"Yes," the man replied with despondence.

"Does that mean you're staying?" The woman overemphasized words, drawing out the last syllable of each into the beginning of the next. Evelyn presumed the glass she drank from was meant for the woman behind the door, though she sounded as if she'd already had too many. Evelyn remembered angry nights like these with David and how terrible she felt the next day. Most of the time it was over something small too, like leaving his laundry all over the house for her to pick up. Sometimes they were more irritating fights like when she'd want to vent about work and he, even though lacked the education, training and experience she had, still had the nerve to tell her how to do her own job—travel journalism—which she was quite successful all on her own. Though it irritated her, how he sought to be the contrarian in all matters, it didn't stop her from loving him. The anger, and the drink, had usually exacerbated the fights, and his stubbornness didn't help much either. The following day she usually felt so much grief for causing such a scene, but David had this way about him: even when it came to subjects he knew nothing about—he had to be right. Even when he was clearly wrong. It didn't matter to him if it under minded Evelyn as a person, a professional, or a spouse. Or even if it drove her to anger or drinking and how it affected her hurt emotions. As long as he made everyone think he was right, he was willing to pay any price. And Evelyn forgave him for that.

"No. I already have a soul mate and it's not you."

Evelyn jumped backed as she heard a door open; a man's footsteps tromp across the room and clanged through another exit.

Evelyn heard the woman approach the door. Evelyn jumped back and sprinted to the bar so as not to be noticed eavesdropping.

No more than a second later, a woman stumbled from the hall into the open room and braced herself against the bar. She wore a tight green miniskirt and tight black V-neck shirt with a shimmering purple lining. Her hair was blonde, like Evelyn's, and just as disheveled, but shorter. Black mascara streaked her pale and pretty face.

The woman snatched a glass from the bar, her knee-high black boots thumped on the wooden floors to the stool and braced herself against the bar where she doubled over in hysterical, drunken sobs. She saw Evelyn from the corner of her puffy eyes. She spoke, her voice calm, but shaky. Silent tears ran down her face.

"It's like no matter what I do, it never seems to be enough for him." She poured herself a glass of whiskey from the same bottle. "He said he loved me. We had plans to get married, but now he tells me he already has a soul mate." She took a large gulp and then slammed the glass down on the bar causing Evelyn to jump. "What the fuck kind of shit is that?" the woman screamed at her own reflection. What hadn't spilled of the whiskey in the glass sloshed around. "I loved him! I fucking *loved* him!" She took a deep breath and ran her forehead along her shoulder. Even from several stools away, Evelyn could see the woman's hands trembling. When the woman lifted her head, her face was calm again and when she spoke, her voice had become quiet. "Why would I even want to marry him if he

Nightmare Eve

thinks I'm not his soul mate? I would've done anything for him. I would've died for him. All I wanted was to encourage him and to show him how truly special he is. His problem is that he just doesn't think he's special. He thinks that wallowing in his own misery is all he deserves. Or maybe it's all he wants. I try to fight for him, but I just don't know why. It just makes me miserable to see him continuously put everyone else before me. I would *never* do that to him. He chose someone else, yet I *always* choose him." The drunk woman sighed and drank the last bit in her glass. "I guess that's why I can't keep him close. I feel like I mean nothing to him. Being around him is just too painful."

Evelyn approached her. She took the glass from the drunken woman's hands and placed it just out of reach. "These things will be okay," Evelyn said, "everything happens for a reason."

"Being around him is just too painful." The drunken woman sobbed again.

"Things get better. Every relationship has issues, but over time you'll see that things aren't that bad." Evelyn put her hand on the woman's shoulder. She could feel the moisture from her body heat dampening her clothes. She felt something drip onto her head. Evelyn reached up and touched her hair, just above the sore spot. It felt welt. A glob of rain dripped again, smacking her face when she looked up. A crack in the wood ceiling allowed the rain to infiltrate the warm bar, and her sweater. A stale breeze siphoned through and then dissipated. The wind howled and Evelyn swore she heard thunder rumbling not too far off shore. The woman sobbed at Evelyn's feet.

"It's just too painful." The drunk woman's voice became muffled by her own hands.

The bar shuddered from a gust of wind. The lamps above began to sway. Water dripping through the cracks above spread wider until it flowed like a backyard spigot. The roof crunched and twisted, buckling under the storm. The walls and ceiling sprung leaks. Evelyn braced herself against the pool table, except it wasn't there anymore. Her hands hit empty space and she started to fall back, but caught her balance. The lights flickered. In a split second of darkness, she heard the woman moan. The light flickered on and Evelyn thought she saw the ripples of the woman's spine through her shirt before the lights cut out again.

"*It's just too painful,*" the woman repeated again, only this time there was something different in her voice, like a raspy gurgling sound. A feeling overwhelmed her, strong enough to force her to take a step back as if the wind had been forced out of her. Except it wasn't the wind. It was as if being suffocated by some evil weight that sucked happiness and hope right out of her soul. Immediately she felt dizzy and weak.

Between each flash of light, the room had begun to change. The stools had disappeared, replaced by tall rusty spikes with wooden tips like a shoulder-high barricade in some industrial nightmare. The shelves of liquor overflowed to the floor like a cascading black waterfall. Where was it all coming from? Above the mirror, the walls cracked, spewing the black foul water. The room expanded, nearly twice the size as before, the walls hidden somewhere in the darkness. At the end of the hall, near the one remaining pool table where Evelyn had been eavesdropping earlier was boarded up. From somewhere in the ceiling, a three-foot wide drainage pipe dropped down along the perimeter of the room where the booths used to be. Rotting wood, mold and the scent of death, like dried blood and rotting flesh invaded her nose.

"*It's just too painful,*" the drunk woman's voice warbled like a melting record. "*So much pain!*"

At the edge of darkness, only when the lights flickered on, she could see the woman crawling on the floor like a human-sized spider, her bones breaking and contorting into a hideous humanoid creature with arms and legs that bent the wrong way that spasmed and jerked with each step closer. Her flesh crawled like cockroaches beneath the surface of her clammy skin. When the lights flickered out again, she became silent. The only noise Evelyn heard was the water tumbling from the shelves.

She held her breath. Listened. Waited.

In a flicker of light, Evelyn caught her own silhouette in the mirror. The woman stood behind her, rising to her feet like a creature emerging from a watery grave.

Chapter 14

Evelyn ducked as the creature swung. Its long, skeletal arms barely grazed her hair. When the thing hissed, thick black fluid spurted from between her narrow, peeled back lips exposing a row of tall, broken teeth.

Evelyn took a step back and collided with the spiked barricade. The snarling creature tumbled forward. She was trapped. It's hollow eyes, locked on her, cried black ink. Just as the creature reached out with long, bony fingers, Evelyn dove to the side, landing in the murky waters. The creature let out another hiss.

Evelyn climbed to her feet and tried to sprint away from the creature, searching for a door, window or some other way out, but the room appeared to be sealed, a door-less, window-less box. She stood near the pool table. The water, which lapped against her ankles, was getting deeper. The lights flickered out. Evelyn froze straining to hear the creatures movements, but heard none. When the lights flickered on, the creature stood in front of her, it's dislocated mouth wide as if to swallow her whole, and eyes purging the inky blackness.

The creature reached for her, but Evelyn snatched the pool cue and swung it against the creature's skull. The creature spasmed where it stood, like a seizure, allowing Evelyn to put some distance between them.

The light above the pool table swayed, making the shadows dance when it flickered on before flickering off again. In the flickering light, Evelyn watched the creature recover and violently twitch as she staggered closer. Her body hunched forward and her arms went rigid. She breathed in raspy breaths and her mouth opened and closed as if she were chewing on invisible flesh. The creature lurched toward Evelyn again, colliding with her, sending them both sprawling to the watery floor. The creature's grip on Evelyn remained firm, pinning to the ground as the water continued to rise over Evelyn's face. She wanted to scream, but the water drained into her mouth.

Evelyn pushed her hands against the creature as it snapped with its vicious jaws. Its weight barred her beneath the water's surface. Evelyn's lungs begged for air. Her arms flailed, splashed against the water and tried to wrench free of the creature's powerful grip, but her muscles grew weak. Her lungs burned and vision blurred. Then her arms fell limply to her sides as the world around her faded to black.

—

The bar filled with gentle stylings of brass and piano. A howl, like a wolf calling the moon, rose above the classy jazz while the others in the room hollered with enthusiasm at the dueling pianists. Their waitress, Maddie, in a black corset and stockings with red trimmings balanced a tray of vodka shots while she maneuvered through the crowded bar. Her dark-chocolate colored brown locks bobbed against her pale round face as Maddie straddled her sexy and voluptuous red headed friend, Robyn Lindscott.

Nightmare Eve

Evelyn Harris watched as her friend downed the shot, topped with whip cream with a big grin on her face.

The others sharing the table applauded and cheered, their comments lost in the dizzying array of commotion. Robyn smiled with whip cream still smeared across her chubby, pretty face. She wiped the sweets off her face and her makeup remained flawless. Robyn was beautiful and she spared no expense when it came to her appearances and her friends.

"No solids for two weeks," Evelyn said. "No drinking for even longer. Enjoy it while you can."

Robyn held up a green Jell-O shot. "I don't know if these really count as solids, but it's my last night before my surgery tomorrow so I won't be able to hang with my drinking buddies for awhile."

"Two months is a long time without seeing you. The bars are going to be so quiet without you."

Robyn picked up a second Jell-O shot and handed it to Evelyn. "I'm so glad you came, Evie. I'm really going to miss you."

Evelyn took the Jell-O shot from Robyn. "I'll visit you in the hospital. I promise."

"No flowers please. I'm allergic to them."

"You are?"

"No, I just hate flowers. If you bring me something, not that you have to, bring a magazine and an *In-N-Out* burger."

"Deal." They both laughed. "Now whose turn is it to buy the next round?"

"I think it's mine." A man's voice came up from behind Evelyn. Robyn's face lit up.

"David! You made it!"

Evelyn's polite smile was casual in the way anyone would meet a new friend, but Evelyn was unprepared for his beauty. He stood much taller than her with sparkling, cheerful eyes that seemed to be hazel, grey, blue and green all at the same time. He had a curved jawline, perfectly pale and unblemished skin with eyelashes any woman would've died for. His lips, thick and bright red curled into a seductive smile that he knew would melt any girl's heart. He dressed in the same semi-formal dark slacks as the other men, with a black button-up shirt with white buttons and a cherry-red collar and hem.

"Another Hurricane?" he asked. Robyn nodded. Evelyn continued to stare as she watched him approach Maddie for another bucket.

"Oh, I'm up next!" Robyn announced. She took a spoonful of the whip cream on the table and ate it before she jumped from her seat, crossed the room and mingled with the other performers until her name was called.

Evelyn had never been to a dueling piano bar before. Jazz musicians and two incredibly talented pianists sat at separate pianos across the stage from each other. They mashed up music, everything from Lady Gaga to Johnny Cash with stand-up comedy routines in between. After several buckets of Hurricanes (a half-gallon plastic bucket filled with an assortment of tropical flavored liquors and served with a handful of crazy straws) and countless more Jell-O shots from Maddie, Robyn finally took the stage and rocked out to *Pour Some Sugar on me* by Def Leopard. The bar was in delightful uproar, but Evelyn was focused on David—the most handsome man she'd ever seen.

Several minutes passed and the bar, filled to maximum capacity, grew stuffy. Evelyn felt disoriented, dampness forming on her forehead, the constant battery of loud music and the roar of people screaming to be heard across the table became overwhelming. She tore her eyes from him but caught his smile as she headed for the door and hoped he hadn't noticed her blushing in the dimly lit room.

She stood on the balcony alone. The hot Los Angeles air felt cool by comparison to the heat of the bar and a few stars could be seen just above the palm trees adorning the hillsides.

The palms swayed in the gentle breeze and Evelyn appreciated being in the moonlight's comfort.

"It's a beautiful night." David's voice made her turn around. "David Morel."

"Evelyn."

They shook hands. When he smiled, his teeth glowed as bright as the moon.

"Is your boyfriend in there?"

Evelyn shook her head. "No, no boyfriend. I've never really connected well with other guys."

"Oh." He thought a moment. "Are you a lesbian?"

Evelyn laughed. "I wish. It seems like it would make life so much easier, but no. I like men."

They both laughed.

"Any man in particular?"

"Not yet." Evelyn smiled again. She hated to look away from his face while his eyes still locked on hers, but she didn't want him to see her face flush with embarrassment. "It's just that every time I try to put myself out there, I always end up getting hurt. I just don't want that to happen again."

David nodded. He stepped beside her and leaned against the railing. Together they watched the clubbers and shoppers bustling along the city walk. "I know what you mean," he said. "It can get lonely sometimes and—"

"—and you just can't ever seem to find the one." Evelyn finished.

He gave a nod.

She smiled a sad smile and returned her gaze to the moon. The wind caught her hair and she tousled it aside before gazing into the stars.

He touched her hand. "Well, maybe I just haven't met you yet."

—

Evelyn groaned as consciousness forced its way into her pounding head. Pain shot like lightning from her skull, striking her chest and shuddering her body. She opened her eyes and saw bright white all around her, like a coffin made from sunshine, but she wasn't dead. Though from the pounding in her head she wished she were. It took her until she reached for the sides and stood up for her to realize she was in an old bathtub speckled with soggy plaster, dust and a couple fly and cockroach carcasses.

Evelyn fastened her grip along the edges of the bathtub to hoist herself out. The room resembled a Laundromat. White and green-papered walls and checkered floors, dusted with a fine powder were signs of many neglectful years. Only a single washer and dryer located in the very back furnished the room. Evelyn eased herself across the room to the exit.

Copious grey clouds tumbled over Amherst. The growing offshore winds teased her hair and cooled her face, her sweater kept her body warm. A deep breath and her headache subsided. The streets and sidewalks remained empty as far as Evelyn could see and she stood between stop signs pondering her direction. With a heavy sigh, Evelyn looked into the clouds just off the coast. Dour weather was appropriate for her mood. She wiped her hand across her face.

"What happened?" Evelyn muttered to herself. "What the hell is this place?" Amherst General, Auntique Annie, and some flower shop with the sign crossed out stared with dark windows like hollow eyes. Stop lights switching between red and green signaled nonexistent traffic and a newspaper, caught in the breeze, danced beneath a movie theatre marquee. A red streak defaced the ticket booth. Evelyn's muscles tightened.

The neatly square-cut blocks offered multiple routes to wherever she needed to go. The marina maybe? Or the mountain? Back at the art store, Carly had talked quite a bit about the University. The town didn't seem big enough to have a university, but maybe students commuted from the other towns near by, though Evelyn couldn't think of any. She didn't even know where she was. The man who donated the Mask of

Flesh to the gallery, Theodore Brook, was a doctor according to Carly's story. He worked at the university. In a small town like this, where everybody seemed to know everybody, it was likely that Theodore Brook and Jack Dullahan knew each other. Maybe even worked together. At the very least she could research Doxepin.

Unsure of which direction the university was located, Evelyn headed sea-bound, occasionally glancing over her shoulder along the way. Already the sun dropped lower into the sky. Evelyn must've been out for an entire day. Or were days shorter this far north? In either case, she thought for certain somewhere along Market Street a vehicle would've passed or at least a pedestrian rushing home to escape nightfall. She had two hours at the most.

The overprotective innkeeper, Mrs. Smith, wouldn't waste a single minute to report her missing if she didn't return back to the bed and breakfast by curfew. Evelyn remembered how frightened Charity Smith behaved that night, urging Evelyn to dispose of the strange wallet and lock herself in her bedroom until morning. The wallet must be important for her to behave that way and the others—Ms. Smith and Dr. Dullahan—trembled with fear as curfew passed. Evelyn felt certain their fears were legitimate as the doctor was now dead. If he had been in such a hurry to get home, he would've taken the path. But the fact that his body had been discovered yards up the hillside made her suspect that someone, or something, had chased him. Whatever made that monstrous growl lurked in the woods, coming out only at night. Something terrified the people of Amherst so that they hid in their homes, and locked their doors and windows to wait out the night in fearful silence until morning. If this beast had killed the doctor, there would've been claw marks all over his body, the grass collapsed and stained crimson with the doctor's blood and violent scuffmarks in the dirt.

But if his killer was human, someone that the doctor considered a friend, he may not have realized he was in danger. Maybe he and his killer had walked partway together. In the darkness, the doctor never would've seen his killer pick up a rock from somewhere along the path. The blow to his head could've stunned him. He tried to escape by shambling up the hillside where the killer finally reached him, or maybe the initial blow was hard enough to cause him to bleed out moments later. The scenario was educated, but still speculation and raised more questions than answered. Who would want to murder Dr. Dullahan and why?

Evelyn continued down Market Street in long, steady strides. She fiddled with the neck of her sweater. Gusts of winds shook the abandoned shops. The crumbling buildings stirred and cracked like brittle bones. Evelyn pressed onward against the wind. The smell of white spindrift and salt saturated the hazy air until she could barely see the marina at the edge six blocks away. Two blocks later she paused in the center of the street when she heard a gentle chorus of chimes quietly drifting through the ghost town.

Past a boat repair shop and a water athletics store, Evelyn approached a French café on the right side of the street. Through the fine white grain mist she saw the figure of a woman in her early forties who sat at a patio table sipping from a ceramic teacup. Evelyn strode closer eyeing her silky golden blonde hair, crimped to frame the elegant angular visage on her grim face. She wore a simple floral print blouse and denim shorts reminded reminiscent of 1980's fashion. Her semblance was that of an all-around country girl with natural beauty enhanced with bold pastel makeup.

Evelyn suspected that in the stranger's earlier years she would've been a mainspring of wet dreams for men of all ages.

The woman appeared to be deep in thought with her head slightly bowed and her vacant eyes lost in foggy space.

"Excuse me." Evelyn stood on the other side of the ivy-lined wrought iron fence.

The grim-faced woman lowered her teacup to the saucer and gently cocked her head to the side. Her movements were sluggish and drawn out. Even her words weighed heavy by a melancholy drawl.

"Where is everybody?" Evelyn asked her.

"It's the knell of those chimes." Her voice was soft and airy like the mist drifting through the streets. "A thirty minute warning until curfew." The woman avoided Evelyn's gaze. "You must be new here."

Evelyn introduced herself. "I'm not from here. I came to find my family."

Her grim countenance cracked under the hint of a wistful smile—then faded. "I'm not from here either, but it's nice to chat with someone new. It's been very lonely since I arrived." The woman picked up her tea and stared into empty space above the teacup. "Associating with someone like me earns a villainous reputation. I'm not well-liked around these parts." She took a sip, swallowed, brought the teacup back to the table. "This town seemed like such a nice place. I thought I'd move here to get away for awhile, but it seems that no matter how far or long we run, the past haunts us."

"I'm just happy to see another living soul. This place is a ghost town."

The woman gave a subtle nod. Her tired eyes filled with depression. Evelyn felt pity for her.

"What did you do that was so terrible?"

The woman chuckled and Evelyn's mouth slightly parted at this unexpected reaction but she continued on in a more lively tone. "You really are new, aren't you? You haven't been around long enough to hear the nasty rumors about me. This town loves to gossip. Everything is everyone's business here."

"You've hurt someone?" Evelyn asked.

Nightmare Eve

"I've hurt many," the woman replied. She took a deep breath and began her story. "I was a model back in my heydays. I showed up on my first day bold and confident. And ignorant. I bragged to the other models portraying myself as a celebrity. I was oblivious to my colleagues snickering. I thought no one could tell me what to do. In a desperate and humiliating strategy I used my looks and body to sleep my way to the top."

"You hurt a lot of people on the way. You broke some hearts and tore apart marriages and now you're feeling their pain. And some guilt?" Evelyn studied the woman's eyes. They seemed to look without ever really seeing, like she was in a constant daze.

"I remember my life in New York and the lives I destroyed in Paris, but I can't remember how long ago that was. I can't remember how long I've been here. I've seen the marina, strolled through the woods, visited the train yards and toured the university, but I've never seen the chimes in the temple. It's a strange religion they have here, but do you think it's too late to ask for forgiveness? And do I even deserve it for all the wicked things I've done?"

The woman's eyes locked with Evelyn's for the first time. They pleaded with her, searching for redemption, but the redemption wasn't hers to give. What did she know about God? So Evelyn offered the next best thing.

"If there is a God, then I'm sure he'll listen. That's what he's there for, right?"

The woman rose from the table and turned away from Evelyn. Over her shoulder she said, "God does not exist in this town. Only the Executioner can free the righteousness and punish those who deserve it. I think it's time for me to go now." She offered a morose wave before she disappeared into the dingy café.

After their conversation, Evelyn speculated she had twenty minutes to curfew without any whereabouts of the university. The town wasn't very big, no more than a few square miles, but the rolling hillsides and sheer mountain cliffs graced with prolific sequoias and winding roads hid the true vastness of Amherst. Without any guidance Evelyn wandered the hazy streets like a nomad, counting down each minute until curfew would force her to claim sanctuary in one of the derelict shops.

Like an executive late for a meeting, Evelyn traversed the streets with determination, the heels of her feet growing tender with every step.

A somber squall advanced toward shore as time ticked away. Trees bristled in the heavy winds. Rain was imminent. She needed to find shelter from the cold, though there were worse things to be afraid of. If her search wasn't completed before nightfall, she'd be forced sleep in an abandoned store or bait shop somewhere.

With only twelve minutes to spare, Evelyn reached the narrow-shouldered road inclining between a sharp hillside and a steep serrated mountain. At the intersection Evelyn spotted a road sign labeled 'University Drive' with an arrow that pointed up the grade across a deep gorge of uprooted trees.

Evelyn tromped up the road, climbing higher and deeper into the woods. The air, leaden with moisture, and the spicy fragrance of wet pine needles invigorated her. She was almost there. Her eyes scoured the edge of the forest, peering into the darkness She stood exposed and vulnerable in the streets, but the woods were no safer.

The road ahead narrowed, and as it curved Evelyn noticed the yellow caution tape stretched from the barranca to the hillside. Just beyond, a wooden barricade stood before the washed out remains of the road. The cliff to her left had collapsed from the torrential waters and brought the road with it. Tree trunks and telephone poles speared the earth like splintered toothpicks. Crossing would be impossible. To her right a vista point overlooked Amherst nestled in the cove. Roads were laid out in a simple grid until the edges of town where they snaked various directions into the pine forests.

Nightmare Eve

Another road arched along the narrow beach, around the sheer cliff side and ascended into the mountain. If there was another road to the university, that would be it. Her eyes traveled University Drive back down to the village streets crisscrossing between the buildings. Just a straight stretch from here to the alternate road.

Through the night, above the rooftops and vacant store windows, echoing through the cove came the haunted melody of the chimes, signaling the start of curfew. Night was upon her and the palpable darkness sifted through the town. The others would be in their homes, the doors locked and windows shut and curtains drawn. They'd sit in silence, surrounded by loved ones among a single candle to keep out the darkness and push away their fear. They were home and protected, and Evelyn could see the rooftops of their home. All she had to do was listen carefully and follow the chimes. Then she began her descent into Amherst, a descent to hell.

Chapter 15

Evelyn followed the road past a decrepit warehouse made of wood and rusted sheet metal that curled around its edges. A segment of the roof had collapsed, exposing manufacturing equipment to the elements. The machinery, with an unidentifiable purpose both strange and mangled looking, had rusted like the roof and the floorboards below had warped and cracked. Virginia creeper tangled its way along the front of the building and then roped its way across the roof and clung to the gutter. Behind the warehouse, a nearly empty lumberyard with cranes and logging trucks could be seen. When the wind caught the hillside just right, a malodorous scent, like mold, decay and cat piss, wafted through the air. Evelyn's nose wrinkled. Other than Evelyn, nothing seemed to live or move. Even the cobwebs in the broken out windows appeared abandoned.

Nightmare Eve

At last Evelyn reached the location of the chimes. She had expected to find some kind of civic building, like a town hall, a clock tower or even a post office, but instead a large cathedral stretched above her. It wasn't like the cathedrals she was used to seeing with beautiful brightly colored stained glass and cheerful pale paint and lavish garden. This one was much different; a temple painted in cherry-brown with black trim and concaved arches embellished with unrecognizable pictographs carved into the wood. Evelyn looked closer. Were they demons? Evelyn stood at the entrance and stared at the dark and forbidden entrance that rose high above her, an obelisk of horror. This was not a temple of godliness, but not Satanic either. Evelyn had seen many temples from all over the world in her travels, and she'd been able to spot the subtle nuances of architectures that revealed their history through every carving and every wooden nail. This temple was used in worship by a religion that pre-dated any form of Christianity, long ago before the invention of God or Satan. This cathedral was her only place to escape the ascending nightmare befallen Amherst. From the entrance, Evelyn heard the chimes in the courtyard. She mounted the steps and reached for the iron door.

Evelyn didn't recognize the carvings in the door or in the iron handle. The rusted metal felt abrasive against her smooth palms. Rusty hinges creaked as the wooden doors groaned. As they opened she was greeted by spicy and sweet incense in a musty room.

The stark interior of the temple was just as she'd expected with rows of blood-crimson carpet over dark brown wooden floors. Rows of pews faced the pulpit, which was lined with purple and gold silk. The stagnant air in the windowless room, engulfed in dancing shadows from lit candles and a luxurious chandelier above, felt heavy with moisture. The smell of mold grew stronger.

Evelyn stepped past a tall stone column that reached the ceiling draped with expensive dark purple and black silk. She gasped when she spotted the figure perched in the second row of pews. She recognized the grim-faced woman from the French café forty-five minutes ago. She leaned forward, her head raised to see the confessional depicting a massive creature, the Executioner, above the door. Below was an inscription of some ancient Asian language.

Evelyn crept down the aisle, her footsteps imprinted in the dust gathering on the floor. She looked over her shoulder at the grim-faced woman, head bowed in glimmering half-light. In the sorrowful atmosphere she appeared like a ghost. Just beyond the grim-faced woman, along the wall, Evelyn spotted a narrow door as tall as any other, but narrower.

When Evelyn brought her foot down over the first step, the chimes went silent.

The citizens of Amherst were bound by curfew, barred from the streets and garrisoned into their homes as refugees of the night.

The grim-faced woman rose to her feet and ambled at the pace of a funeral march to the wooden booth. She closed the door behind her. The sound of the latch echoed through the cathedral. Her soft whimpers echoed throughout the room.

Just knowing she was in the presence of another human calmed her, but standing alone now, a shadow passed over Evelyn's bereaving heart and she became overwhelmed with a deep sorrow and a tinge of fear.

She grasped the spherical door handle, cool and damp in her hand, and pulled open the narrow door that journeyed into another section of the cathedral with smaller rows of pews and a second pulpit used for private religious ceremonies. While the main room held approximately thirty pews, this private hall contained only seven and was lavishly decorated with fresh ferns and ancient black and gold symbols embroidered on decorative royal purple silk tapestries. A faint shuffling sound followed by a wheezing made her pause. She wasn't the only one in the room.

Nightmare Eve

Mr. Morgan appeared from behind the podium.

Evelyn relaxed.

"What are you doing here?" Mr. Morgan scolded. "Don't you know it's past curfew?"

"I was looking for the university, but—"

"The road to the university is closed," he said. "It's this damn weather. There's an evil breath in the air and it's changing things. Not just the town, but the people too. I thought I was the only one, but you're starting to see it too, aren't you, Evelyn?"

Evelyn didn't know what to believe anymore. There was definitely something abnormal about the other townspeople in both patois and ethos. Even Mr. Morgan.

"I don't know what's happened to this town," Evelyn clenched her arms at her side. "I just want to find my fiancé and his little girl."

The old man pointed with his bony finger to the end of the dark hallway. "If you're hoping to find them at the university, there's a back door at the end of the hall that will lead you to a path. Follow the path to the only other road to the university. The other roads are washed out. I don't suggest you go. At least not tonight."

"Do you think it will be dangerous?"

"These coastal storms aren't like the ones inland. You don't want to be caught up in them. The roads could crumble and you might find yourself buried in a mudslide or sinkhole or swept away in a flash flood. Or worse. The church isn't the most inviting place to be, but it's warm and out of the rain. Plus you're with good company."

Evelyn cracked a smile. Though her feet ached and her legs felt rubbery from exploring, she'd never be able to sleep knowing that David and Ivy were out there somewhere in this hellish nightmare.

She glanced to the strange statue of a man bound in chains, his mouth twisted open in an agonizing scream. A chill quaked her spine.

Mr. Morgan caught her staring at the other paintings between the tapestry-lined walls. "This town was founded on a religion that predates Christianity by thousands of years. It takes more than prayers to find answers here. It takes a will to survive. You learn to fight. This place is a hungry little town that feasts on the flies of guilt that buzz around your head, much like our friend in the confessional booth. The key part of recovery and healing is forgiveness. That we forgive ourselves and we forgive those who hurt us."

Evelyn looked at the confessional booth. Faint whimpers and an occasional sob permeated the silence.

Mr. Morgan said, "She'll find solace soon enough." He turned to her, his knuckles white as he gripped the cane. "We all will eventually. You'll find what you're looking for through the exit in the back. When you're ready, follow the street up the hill."

Evelyn nodded and turned away from the old man, but before she exited the room he called out to her. Evelyn stopped and glanced over her shoulder.

"I hope you find the answers you're looking for," he said. "And be careful out there."

Evelyn faced the door. With a slight nudge, it swung open with a rusty scream. On the other side was a narrow hallway too dark to see more than a few feet ahead. The walls were made of rough concrete and stained with rust-colored water.

Once she stepped through the door, it closed behind her and Evelyn continued her decent into the darkness.

Chapter 16

Evelyn braced herself against the wall's rough surface. She used her fingertips to guide herself forward, taking each step with caution. The eyes could never adjusted to this kind of darkness, like being in a narrow cavern a hundred feet underground and just as dank too.

The door at the end led into another room. The first thing she noticed was the damp odor, stagnant and musty, the smell of soggy carpets and rotting trees.

She neared the end of the hall, which opened up to a large room with grey rafters that had splintered and crumbled to the broken pews below. Water streamed from the cracks in the roof. Above, Evelyn could see the stormy night sky and below puddles collected on the warped floors. The odor became a miasma of sour decay.

Near the back of the room, where a pulpit once stood, the wall had caved in and filled the room with mud and boulders the size of a truck from a mudslide. The entire back section of the cathedral had collapsed under the encroaching earth, slipping down the mountainside.

She moved along the row of pews. Plaster crumbled from the wall on her right. Ahead, muddy water tricked out from und the doors. A rock the size of a bowling tumbled down the wall of mud and crashed into the ground. One wrong step and she'd be crushed.

Evelyn stayed close to the wall when she could as she crawled over broken timber, chunks of cement and tangled wires. She struggled when one of the wires snagged her shoe and she reached back to free herself.

When she came to her feet her eyes fell on a horrendous version of the confessional in the other side of the cathedral. This booth was taller now, stretching to the remains of the cathedral's ceiling. At the top, razor wire and wooden spikes crowned the both. The front was stained with blood. Inside, the woman's sobs echoed up the chamber and into the night sky.

Evelyn knocked. The sobbing continued undisturbed. Evelyn was about to turn away when the door creaked open and Evelyn found herself staring into an empty confessional booth splattered and dripping with fresh blood and rain through the exposed roof. The stench of death that came with it made her gag.

Water droplets continued to dilute the crimson to dark pink puddles on the gritty wooden seat. Evelyn slammed the door closed and listened. The room was silent. No more sobbing. The room shuddered against the whirl of ocean breeze and a light sprinkle wet her face. Her eyes darted across the room to the door where she had entered, but now the door was gone, replaced by a solid wall.

She pressed her hand against it certain there was a door there.

Nightmare Eve

Looking around the room, Evelyn saw the support beams had broken in half and crushed the only other door in the room. The busted walls and piles of mud had broken in through the wall leaving a space just big enough to fit through. If she could break through the flimsy booth wall, she might be able to stand on the bench and bust through the back of the booth. She returned to the booth and reached for the second door where the priest or whoever was in charge would sit and her the confession. She pulled open the door expecting another gruesome sight. She was surprised to see the booth had already been damaged. All Evelyn needed to do was break off a single thin piece of wood to climb on the bench and crawl through the gap.

Usually rain made everything smell fresh, but not here. It still felt polluted. Clouds churned like a raging black river in the sky.

Evelyn lowered her left foot onto the step. The porch groaned again. She eased herself down the stairs to the stone path below. As she pressed onward, the temple was lost in the darkness behind her. Evelyn grew uneasy. All normal sounds of forest nightlife, like chirping crickets, hooting owls and bleating frogs were absent. Evelyn hoped that was due to the approaching storm rather than from predators. It was unnatural for a rural town to be so dark and silent. Evelyn hesitated moving any further. The eroded stone path beneath her feet had been washed over by mud. She looked behind her. Which direction had she come from?

Unable to turn back, unsure of where to go next, Evelyn tried to remember Mr. Morgan's directions. There should be one road still open that would lead her up a slight hill to the university. She couldn't miss it. Mr. Morgan was sure of it. As long as she moved on she'd eventually find it.

After tromping through the mud, past rows of houses on the outskirts, violin music rose from the silence. She listened in hopes to determine the source. It was coming from somewhere ahead of her.

Ten more steps and she jumped at the sound of rustling from somewhere close. An image of Dr. Dullahan's body flashed in her head, his bloody body saturated from rain and streaked with mud and wet grass.

Her skin pricked with nervousness. The veil of night obscured her visibility, but she stared deep and ignored the instincts that urged her to run. Was this how the doctor felt before he was murdered? The silhouette of a man appeared at the edge of visibility. He stood immobile, almost as if he were frozen in place. Even though the darkness obscured his features, his figure was unmistakable.

"David!"

Evelyn lunged for him, her face flushed with the sting of tears, but when he turned around she saw she'd made a mistake.

"Oh. You're not David. Sorry, I thought you were someone else." Evelyn dropped her gaze to her feet. She felt foolish, but with his tall and muscular frame, fair skin and dark eyes beneath cascades of black eyelashes, he displayed uncanny resemblance to her fiancé. Their differences were apparent. David often kept his hair buzzed and face smooth in accordance to the United States Naval codes. This man had fashionable caramel-colored hair parted slightly off to the side that grew down to his earlobes and thick, dark brown stubble from his neck to his cheekbones.

He ran his fingers through his neck-length brown hair while his other hand rested in his pockets making him appear casual and relaxed—a strange contrast to Evelyn's heightened state. Evelyn grew tense. It seemed there were only two people who stayed out past curfew: victims and killers. Which one was he?

"You're looking for someone too?" he asked from several feet away.

Evelyn gave a suspicious nod. "Yes."

Nightmare Eve

He gestured toward the empty streets. "I'm surprised to see anyone out after sunset."

"I'm looking for a way to the University." Evelyn said. "Do you know where I could find it?"

The man cocked his head to the side and raised a curious brow. "Haven't you heard? All the roads are closed due to the mudslides. If there was an open road, it'd be that way"—pointed behind him—"just beyond the fence. You're not going there tonight are you?"

He lowered his arm and turned to face her, his face scrunched with concern.

"I have to try."

The man frowned, but he must've seen the determined expression on her face because he took a side step allowing her to pass. "Be careful though. I know this town inside and out and it's easy to get disoriented once the marine layer settles. If you get lost, just keep an eye out for the lighthouse. It'll keep you pointed west."

Evelyn glanced in both directions and reluctantly gestured to the right.

He shook his head, smiled, and then pointed in the opposite direction.

"Thanks."

She proceeded to take a few steps in that direction when he jumped forward, startling her. He stopped a foot from her.

"You know, I was supposed to go to this recital at the auditorium with someone, but I think I've been stood up. The walk isn't very far, but perhaps you'd like some company? I could show you the way. Safety in numbers."

"A recital? After curfew? Who'd attend?"

The man shrugged and held up a pair of tickets. "Me. And you I hope."

She took a moment to make up her mind. Her eyes switched between the darkness ahead, dreading to face it alone, the tickets in his hand, and his eyes, which glanced nervously when she took too long to decide. He shifted his weight from one foot to the other and Evelyn realized he too was nervous to go alone.

"Alright. Lead the way," she said.

"I'm Hunter." His smile was genuine.

Hers wasn't. "Evelyn."

Just as Hunter predicted, as they walked, the marine layer draped across the seaside town creating a fine white curtain that gave the hillside a ghost-like atmosphere. The treetops rustled and swayed but the surrounded mountains acted like a shield blocking the stronger gusts. The sprinkle of rain continued and Evelyn imagined it would soon become torrential. They reached the fence Hunter had mentioned, made of thin boards with sharpened points like medieval wooden daggers. Beyond the fence, chunks of pavement crumbled into a washed out sinkhole.

"Wait." Hunter instructed.

Evelyn stopped at his outstretched hand. It took her a moment to notice the slimy-looking red heap in the road up ahead.

"What is that? Some kind of animal?" Patches of fur was matted with sticky red blood from its red bloated hide, mangled beyond identification. The creature's blood flowed into the pavement cracks down into the sinkhole.

Hunter looked to the woods. "These mountains are full of wild animals. Someone probably struck it coming down the road."

"Could it have been attacked by a cougar? Or something else?"

Hunter thought a moment. "What kind of animal could skin it like this?"

A thunderous boom resonated in the distance followed by more raindrops. The whisper of leaves rustled through the branches. Hunter raised his head to the violent skies. "We need to keep moving."

Nightmare Eve

Usually storms brought in fresh air, but there was something different about this approaching storm. The air remained stagnant somehow, like breathing the same recycled air, circulating with nowhere to go. They moved onward, scanning the road ahead for dangers until they came across the sign wobbling in the gusty air.

Westminster University.

An arrow pointed up to a sharp left curve between a pair of stone pillars.

"Come on, we're almost there," Hunter breathed.

Over the ocean, lightning cracked the sky. Evelyn saw the landscape illuminated by the pale blue flash: many large branches snapped from trees and were scattered across the muddy trails. Entire trees had toppled over, loosening the soil, which spewed like a muddy geyser over the roads, liquefying the mountainside. The thought of being buried alive was suddenly a very real possibility; she stood close to Hunter, trusting him to guide them safely. As they neared the apex of the mountain, the winds grew stronger and her clothes did little to keep her dry. Each lightning strike gave the marine layer an ethereal glow.

They moved quickly while the sprinkle turned to rain and they stood at the entrance to a vast parking lot. To their right, a small ivy and fern-laden wooden toolshed housed rakes, shovels and other tools.

"It's too dangerous to cross the parking lot now," said Hunter. "We'll be lightning rods in this storm. We can probably reach the front entrance by following the paths in the woods and staying low. I'll go first to make sure it's clear and then come back for you."

Evelyn's chest tightened.

"It could be dangerous. You'll be safe here." Hunter reassured. "Stay low and don't let anyone see you."

Before Evelyn could protest, he bolted around the tool shed and cut the corner of the parking lot before launching himself above a row of ferns and landing out of sight in the woods. More lightning illuminated the sky.

Evelyn pressed her back against the tool shed, blocking the wind and rain. She lowered herself to her knees and shivered despite the tepid air and wondered why everything still smelled so stale.

It was the darkness, she feared. It's coming.

She hugged her legs and thought of David's smile and how badly she wished to see it again. She pictured Ivy as she sometimes sat at the dinning room table, hunched over a piece of construction paper with crayons scattered around her. She'd watch Ivy until the moment David would come home from work and she'd leap across the room to hug and kiss him. It was the second best part of her day, the first being those moments in bed with him every night, curled under the weight of his arms as they waited for sleep. Those memories seemed like a dissipating dream now, like the rain-corroded landscape around her. She felt lost, plunging farther into this woeful nightmare.

Evelyn sensed movement and released her legs in order to slide behind a large cinnamon fern.

A horrific scream sliced through the howling wind followed by heavy thuds and the sound of rapid footsteps on pavement.

Staying low just as Hunter instructed, Evelyn maneuvered around the fern for a better view of the woman fleeing across the parking lot. Raindrops pattered against her face.

A woman approximately forty-five years old with wet hair matted against her face shrieked as lightning illuminated the sky. She flailed across the parking lot and glanced terrified behind her. The woman looked familiar, but Evelyn couldn't remember where she'd seen her.

Evelyn rose to her feet, about to step out of hiding to assist the poor woman but froze when she saw the silhouette of an enormous creature, at least ten, maybe twelve feet tall,

Nightmare Eve

hunched over plowing forward on two sturdy legs as thick as tree trunks. Even through the rain, fog and flashes of lightning, she recognized the monster as the one that chased her off the path on her arrival. The Executioner, they had called him.

In its bulging hand, a long metal rod with a crescent blade at one end and a long chain with a massive spiked ball at the other dragged along the pavement. The screeching sound cut through the night.

In long, swift strides the Executioner advanced on the woman. A loud clank and something shot through the fog. The woman screamed again. Blood spurted from her mouth. The Executioner let out a grunt as it gave a strong yank to the chain, causing the woman to fly backward. She hit the pavement hard enough that her skull bounced off the surface three times, each leaving a red splatter bigger than the last.

Her scream faded into a dull, pathetic whimper and even in the darkness and through the fog, Evelyn could make out the glint of the crescent blade.

She *had* seen this before—in an article from the local newspaper back at the Shady Nook Lodge. Mrs. Rosecrans, who'd been discovered the next day by hikers had been murdered—her body sliced in two.

Evelyn knew it was impossible, but here she was seeing it with her own eyes.

The monster raised its massive arms, gripping the pole. The blade at the end made a whistling sound as it first traveled through the air and then into Mrs. Rosecran's torso. The woman's viscera tumbled out from her severed torso like a bowl of spilled pasta and then let out a final whimper as she frantically tried to scoop her entrails back inside her torso. A moment later, Mrs. Rosecrans was dead.

Evelyn would've vomited if her hands weren't still clamped over her mouth. She forced herself to breath and remained still, watching as the killer's silhouette continued across the parking lot. Where the asphalt met the woods, the Executioner suddenly stopped.

In the thick fog, the Executioner appeared to grow bigger.

No, Evelyn thought. Not bigger.

Closer.

Chapter 17

She turned and immediately slipped in the mud, but caught herself against a tree. Below, Evelyn could see a steep ravine scattered with sharp rocks and broken branches.

The executioner barreled through the trees like a bulldozer, his shoulders busting and ripping off the bark, splintering wood and crushing everything beneath his thunderous footsteps.

Without thinking, Evelyn swung open the shed door and dove inside and then immediately cursed herself for knowing that the Executioner could easily rip through the shed just as he easily as he ripped through the woods. There was nowhere else to hide and she dared not to outrun him. His movements were slow, but his strides were long and could easily reach her if she tried.

Inside the storage shed she found a variety of rakes, a rusty wheel, probably from a bike tire, a chainsaw, garden hose, cables and a power generator. She didn't have a plan when she moved, fueled on adrenaline. She flipped the lever and the generator grumbled to life. Sparks flew to the two power cords, one black, one red with a clamp at each end.

The monster let out a deep angry snarl, as he swung the blade. She screamed. Splintered wood exploded around her as the Executioner tore the shed apart. The medieval blade struck the wall, the attached chain wrapped in his beefy hands.

Evelyn launched forward with the cables and clamped them to the chain. A loud snap of electricity lit up the air in hot blue and white, the current traveling down the chain and into the Executioner.

Evelyn hobbled through the shattered remains of the wall and hurtled across the parking lot ignoring the lightning and rain. She locked eyes on the woods not wanting to see Mrs. Rosecrans' disembodied torso and wide, dead eyes staring back at her.

Evelyn didn't stop running—past the parking lot and into the woods until she descended into the suburban valley of the University District. Her lungs burned for air, her legs stumbled and she collapsed into the muddy earth.

Her heart still racing, she climbed to her feet and waited for the Executioner to emerge from the marine layer, but he was gone.

She choked for air and walked in small circles letting her heart have a chance to catch up. When she caught her breath she stood and surveyed the neighborhood. The fog came in thick and clung to the ground leaving only the rooftops exposed to the sky. A break in the storm clouds had allowed a bit of moonlight to shine through, illuminating the neighborhood in ominous ghostly white. Evelyn could see by the surrounding clouds and occasional flash of lightning this break would be brief.

Nightmare Eve

She moved from block to block. Homes were dark and the street lamps were out. Each road intersected at a four-way stop in perfectly symmetrical blocks. Carefully groomed yards and unvaried landscape reminded her of *The Stepford Wives.* She figured this neighborhood housed families, faculty, students and alumni of Westminster University. Evelyn crossed to the adjacent block. Water flowed in rivulets through the gutters along with leaves, pebbles and other debris. She scanned the sidewalks for any sign of movement, either from the Executioner that might be tracking her, Hunter, or anyone else brave enough to break curfew.

Through the fog, she spotted a dim warm light from a house at the end of the block. As she stood at the end of their driveway, she could see the family inside. The number on the mailbox read *Norris 225.*

A young boy approximately Ivy's age played rambunctiously around the living room with toy airplanes, swooping them close to his father's face and then across the riving room before crashing it into a stack of blocks. Mr. Norris, a handsome man in his late thirties or early forties rocked in a billowy chair reading a book about biomechanics. Strange their lights were on past curfew.

From somewhere close, Evelyn heard the Executioner's distinctive growl. She had to warn them. She had to call Sheriff Rhett.

Evelyn raced up the steps and pounded her fists against the door, shouting to the residents. She heard movement inside the next rom, but no one came to the door. She knocked again, louder this time.

When they still didn't answer, she moved along the porch to the wide picture window facing the street. Just before she peered in, she caught a glimpse of her reflection. Her scratched face was streaked with dried blood and dirt, dark circles beneath her eyes and saturated hair matted to her skull. Was she really as crazy as she looked and sounded? Her eyes focused back on the child playing so sweetly and innocent on the carpet. Evelyn balled her fist and pounded them against the window.

"Hey! Please, I need help!" She screamed at the window. A glimmer of hope sparkled within her as the young boy with his pudgy round face and eager eyes looked up from his airplane.

"Yes! Over here!" Evelyn called out.

The boy rose from the floor and scrambled to the couch at the window. He steadied himself just an inch from the opposite side of the glass and peered through her. "Please, I need to use your phone!"

He tilted his head curiously, lips twisted into a deep pout.

Then an image flashed in her mind: the missing boy on the poster. Outside the Laundromat when she came across all those flyers for missing people. She couldn't remember his name, but she distinctly remembered his chubby face.

"No," she muttered. She covered her mouth with her hand. A knot formed in the pit of her stomach. She flipped over the doormat in hopes of finding a spare key. She reached for flowerpots and checked the doorframe among other places spare house keys are hidden.

"Did you hear something?" Evelyn heard Mrs. Norris ask from inside.

Mr. Norris replied, "I don't hear anything. Probably just the storm."

The woman nodded and returned to the room with a stack of folded washcloths in her hands, sat them on the chair, then took a sip from a white ceramic mug.

Evelyn banged on the window again, as hard as she could. "Please you have to open the door!"

Mr. Norris looked up from his book as his wife poked her head around the corner into the living room.

Nightmare Eve

"I'm sure you heard that." Her face tightened with concern. She glanced at the front door.

Mr. Norris placed his book on the table beside him and strolled across the room. He approached the front door. There was a click. The door swung open. He stared at her.

"Please, I need to use your phone. I need to call the police, there's someone trying to kill me and your son—"

"Is someone outside?" Mrs. Norris interrupted. "Who on Earth would dare to be out in this weather? Especially after curfew."

Mr. Norris shook his head. "There's no one out here, hon. Good news though, it appears the rain has let up."

Evelyn's mouth fell open. He couldn't see her! He turned away from the door but before he could shut it, Evelyn stepped inside the home.

The first thing she noticed was the scent, like spiced apple and cinnamon tea and with a juicy roast beef. The temperature was warm and full of life, not at all like the stagnant air outside. In the kitchen, Mrs. Norris returned to her mug while Mr. Norris settled back in his chair and retrieved his book.

The clank of metal against pavement echoed from the street. It was too late, the Executioner was already here. There was nothing she could do now except watch history repeat itself. The family was already dead and Evelyn was here to witness it, just as she had with Mrs. Rosecrans.

Mr. Norris's eyes grew frantic. He shot up and bumped his wife's mug off the side table. It didn't break, but the tea inside sloshed, spilling over the carpet. The young boy looked up, startled.

"Daddy?" The little boy scrambled to his feet and rushed over to his father. "What's that noise?"

A heavy thud shuddered the porch.

"Get away from the door!" Mr. Norris shrieked at his wife.

Nightmare Eve

It was the back door that exploded inward like a bomb, shattered to hundreds of sharp fragments.

"*Run!*" Evelyn screamed and dove to protect the child.

In a cloud of dust and splinters, the hulking creature, as wide as the hallway, appeared.

The room filled with screams. The child, just out of reach darted for his father. She raced to the hall door and slammed it closed. It wouldn't hold, but she hoped it would buy them some time.

Mr. Norris rushed for the nearest object—a fire poker—and Mrs. Norris sprinted across the living room where her son let out a high-pitched shriek. The Executioner exploded through the hall door and in a clean swipe, severed Mrs. Norris at the waist. She continued to take another three steps before her torso slid off her waist and hit the carpet with a wet *smack!* She reached for her son and emitted a wet choking sound as blood spouted from her mouth and puddled around her. Her legs staggered forward like a drunken walk at the end of an all-night party, and then fell to Mrs. Norris's torso.

Evelyn screamed and pointed to the kitchen. "This way!" Still, the Norris family couldn't hear her and Evelyn watched helplessly as the father swung the fire poker in vain.

The Executioner's right eye twitched furiously beneath the eyehole cut from the burlap sack tied over his head and around his neck. He flicked the chain, which caught the father's wrist, and then yanked, popping Mr. Norris's hand off with a swift snap. His hand thudded to the floor and Mr. Norris let out a painful screech. With a hefty swing, like a mallet at a carnival game, the Executioner brought the blade down vertically through the man's skull, sliced through his torso and stuck into the floor between Mr. Norris's legs. He froze, completely immobile, his eyes swiveling frantically in his skull. A small line of blood dripped from his nose, and his lips parted as if he were trying to speak. He let out a small croak and his left side peeled

Nightmare Eve

away followed by his right, both landing in a gory heap beside both halves of his wife.

The room, including Evelyn, was painted red. Evelyn reached again for the boy who was shocked into silence.

Without mercy, the Executioner snatched the boy before Evelyn could. She screamed, reached for his kicking legs to free the young Norris boy. Using his left hand, the Executioner's balled fist slammed into Evelyn. She landed hard against the table knocking the lamp to the floor shattering it. The room fell into darkness. She couldn't see and she didn't want to. The sounds of the boy whimpering were terrible enough. There was a sharp gasp, a quick yelp, and a sickening crunch. It all lasted no more than a split second, but the sound echoed horribly in her head.

There was a moment of stillness before the heavy crunch of a massive footstep over broken furniture. He was coming for her next.

Blindly, she dove through the debris, somehow managing to evade a blow from his powerful arms. She stayed on her hands and knees, wooden splinters, broken glass and sharp wires piercing and tearing her flesh. She lunged forward, bringing herself to her feet and leapt through the gaping hole where the back door once was. She tumbled across the wood porch, her heart pounding so hard she thought she'd succumb to cardiac arrest. She couldn't stop now though. She looked back expecting to see him barreling over her in mid-swing, but instead she saw the empty doorframe of a weathered house that appeared abandoned for decades.

Dust swirled in the doorway. The only sound was her rapid heartbeat and deep breaths. Around her, the neighborhood had welcomed the sopping nightmare city made of water and wood.

She pounded her fists into the wooden porch, drawing blood. "What is going on?" She screamed.

Nightmare Eve

Each window appeared busted out of the withered old house. Even from the porch she could see the room was empty, free of any furniture and the roof had collapsed in the kitchen causing the walls to bubble with moisture and the tile to fade. Around her, massive poles stretched into the sky. Some were made of wood, like the beams beneath the pier while others were made of metal, corroded with copper-colored rust. The roads were no longer asphalt, made of long stretches of wooden planks stretching endlessly into the night. The marine layer remained thick, and from above, rain fell from a crystal clear sky. Frustrated, she kicked her heel against the banister. The beam was soft enough that her foot burst through. The beam crumbled and pieces fell between the wooden planks. Evelyn heard the splash as they disappeared in the ocean below.

Get it together, she told herself. Her eyebrows angled sharply down, her scowl deepened. This world was exactly like the one she had dreamed. Soggy and wet, the very same stench of rotten wood. Same fear, same anger and same hurt. Only unlike her dream, this time she wouldn't give up so easily. She was going to stop the Executioner from murdering again and unearth the truth about her and this town. The answers were out there and nothing was going to stop her from getting them. Not even the Executioner.

Chapter 18

The image of the young Norris boy haunted her mind as she strolled down the pier, lonely and afraid of the alternate cityscape around her.

The black sea roared and crashed against the massive wooden pillars below. The houses now resembling abandoned wood cabins, a city of wood and rust. As Evelyn continued along the creaky boardwalk, she could feel the hungry eyes of the killer watching her from somewhere in the mist. He was out there, she knew. Somewhere in this sleepy village, stalking the alleys and streets. He would inevitably cross paths with her again like a murderous game of chess. Her fiancé was out there, too. She remembered him, losing her in the fog before waking up at the lodge. How could he leave her like this?

She wasn't helpless, she'd demonstrated that before with the crazed woman in the bar and then again with the

Executioner in the storage shed. He was much too powerful for her to kill with her own hands. She'd need some sort of weapon, like the power generator, except stronger. Something that he wouldn't come back from. As for the poor family, there was nothing she could do. The murders had already happened and somehow, through a vision maybe, like a glimpse into the past, she had witnessed their brutal slayings. She'd meant to see it for a reason, but why?

Between fastidious steps, she saw the churning waters between the cracks in the boards. Some of them creaked and groaned under her weight and she hopped over them in case her weight caused them to buckle. If she fell into the waters below, it would mean her death.

She strode past the dark windows of an old building, one of those seedy motels that probably rented by the hour. She cringed. She needed to sleep, but couldn't not knowing David and Ivy might be in trouble.

She walked slowly, trying her best to cope with the tornado of thoughts swirling in her head. She wished her memory would return so she could put all this behind her, but a piece of her refused to let go.

She stopped again and looked at the houses peeking above the marine layer of the University District. Yes, she was sure she was still on the right path, despite the change of the city's aesthetics. The houses still lined both sides of the street, however now they appeared weathered and abandoned like an old western built impossibly over the ocean.

She moved to one of the neighbor's houses and scrambled across what should've been a yard that was now just rows of planks, similar to the boardwalk-like suburban streets, except the property was elevated by a single step. She crossed the planks clunking beneath her feet and approached the window with more conviction than she'd had at the Norris residence. She was sure nobody was home. As far as Evelyn had seen, only a dozen or so people remained in this city built for

Nightmare Eve

more than twenty-thousand, much bigger than she originally thought.

The living room appeared like any other, a couch and a love seat. An over-stuffed, lumpy rocking chair and an old, dusty looking television set that might be found in some grandmother's kitchen somewhere. The doors were jammed shut and splinters of wood had been chipped out of the frame by relentless storms and weight of the sagging edifice.

There was nothing else left to be learned about the neighborhood. Just rows of empty houses. Real life or aqueous nightmare. That was, until Evelyn drew near the end of the block which opened into the wide mouth of Cemetery Park scattered with sepulchers and above-ground grave sites much like in Louisiana, except these graves were encased in wood and adorned with tarnished, serrated wires in a disfigured, rust and wood-filled landscape. In the midst of salty-tepid fog, Evelyn heard the faint sobbing of a woman in bereavement between two grotesque, crumbling caskets splattered crimson and tarnished yellow.

The woman's head bobbed in her hands and rainwater dripped down her chin and puddled at her knees. Evelyn approached her with great consternation.

"It should've been me," she sobbed into her hands. Evelyn noted the flowers on each gravesite were shriveled to black and bound by wire.

Before Evelyn stepped any closer, the bereaving woman climbed to her feet. She didn't seem to notice Evelyn standing only a few gravesites away. The bereaving woman stood and turned her back towards Evelyn before sulking into the murky cemetery atmosphere.

Evelyn strolled over to the grave where the woman once stood and read the names carved into the wood. Selena Lupez had died at age seven and Enrique Lupez, Selena's father, passed away at forty-seven.

Lupez.

Nightmare Eve

She remembered with the clarity of daylight reading in the paper at Shady Nook that Mrs. Maria Lupez had been the only survivor of a horrendous train wreck on the outskirts of Amherst some time ago. She remembered reading that Mrs. Lupez had been on a vacation with her family on a northbound train when intense seasonal weather caused the train to derail and slide into a ravine below. The newspaper had called it a miraculous story of survival, but seeing Maria now looked more tragic than miraculous. It was a mind-shattering experience no one should ever have to live through, not even her worst enemies. Evelyn knew first hand how difficult it was to lose her family, but now she had the chance to get Ivy and David back. There was still hope for her, but for Maria, there was nothing.

Evelyn looked around the rusted cemetery. First the vicious razor wire that curled around the perimeter and then the metal and wood sepulchers streaked with rust and black mold to the scraggly trees with thin black trunks and gnarled leafless branches. Evelyn backed away from the graves and stumbled when her heel caught a warped plank. Her arms shout out while her right palm caught the edge of another barbed wire lined grave and decayed flowers. She yelped in pain and brought her hand to her face in time to see the ruby red pearls of blood seep from the wound.

This wasn't a dream. The city looked the same, but only it was real. Something was wrong with Amherst. Was it some kind of alternate dimension? Evelyn didn't believe in curses, but if such things existed, Amherst was it. There was no way to rationalize it. No scientific explanation so far. She just had to survive.

Evelyn dashed through the cemetery. She didn't care where she was running except that she wanted to get away. She didn't know why this was happening to her, or what she'd done to deserve to be in this living nightmare.

A sick emptiness churned in the pit of her stomach when she thought of the missing pieces of her memory. Maybe there was a reason why she didn't remember everything. Why David had left her—no *abandoned* her. Evelyn made a promise to find David and Ivy and stop the Executioner from hurting anyone anymore. Hell or not, she had to keep going for their sake.

Outside a small bistro, oversized wooden spools replaced the patio furniture surrounded by chairs resembling torture devices. Sharp rusted nails protruded from the armrests. In the middle of the street ahead, a large puddle of dried blood had been smeared across the street. Whatever had been killed had been dragged across the street and into the open doorway of the yogurt shop, leaving a bloody trail of gore in its path. A few steps further, a small storage shed with industrial chains locked the wooden doors in place. The cracks seeped with blood. When she passed, the doors shook violently. Evelyn let out a startled cry and sprinted forward, glancing over her shoulder until whatever nightmare creature behind the doors was lost in the fog.

The towers of Westminster University broke above the mist beyond the train yard. She hoped Hunter had made it safely inside, worried that he'd returned to get her but instead found Mrs. Rosecrans's dead body and Evelyn, missing.

Another blood trail led to the gutter where the upper-half of an animal torso, its dog-like head to its two front paws, lie skinless and eviscerated. The dog-thing's wormy lips curled back and growled while its hallowed out eyes twitched. As she ran passed, it quivered and tried to use its remaining two legs to drag itself across the sodden planks. Looming inside the nearest house, a dark silhouette of a man swayed side-to-side from a noose, his limp arms dangling lifelessly at his side. Evelyn could see the windows in the next room over where a television screen displayed black and white static with sudden flashes of a human eye. Sharp hooks pierced the eyelids, forcing them open. The eye frantically darted, looking in all direction. As Evelyn rushed by, the pupil focused on her and continued to follow her until she was out of sight.

Evelyn's legs grew fatigued. Ahead, the train yard looked foreboding. Whatever creature lived inside, she hoped it was small enough to fight because her legs were too weak to carry herself much longer. It'd been at least a day and a half since she'd eaten and about the same since she last slept.

Train cars, no more than rusted boxes of sheet metal and wood bracings were scattered through the yard in a sinister maze. The wood and metal railroad crumbled in spots; the railroad crossing guard was stuck at a 45-degree angle. She ducked slightly, stepping under. The first passenger car was empty and dark and the second one leaned slightly to the side with cracked windows and smeared with coagulated blood. A huge dent in the side prevented the door from closing properly and was pitched downward from bent hinges. She hated to imagine what horrific creature had been responsible.

She stepped around the final car in the first row and stood between the tracks. The second row was back-to-back with more rusted passenger cars like a wall of metal and wood. Each car appeared vacant and dark except one near the end lit by fluorescent lights and a wide open door. As she drew nearer, she could hear Mrs. Maria Lupez's distinct sobbing from inside. Evelyn reached for the creaky banister, the rough metal scratching against her soft palms, and hoisted herself into the cart.

Evelyn sucked in a deep gasp at blood-splattered car, her eyes falling first on the bereaving woman, Mrs. Lupez, sitting in the back, then to the mangled body of a man in the seat across from her. His skull had been smashed open and hallowed out with strings of gore, bits of flesh and fat stretched out like taffy. His severed left arm, wrenched from his shoulder socket, lay in a bloody mess on the floor. There was a large mound of shredded flesh in the lap of the man. At first Evelyn thought it was his distended belly, but it was too large. She

Nightmare Eve

didn't want to look, but she couldn't tear her eyes away. The small child's head was barely recognizable, huddled against the dead man's chest. With sickened realization, she knew this lump of flesh was Maria's daughter and husband.

Evelyn cried out and covered her eyes, opened them again and looked away. There was no safe place to rest her eyes. "Oh God," she muttered. Bile rose in her sore throat. "Mrs. Lupez, you shouldn't be here. You shouldn't see this." Evelyn fought the dizziness that grew inside her and reached out to tug Mrs. Lupez away. She didn't need to see this.

"It should've been me," sobbed Maria. She sat in the seat in the back "Why did it have to be them? Why couldn't it have been me? Why was I the only one who survived?" She muttered just above a whisper in incoherent thoughts.

Evelyn crept further down the aisle and cautiously approached Maria Lupez. "I'm sorry about your family—"

"I lost everything. Why couldn't I have died with them? Everyone is gone. Everything."

There was a pause where Evelyn was unsure of how to respond. She was never very good at consolation and found it very uncomfortable when people cried in front of her, but she couldn't leave Maria out here in a place like this.

"I know it's hard, but they would've wanted you to go on. They were your family and they loved you. This place, there's something wrong with it. It's dangerous. Think of your family and how happy they'd want you to be. Don't let them down."

Maria Lupez raised her eyes for the first time, her eyes a burning glare. "And what do you know about family?" she hissed.

Evelyn was taken back by the woman's feral tone.

"Where's *your* family?" She stood up.

"I—I'm not—" Evelyn's voice wavered.

"You didn't love them anyway!" Maria screeched. "I loved my family, I would've died for them! It should've been me!"

Her voice warbled, stretching low and deep then speeding up in a high frequency, then dropped low again like a warped record, much like the drunk woman at the bar.

"*It should've been me!*"

Her eyes grew black as if a dark curtain had befallen them. The tears streaming down her face became black and inky against her white skin. Purple and blue veins throbbed beneath her translucent flesh.

"*It should have been me!*" She screeched again and reached out with her decayed hand to Evelyn's throat.

Evelyn ducked low and scrambled back toward the exit, slipping on the wet passenger car floors. The woman advanced on her, but Evelyn recovered and lunged out the doorway, leaping from the rear of the car and landing on the wooden ground with a heavy *thunk!*

She could still hear Mrs. Lupez groaning as she stalked down the aisle toward the door.

Evelyn searched the train yard for anything to defend herself with, but there was nothing on this side of the wall of train cars. She sprinted forward gasping for air, hoping her legs would stay strong enough for another battle. Her eyes scanned the wall of train cars, hoping for a break wide enough for her to slip through and escape the creature that Mrs. Lupez had become, but the wall of cars ended abruptly along with the intersecting planks that made up the ground. Even though the air was somewhat calm, down below, the waves thrashed as if a heavy storm had tore the ocean. Behind her, the thing that had once been Maria Lupez grunted and hobbled closer, dragging her clunky feet against the wooden planks. Without any other place to run, Evelyn fell to her knees, slid on to her belly and pulled herself under the train car and waited in silence.

Maria emerged from the fine white mist.

Evelyn held her breath as she watched the creature's broken feet stop in front of her. The creature stood for what seemed like an eternity before she continued forward.

Evelyn exhaled and shut her eyes and allowed her forehead to rest on the cold, harsh texture of the wooden ground. She drew in another deep breath while enjoying the moment of rest and relief. Part of her wished that she could fall asleep here and wake up in her own bed with David, but she knew that wouldn't happen. Feeling confident, she opened her eyes and screamed.

Maria Lupez scrambled under the rows of cars, shooting toward her with the agility and quickness of an insect, her limbs working mechanically like a spider, one over the other.

Evelyn yanked herself from underneath the car and stood in the maze of trains unsure of where to run. She bolted to the left as Maria scrambled from underneath and stood, her feet bending, body contorting and bones cracking. Maria moved quickly, too fast for Evelyn to outrun.

Evelyn's eyes darted between each row of train cars until she spotted a break, barely wide enough to squeeze through. She sprinted towards it. Behind her, the monster clawed the air and Evelyn felt the brush of her rotting fingers against her hair.

Evelyn bounded through the gap and ran between the tracks of another row of train cars. She couldn't keep running forever. She'd inevitably back herself into a corner, but another break in the train cars revealed a lever. She darted to the right, evading another one of Maria's swipes, and grasped the lever tightly, and pulled.

There was a sharp crack. Just as the creature darted between the train cars, the entire train rolled backwards. A sickening crunch echoed through the train yard as Mrs. Lupez monster was crushed between them. Blood spewed from the creature's mouth and nose, her crushed ribs punctured her internal organs. She shook violently and let out a mournful garbled wail of defeat and then slumped forward, dead.

Nightmare Eve

Pure luck, Evelyn told herself. She was grateful to have it. She inhaled a relaxing sigh and tilted her head back to let the light rain fall directly on her face. When she opened them again, the world around her melted away into the sea, washing away the dilapidated textures of the wooden buildings and revealed normal asphalt roads and grassy hillsides once again. The cars in the train yard appeared normal with large breaks between, opening up to a pathway to a normal, however vacant looking university.

Evelyn felt her spirit lift slightly. Even if she couldn't save Maria, at least she tried to help as much as she could. Like so many others in this town, Maria suffered from a great loss, a terrible tragedy that corroded away her consciousness and pushed her to the desperate brink of sanity. A tragedy like that would consume anyone, no matter how strong or brave they were.

Evelyn, grateful to be alive, felt cheered by the soft melody of a violin that suddenly rose from somewhere in the town. It sound so faint, it disappeared with every crunch of pavement beneath her shoes. She turned around listening carefully. It sounded strange for her to hum along to the music as she nervously eyed her surroundings for any dangerous creature that may strike.

She felt less like humming when she saw in the yard of the suburban home to her right, a stretcher overturned in the grass and a body tangled, mostly covered with a white sheet on it's side. A bloodied hand protruding from the stained sheets wriggled its grass-stained fingers, beckoning her closer.

Chapter 19

Amherst had not returned to the normalcy that she'd hoped for.

Sure, the quaggy boardwalk of crumbling edifices and spongy, rotten wood had been washed away by the cleansing rain, but the overturned stretcher laying in the yard with pale, decomposing fingers fluttering in the grass meant nothing had returned normal.

A nervous whimper croaked from her dry throat. Barely visible through the pine and maple trees, was what looked to be a vast medical facility rather than a university. She stared in brief silence at the mysterious building looming above the trees and she felt discouraged by the formal, but sinister decorative columns standing like guards to Victor Frankenstein's castle.

She caught a glimpse of a photograph approximately the size of a full sheet of paper, framed, and propped up on a card table adorned with wilting flowers and melted candles. The dusty picture frame appeared to have been neglected and long forgotten.

Evelyn ambled up the flight of stairs to the front door, more nervous than her first day of school. She sucked in a deep nervous breath, reluctant of what she might find inside. Monsters? Zombie students? Severed limbs? Her imagination went wild. She wanted to believe it was just a regular university like any other, but she knew that was not the case. Nothing in this town was normal and she doubted Westminster University would be any different.

She pulled open the door and stepped into the sterile hallway of the university.

The narrow *L* shaped lobby branched into other corridors and offices. Directly in front of Evelyn was an empty receptionist's desk with various folders and stacks of paperwork. Meetings, dates, times, room numbers were scribbled across notepads, none of which seemed relevant, but her heart leapt when she spotted the phone.

She picked it up. Just as she expected there was no dial tone.

At the end of the corridor she noticed the stone texture of a fountain, dry of water. Her footsteps echoed off the yellowing tile floors and dingy white walls. It seemed so formally organized like a mental institution rather than a university dormitory. More corridors in strange layouts with emergency exits added to case that it was, in fact, a mental institution.

After she had made a large square, Evelyn returned to find a young woman sitting at the dried up fountain. She sat on the ledge her ankles crossed, her body angled away from Evelyn so that she didn't see her approach.

"Excuse me," Evelyn said soft as to not startle the poor girl.

She spun around and Evelyn saw she was no older than nineteen, very pretty in a simple way with creamy pale skin and

Nightmare Eve

a pink flush in her narrow cheeks and leggy, wearing fitted denim jeans and a simple brown blouse, several shades darker than her light blonde hair. Her entire appearance from the clothes she wore to her complexion appeared desaturated with color.

"Sorry," Evelyn said. "I hope I didn't startle you."

The girl shook her head. "I just didn't expect to see anyone today. What are you doing here?"

"I'm a bit lost," Evelyn confessed. "I'm looking for someone."

"All the way out here?" The young woman leaned toward her, her face jutting forward like a rooster, her eyes wide with disbelief. Then she shook her head and pulled back. "You won't find anyone. Not here. Not this time of year. Everyone is gone."

The student's constant fidgeting and twitchy movements made Evelyn nervous. She was acting erratic and stumbled over her words, and when Evelyn tried to look at the student in the eyes, the student would divert her gaze elsewhere then shift again, stepping on her own feet or twirling her hair in her fingertips. Between her sporadic movements, Evelyn could make out the details of her red-rimmed eyes and puffy cheeks and she knew the student had been crying before Evelyn approached.

"Do you have a cell phone I could borrow for one second? The phone lines around here seem to be down." Evelyn asked politely.

The student shook her head. "I have a phone, but it doesn't work. No one gets cell service in this area. None of the phones on campus are working either. The storms keep knocking out the power and phone lines. They won't be fixed until this storm is over."

"What about the medical buildings or the library? Can you tell me how to get there?"

The student looked back over her shoulder as if she was paranoid someone was watching her. "There's a campus map at the front desk, but it's dangerous to go exploring on your own."

"I know. My fiancé and his daughter are missing and I'm not leaving until I find them."

"You think they're here? In Amherst?" she asked.

"I don't know. Maybe. I mean, I think so." Now Evelyn wondered if she sounded just as crazy to the student.

"When I want answers," the student said, "I usually start with the library."

"The library?" Evelyn thought for a moment. She could find more about Doxepin. "Is it up that way?" Evelyn pointed to the stairs that lead up a walkway that weaved between several four and five story university buildings.

The student gave a smile, both sad and sweet. "Just stay on the path and you'll find it."

"Thank you," Evelyn said and introduced herself.

The girl introduced herself as Nora Brooke. "I'm a freshmen here at Westminster."

Evelyn cocked her head to the side and frowned. She studied the student's sullen features: the long bridge of her upturned nose and shoulder length blonde hair and dark somber eyes. Evelyn touched the Mask of Flesh in her cargo pockets and remembered the paintings of the lighthouse.

"You painted the lighthouse scene at Pan's Art Gallery." Evelyn stated.

"I paint sometimes," Nora Brooke replied.

"Your father—" Evelyn started to say, but paused to reach in her pocket. She felt the dried leather between her fingertips.

"My father?" Nora became shrill.

"Can you tell me anything about this?" Evelyn retrieved the Mask of Flesh from her pocket and held it out for Nora to see.

Nightmare Eve

Nora jumped to her feet, sucking a whoosh of air into her lungs. Her eyes filled with fear.

Evelyn, startled by Nora's reaction, inadvertently took a step back. "Your father donated this to the gallery. What is this? Where did this come from?"

"Y-you've got the Mask," she stammered, still cringing. Her fingers gripped tight against the stone fountain until her knuckles turned white. "Do you have the others too?"

Evelyn nodded, showed Nora the wallet.

Her mouth fell open and her eyes widened even more. She looked around, panicked. She let go of the stone fountain and gripped Evelyn's wrist so hard it hurt.

"Have you seen him?"

"Seen who? What is going on here, Nora?"

"Then it's true. The Executioner has returned! He's going to kill us all!"

"Nora, please just calm down and explain. What is going on here?"

Nora let go of Evelyn and quickly gathered her belongings. "We've all made mistakes. I'm sorry for what happened, but I just can't. . . I hope you find your family." She flung her backpack over her shoulder and ran from the courtyard leaving Evelyn alone wondering what the hell had just happened.

The main corridor of the Westminster University Welcoming Center guided Evelyn past rows of empty offices on both sides of the hallway. Past the receptionist's desk, she stood in front of a locked door. Bold, black words were painted across the wall and as high as the ceiling: *I dare you.*

Evelyn frowned and wrinkled her forehead. The challenge taunted her. She was certain there were no words there a second ago. When she brushed her fingertips against the words, the paint cracked and pealed away as if it had been there for years.

She turned her attention to the front desk looking for the map Nora had mentioned.

Among various files was a basic outline of Westminster University that included a basic map of the surrounding neighborhood. The other end of the map showed the Performing Arts building at the edge of campus near the library along a road that looped back to University Drive—the only open road.

She found her location at the western most building from the train yard. All she would need to do is exit back through the doors and cut across the plaza—the same place where she'd met Nora, and then follow the straight-shot path between the science labs and the Humanities building, past the gym, a courtyard, the concert hall and finally the Westminster University Library.

She stepped away from behind the receptionist's desk and wandered over to a cluttered bulletin board. As she strolled by, barely paying attention to the row of headshots from various faculty members she paused when she recognized the smiling face of a middle-aged man in a simple black polo shirt with a whistle and stopwatch dangling around his neck. Although his smile was wide and appeared genuine, the wrinkles around his puffy eyes indicated that he was probably more short-tempered on the courts and in the field. The name on the plaque below was Coach Norris. Head of the fitness department. The same man Evelyn had seen murdered in his own home by the Executioner.

Beside Mr. Norris's photograph was a photo of Dr. Theodore Brooke—Nora's father and head of the Chemistry department. Evelyn stared closer at the bulletin board. This wasn't just a coincidence, was it? Her eyes fell to the slip of paper stapled to the cork board beneath the faculty photos. It was a memo to all the students.

Attention all students:

Nightmare Eve

Due to the recent graffiti and vandalism of university property, all rooms will be locked before and after class. For extracurricular activities, including but not limited to, use of the gymnasium, science labs, art studios, theater, and library. Appointments will need to be made by contacting the head of the appropriate department. At Westminster University, we strive for excellence and professionalism in a healthy and professional facility. If you have any information regarding the recent issues on campus, please contact any one of our faculty members.
   Dr. Charles Greyson
   Dean of Westminster University

Evelyn eyed the faces and read the plaques again trying to memorize each of the instructor's names and their corresponding departments. If she needed to get into the Library, she'd hate to make it all the way across campus only to find the door was locked. Calling to make an appointment would be pointless. The campus was practically deserted and the phones weren't working. Finding a key was going to be more difficult than she realized.

Evelyn eyed the faces and read the plaques again trying to memorize each of the instructor's names and their corresponding departments. If she needed to get into the Library, she'd hate to make it all the way across campus only to find the door was locked. Calling to make an appointment would be pointless. The campus was practically deserted and the phones weren't working. Even though she hadn't been impressed with the size of the campus, finding a particular key would prove more challenging than she originally thought.

With the teachers and their corresponding departments on repeat in her mind, she exited the building using the double doors at the southern end of the corridor but was forced to abandon her path when it dipped low into a flood zone. The soggy earth had cracked open and murky water flowed upward at an alarming rate responsible for the collapsing walls. This school had bigger problems than a bit of graffiti. Evelyn sighed heavy with grief. Once again she found herself at a dead end and now had to find another way across campus, in the dark. Evelyn cursed under her breath.

Past the Science building, Humanities, labs, beyond the courtyard and rising above another two rows of university buildings and stretching even higher than the shuddering pines was the clock tower. According to the map, the clock tower was the tallest structure on campus and was placed directly between the library and the concert hall. It was further than she would've liked to walk, considering she'd already hoofed around the entire town, and the university buildings along with the fog had obscured her direct view of the path, but she knew as long as she could see the clock tower through the marine layer she could keep herself from getting turned around. The landmark offered a sufficient reference point from nearly anywhere on campus.

According to the map the only clear path to the library cut through the labs and around the gymnasium, and bring her to the courtyard. It was a wide loop and order to make it through the labs, she'd have to find a way inside somehow. Only the instructors had keys, according to the memo.

She shifted her weight from one foot to the other and, upon hearing a crunch, looked down at the chunk of concrete that wedged loose from sidewalk. Around her were other bits of tile and soggy plaster that had washed down from the collapsed Humanities building. Whatever architectural beauty Westminster University had before, had been washed away.

She backtracked to the Welcoming Center, past graffiti-painted offices and located at the end of the easternmost hall where a whoosh of air vibrated the doors. She counted the doors until she stood outside the final door on the right. The handle turned easily in her grip and the door swung outward stirring up dust. Evelyn coughed and then cleared the dust from her face with the back of hers sleeve. Once it had settled and her eyes adjusted to the dark interior of the janitorial closet, she poked

Nightmare Eve

her head and searched each wall for a row of hooks, hopefully with a key ring or at least one master key, if such things exist. Inside was a mop and a yellow bucket, bottles of cleaning supplies, brushes, sponges, and stack of dusty magazines on top of some milk crates, nothing useful, but in the back she spotted a fire axe.

A few minutes later Evelyn toted the axe across the courtyard toward the science lab. She stared at the graffiti letters spray painted above the doorway. It read: *Don't go through this door.*

Evelyn, unnerved by the warning, sucked in a deep breath. They can blame it on the storm. Then she heaved the axe into the doors. The weak doors caved inward like soggy graham crackers that had been saturated in milk. Another swing and a gaping hole formed, large enough for her hand to squeeze through and open the door from the inside.

The door creaked open and she stood in the dingy corridor over broken tiles, chips of drywall flaking to the floors and cracks zig-zagging along the deteriorated ceiling. There was also a faint chemical smell like cleaning fluids and anesthesia. After seeing the piles of broken glass and other bits of crumbling debris she felt less guilty for chopping a hole in the door. She moved forward with silent reluctance.

The long hallways were dark except for bits of light that filtered in through the dirty windows. Evelyn wished she would've remembered to snag a flashlight from her room back at Shady Nook, but how could she have known she'd be breaking into science labs when she left? She thought this ordeal would've ended by now. How much more of this would she have to endure? At least she was inside now, sheltered from the wind and possibility of rain.

She craned her neck first to the left and spied the rooms at the end of the hall. Then she looked to the right and into the dark windows of a classroom, cleared of books and lab equipment. Empty rows of desks faced the podium at the front of the room. Evelyn wondered if all the rooms had been cleared.

Then a deep, drawn-out groan rose from somewhere in the building, echoing down each of the corridors. She paused for a moment and stared up at the ceiling. Perhaps it was just the building settling. The metal pipes were probably old and if the rooms had been cleared of books and computers then the building was probably condemned and deemed unsafe. She'd have to continue with caution, being weary of any holes or weak spots in the floor that could send her tumbling to the floors below.

As seen through the next window, not all the rooms had been totally cleared. She saw a dark office near the back of the corridor with a flickering light and a computer beside a stack of papers and folders. The walls were lined with fully stocked bookshelves and a watercolor replica of pale green and soft yellow carnivorous pitcher plants. The shelves contained self-help book titles and office advice, textbooks of forms and office temp work sheets. Not exactly the kind of information Evelyn was looking for but she was grateful of the possibility that life still existed in some form in this building. She checked the door.

Locked.

She looked at the axe still in her hand, and for a brief moment, contemplated using it on the office door, but the idea quickly passed. What she was looking for wouldn't be found in there.

The double doors behind her were unlocked though, and a flight of stairs ascended to another set of double doors on the second floor. There was gentle current of air flowing through the stairwell and a single window permitted just enough light to keep Evelyn from tripping on the steps.

The second story floor plan was identical to the lower level with rows of classrooms on both sides, and like the first floor, this hall was equally dingy with cracked walls and an occasional softball sized hole in the floor. Evelyn tried the first

Nightmare Eve

few doors, but they refused to budge, even when she used her shoulder to press against them. She peered into the next room and was relieved to see the pale flickering of a fluorescent light. It was weak, casting the room in dancing shadows, but it was enough for Evelyn to make out the rows of books placed neatly on the shelves and along the countertops organized with microscopes, terrariums and aquariums. The chairs were pulled out from the desks and arranged in clusters as if the students had been working in groups. She reached for the door handle and pulled. The door swung open with ease and she stepped into the science lab.

It wasn't until she moved among the rows when she remembered the memo in the receptionist's office. . . . *appointments will need to be made by contacting the appropriate department head.* . . The doors should've been locked, but they weren't. Someone must have made an appointment to use the labs and dodged out in a hurry, leaving the classroom unattended. Books about botany, oceanography, meteorology, human anatomy lined the shelves. Evelyn paused at the bookshelf, a slender gap where a book had been removed. After moving to the front of the classroom she saw the missing textbook laying flat on the desk surrounded by an assortment of research papers and student essays. Among them were files, the name on the files catching her attention. These files belonged to Dr. Jack Dullahan.

The first file showed a charcoal etching of a plant leaf. A photograph of the same plant was paper clipped to the file. She browsed through the report reading about the plant indigenous only the ocean side community of Amherst and the surrounding coastal mountains. The plant, used for medicinal purposes, was being studied by Dr. Dullahan and according to his reports, discovered it possessed similar qualities as hemlock and contained atropine and hallucinogenic properties like the desert flower, Datura. And similarly to hemlock, can be highly toxic and possibly even fatal if too much is consumed. Victims, after ingesting the bright green leaves, show signs of asphyxiation and convulsions before death. Evelyn lowered the doctor's plant analysis and looked up, deep in thought. She remembered passing the upstairs bathroom at the Shady Nook Bed and Breakfast and hearing Charity throwing up in the upstairs bathroom. Ms. Smith also had mentioned that she wasn't feeling well, causing a delay in breakfast. Wasn't there a salad served with dinner that night? Evelyn suddenly felt grateful for her lack of appetite that evening.

After replacing the files she picked up the missing text book—a medical encyclopedia. It didn't take her long to browse the table of contents where she found a brief description of Doxepin, the prescription rattling in her pocket. Doxepin was used as a drug used to suppress nightmares, often given to patients who'd experienced something traumatic like the loss of loved ones, and even war veterans suffering from shell shock but the side effects were severe causing memory loss, headaches, kidney failure. . .The list of side effects continued to the next page where she found a folded piece of paper with Evelyn's name scribbled across it. Below was a memo written by Dr. Dullahan: *The feelings of persecution in a nightmare are identical to feelings of persecution in acute paranoid states. The delusions are the same."*

Beneath the words was a prescription number, same as on her bottle of Doxepin.

So it was true. Dr. Jack Dullahan had been her doctor and was writing her prescriptions for a pill that would suppress her nightmares and causing her memory loss. But why? What else couldn't she remember? She could still picture David and Ivy lying in bed and reading stories. She remembered how David had told her he missed going to bed without her when she had to work late and he'd pull the pillows close just to catch her lingering scent. Those sweet moments seemed like only days ago, but the files dated months ago.

Nightmare Eve

She placed the Doxepin on his desk. He wouldn't be coming back and she didn't need them anymore. It was time for her to remember.

She backed away from the desk and browsed the contents of the terrariums along the countertop. The plants in each were about the same height, each budding leaf the same silky texture and shade of deep green as the next, the same as those indigenous toxic plants from the science book. One tank stood out from the others, filled to the brim with clouded, murky water. Stuck in the sludge-covered rocks came the gleam of a key with Mr. Norris's signature labeled on the identification ring. Evelyn had found the key to the gymnasium.

She inspected the map in her pocket. The gymnasium separated the labs from the library and performing arts theatre. The fastest way to get there would be out the way she came and, once outside, make an immediate left, but Evelyn remembered part of the Humanities building had collapsed, blocking the direct path with a wall of rubble and a river of gushing water. By using the gymnasium key however, she could cut through both buildings to reach the theatre to meet Hunter.

She looked down at the axe still in her hands and contemplated making a new route. But then she thought: no, Evelyn, not all your problems can be solved by smashing.

For her plan to work she needed the gymnasium key from the tank. She rolled up her sleeves. Her face twisted into a disgusted frown as she reached up with her right hand and dipped it slowly into the rancid water. The surface was thick with sludge. She leaned her body in, her face inching closer to the water. She tilted her head away and held her breath. Then her fingertips found the key ring and she pulled her arm from the foul water. She looked at her hand, repulsed by the much that clung to her skin. There was plenty of fresh water outside to clean up with. She strode across the room entered the second floor hall. It was too difficult to be sure in this darkness, but Evelyn thought she spotted a man's silhouette, motionless at the end of the hall. When she took another step, the rushed sounds of someone—or something moving through the long corridor startled her. She clutched the axe ready to strike. She felt the rush of air move behind her and she spun on her heels, ready to swing. When she turned around again, the dark silhouette was gone.

She remained still, her heart pounding. Something was present with her in the corridor. She felt rush of air as it sped past her, and suddenly it was gone. The thin white hairs on her arms stood on end.

After a few still moments, her heart rate steadily dropped and her muscles relaxed. She remained alert as she continued to descend the remainder of the corridor and down the stairs to the first floor. With the axe still braced against her chest, she pushed through the set of double doors and exited to the stagnant night air.

Chapter 20

The foyer was nothing more than a well proportioned room with a leaky drinking fountain at one end and two doors, one for men, the other for women, separated by a glass case with five trophies.

Multiple rows of team photographs were mounted on each wall leading to the entrance to the basketball courts. The doors were locked and she was sure Mr. Norris's key would solve the problem, but upon hearing voices rising from the men's locker room, she hesitated, leaning in to hear better.

Two distinct voices tumbled over each other.

"Hold 'em! No, I said hold his arms back!" said the first one with an angry, commanding tone.

The other voice, higher pitched and lacking confidence grumbled something followed by a soft thud and another grunt. A cry of surprise was cut short by a heavy clang.

Evelyn snuck into the men's locker room, ready to strike with the axe. When she rounded the corner to the center of the square she saw she was alone, even as the sounds continued around her.

"Hold him down! Get his arms!"

She heard the scuffle as if it was happening directly in front of her. She heard the sound of fists beating against flesh, the sound of an unseen victim falling into the lockers with a loud crash. Evelyn jumped as the dent, the size of a young man's head, formed in the locker to her left.

"I'm going to fuck him up good," said another.

Then came the sound of a door opening. The man with the high voice shouted, "Someone's coming! Dump him!" followed by the thud of an unseen body collapsing on the tile floor. A breeze rushed past her. When she turned around she saw the fresh blood spackling the locker where the victim struck his head. Evelyn reached out with her fingertips and touched the sticky fluid. Still warm. At her feet, a puddle of blood began to form, coming from the invisible victim. The puddle grew until it streamed in a narrow line to the drain in the middle of the room.

In the center of a puddle, Evelyn noticed something black, about an inch and a half in diameter. She plucked it out of the blood and saw it was just a simple square battery. How strange! She was sure it wasn't there a moment ago, but neither was the blood or the dent in the locker.

Evelyn placed the battery in her pocket and then moved into Mr. Norris's office at the back of the locker room. His desk was perfectly organized with a photo of him and his wife and son on the basketball court at Westminster. She reached for it. They smiled brightly at the camera. His son's lips grinned wide and cheerful exposing a goofy row of teeth, much like his fathers. His son's eyes were definitely his mother's. It was clear they were a proud family, all very attractive with knock-out curves and smooth olive skin. Mrs. Norris was probably prom

Nightmare Eve

queen in high school. Evelyn put the picture down. The only other peculiar item in the room was a bizarre photograph stashed away in the top left drawer of his desk. In the image, a beefy-looking man with empty black and puffy eyes stared back so cold and alert that Evelyn thought he might actually be seeing her. She flipped the image over and read the words scrawled on the back.

Wallet. Book. Mask. Scarf. Bowl.

Evelyn replaced the photograph precisely as she found it and speculated the origins of the mask in her pocket. The leather was unlike any she'd ever seen or felt. She cringed at the thought of these objects being made from the madman in the photograph. Why would Mr. Norris even have these in the first place? What connection did he have with the man in the photo?

She shuddered at the image of Mr. Norris peeling the man's face off and drying it as a mask. Shaking it off, Evelyn weaved between the row of lockers to the back of the room where she faced two similar-looking doors. In each door, a square window with interlacing wires looked into a weight room while the other, a basketball court. Evelyn spotted Nora Brooke and Charity Smith sitting on the first row of the bleachers. Evelyn considered joining them, but due to the their shrill shrill and sibilant tones and the nature of their clandestine rendezvous Evelyn resisted her confrontational urge and listened, hidden from view.

"I know it's been more than a year, but I still see him sometimes." Charity Smith sounded frightened.

Nora Brooke leaned forward with eyes as gaping as a full moon and an expression like a housewife drooling over scrumptious details of scandal. "Oh no, and Jack?"

"Of course I didn't tell him," Charity spat. "He could tell something was wrong, but I blamed it on the lodge. Things weren't going well at home and business was bad. People were always getting sick or going missing."

"You'd know better than anyone, Charity." Nora's voice took on a more acidic tone and Evelyn wondered if part of Nora blamed Charity for Jack Dullahan's death. "Anyway, I think you can still pick up your homework from Dr. Dullahan's office. But I suppose the time is irrelevant to you."

Charity casually held out a set of keys pinched between her finger and her thumb. Jack Dullahan's keys, Evelyn realized. She'd been the one who'd unlocked the labs and unknowingly gave Evelyn access to the room.

"I swiped it when he came over for dinner. But I didn't know he'd be murdered! I can't tell anyone, could you imagine?"

Nora nodded. "No. I have no idea what you're talking about."

Nora shifted with the same erratic uneasiness that plagued her during Evelyn's conversation. She always seemed so nervous. Constantly fidgeting, both carried themselves with a guilty countenance.

Did they murder Dr. Jack Dullahan by mistake? Was it an accident? She hadn't considered the possibility that he was poisoned using one of his own plants, which caused him to hallucinate the monster that chased him off his path.

Charity rose to her feet and waved goodbye to Nora and then strolled off. Nora continued to sit, her face buried in her hands.

The next door brought Evelyn to the weight room. She stepped inside and knew right away this was not a typical gym. Even though she barely spent time in gyms, she chose to stay in shape by jogging in the evenings and properly dieting with a sold balance of carbs, meats, fruits and vegetables. She wasn't a knock-out, but she had a decent figure. With more exercise she could've been, so she was lucky that David had fallen for her with his crystal good looks and gentlemanly behavior. This gym, however, was more like a rusted medieval torture chamber with

Nightmare Eve

heavy rusted iron and wood devices meant to break bones, rip flesh and dislocate joints.

One particular machine's headpiece was a heavy iron device, bloodstained and rusted. From the seat protruded long iron spikes strategically placed to pierce organs without killing the victims.

Standing among the various devices, Hunter scribbled something in a pocket-sized notebook.

Evelyn approached him, delighted to see him, but confused.

"Evelyn, I thought something happened to you," he said. His voice was sullen, his movements swift. He moved to her and grazed her elbow with sensitivity. "I couldn't find my way inside. The rain had washed everything out. The trails are impossible to get through in this weather. I had to find another way. When I came back to get you, you were gone."

"I thought you were dead!" Evelyn cried out. "After I saw that thing, that *monster*, kill Mrs. Rosecrans—"

"Wait, slow down Evelyn. What are you talking about?" Hunter stood a head taller than Evelyn. He placed a concerned hand on her shoulder. "Mrs. Rosecrans has been dead for months. Are you sure you weren't just having another nightmare?"

His hands were like ice on her shoulder. She withdrew from him. What did he know about her nightmares? Did Dr. Dullahan tell him something? She must've been eyeing Hunter with the venom of a pit viper because he surrendered his hands above his head.

"Whoa, whoa, okay." Hunter took a step back, extending the gap between them. He looked down at the axe in her hands. "I don't know what you saw, but I believe you must've seen something and it frightened you. We'll figure it out."

Evelyn gestured to the axe. "This isn't for you."

Hunter gave her a questionable look and then glanced around the room. His expression changed from defensive to thoughtful.

"I know the equipment here is outdated and doesn't look by much but they get the job done." he said changing the subject, "The gym was everything to me. If I missed a day, I would hate myself for it and try and compensate. There's a kind of honesty in the gym. You can't brag because the weight is crushing. There's truth in the weights. You know it can hurt you." Then his voice went dark. "And you have to be at least some kind of masochist to cope with the pain of weight lifting. The muscles literally rip and tear. Confronting that kind of truth makes us grow. It makes us stronger."

Was he seeing something different? This place wasn't a gym, it's a torture chamber! As they strolled between the rows toward the back door, Evelyn saw bits of torn white flesh clinging to the gears of a particularly wicked device that placed the unfortunate victim between two bars that held him in place as the limbs were bent in the opposite directions until they snapped.

The room was ripe with death and Evelyn could practically taste the sour putridness and rust in her mouth like sucking on penny-flavored candies. *Flesh candy,* Evelyn thought with a shudder. She shook the image away.

"Look, I don't know what's going on. I just want to find my family and get out of here."

"You still don't get it, do you?" Hunters callous laugh fueled Evelyn's fury.

"You search through this town with the paradigm that we're all strangers, yet we've been here much longer than you. In your arrogance, you never considered that *you* are actually the stranger in this town and it's your stubborn attitude that's preventing you from seeing the truth."

"You don't know anything about me." Evelyn snapped.

"That's exactly what I'm talking about. You can't accept that someone may actually know a little more than you. The facts are heavy, like these weights and they'll both crush you. Soon enough you'll see, it's not the town that's haunted. It's you."

Hunter walked through the set of doors in the back, leaving Evelyn to stew in her own fury.

She glanced at the pieces of flesh clinging to the grates at her feet and rusted machines that filled the room and realized she didn't want Hunter to leave her here.

She followed until she reached the door. From the corner of her eye, in the darkest region of the torture chamber, Evelyn heard a groan.

A stifled cry disrupted her thoughts. Her anger and confusion faded only slightly as she moved through the metal catacombs looking for the source.

She half expected to see another monster lurking at the edge of the hard shadows, but instead of the monster, she saw one of the men from the dumpster behind the convenient store. What was his name? Eddy, she remembered. He shook with fear. A leather strap pressed his head against the back of the chair. Corey was standing behind him attempting to remove the straps.

Eddy's arms were extended out to his sides and clamped to a metal bar. His eyes were filled with panic and he was sweating profusely. His expression was pleading, but Evelyn was trying to make sense of it all. His mouth was gagged by a leather strap with tiny, rounded spikes pressing into his mouth. The more he struggled, the deeper the spikes bore into his mouth, shredding his mouth until his were ground away. Blood poured from his face into his lap. Even followed the straps to his legs that were chained to gears of various sizes and girth.

It was like trying to untangle a ball of electric cables behind an entertainment set. She didn't know where to begin or how he even managed to get entwined in the device.

Looking down Evelyn could see he was crouching low behind the machine trying to unlatch his friend from the back.

"Please, help me!" he pleaded. Sweat had matted his long blonde hair to his beat red face. These men, possible murderers who had attacked a man and nearly her too, were seconds from death.

She studied the complex mass of leather straps, chains and gears, difficult with them both screaming. Droplets of blood fell to one of the leather straps and Evelyn raised the axe, prepared to swing, then lowered it. If she cut that particular strap, the gears would loosen and crush his skull. No, she couldn't just chop her way through this problem.

Corey, on his hands and knees pleaded through a constant stream of tears. He frantically tugged and pulled on every part of the device but found no leverage. In the contraption, the spiked leather straps constricted around Eddy's head, tearing at what remained of his lips, teeth and gums, little more than pulp.

More chains, tangled with straps. The gears cranked more. Voices screamed in her head. Corey let go of the straps and started grabbing at his own skull in frustration.

From her knees she looked up at him helplessly. That's when she noticed the poem scrawled in blood on the wall behind him:

Mercy
A young soul to old
Lives in putrid sins of flesh
For 170 pounds of rust
On the weight of his chest
Everlasting darkness
Is mercy granted
Only by the hand
Of the Executioner

Nightmare Eve

This had to be a clue. There was a formula to this place.

She took another look at the gears, still uncertain how the poem was supposed to help her. The levers turned, pulling the straps and chains until his eyes bulged and ribs cracked. Then his skull caved in like a rotten jack-o-lantern and broke through his ribs until he appeared deflated.

Drenched in cranial fluids and painted red from head toe with filigrees of brain matter dangling from her cheeks to shoulders, Evelyn fell to her knees forcing herself to believe it was out of her hands. This was his consequence for whatever poor decision he'd made and there was nothing she could've done to save him.

Saturated with blood, she stood up and shambled down the aisle ignoring the cries of his friend.

On the floor at the end of the isle was a bowl, similar to a breakfast cereal bowl, except cracked. It was strangely out of place like the other objects she found. It was as if the objects had been placed with the obvious purpose of her finding them. As she drew nearer, she knew why the bowl seemed to have such an unusual texture. It had been carved from a human skull.

Evelyn stared at it with sharp eyes and reached for it. When she did, the Executioner emerged from the back of the room. He stood in front of the dead boy and switched his gaze to her. She could only see one eye peering out through the cutout of the burlap sack, and it was studying her.

He watched her tremble, covered in blood, the hollowed out skull in her hand. And then she understood why he was here. The dead teenagers survival was placed in her hands. She had the choice to live or let die, grant mercy or condemnation, and the Executioner had come to judge.

His chest heaved and he raised his blade high.

Evelyn lurched to the side.

The blade sliced through the air and struck the floor between them. Wires in the wooden floor snapped and curled like broken guitar strings. He could've easily cut her in two—he had missed on purpose. He was toying with her, she realized. The real battle had not yet begun.

Another swing. The blade smashed through the metal device. Shrapnel exploded around her. The teenager's body was eradicated in a cloud of dust, blood and fleshy chunks. His jaw lopped to the right and only his feet remained.

The Executioner bounded forward. Machines splintered and snapped around him.

Evelyn shuffled along the floor, arm-over-arm like a military man in the trenches as shrapnel flew overhead. She evaded another swing, closer this time.

The gymnasium door swung open. Someone shuffled into the room.

A voice called out. "Hey, over here!"

Evelyn looked up. Behind the Executioner, Mr. Morgan shambled toward them, tossing rocks and chunks of wood at the monster. A blow to his masked head and he finally turned to face the withered old man. Evelyn felt grateful for the opportunity to escape but now Mr. Morgan would be killed.

He was too old. Too slow.

In his last moments before the Executioner stepped between the metal beams, cornering Mr. Morgan between the blades and the wall, he shouted, "Love is not selfish and those who are never find it. We make mistakes. Some people are lost. We can't save everyone. Not even those who deserved to be saved."

Evelyn reached for Mr. Morgan. The blade came down, slicing him in two.

Mr. Morgan's upper body slid to the side and struck the floor with a wet, *slop!* His lower body stood for a few seconds, wavered, collapsed.

It had been a trap, Evelyn realized. Mr. Morgan sacrificed himself to lure the Executioner near one of the strange metal devices in the center of the room. She hadn't noticed before, blending in with the wicked décor. Chains, like a net, wrapped around him and he squirmed. The Executioner fell to the grate, his weapons clattering beside him. He continued to struggle. The chains wouldn't hold him forever, but she'd be able to escape now.

Mr. Morgan saved her life, but the Executioner had taken another.

—

Evelyn wanted to run forever, but her body weighed against her, heaving down the sidewalk like a bumbling sack of potatoes. Her lungs burned and her sleepless eyes blurred over.

No matter how far she could carry herself, it wouldn't be far enough.

It was daylight now, but the sky was steeped with clouds and the suburban blocks were shrouded in the early morning marine layer. Her skin was damp from a mixture of sweat and the morning's dew and her face and clothes were stained red.

On the next street right on the sidewalk, she ran past a blood-splattered surgeon wearing a mask slicing through Corey's fleshy belly with a scalpel. Corey shook on the stretcher trying to free himself.

With a scalpel in hand and elbows deep in blood, the doctor raised his head to Evelyn when she ran past. She had to stifle a gasp when she saw that the doctor's eyes had been cut out, eyelids crudely stitched together. He did not follow her. He tilted his head back down to Corey and swiftly jabbed at his nerves manipulating his spasms like a sadistic puppeteer.

She ran past another poster mounted to a lamppost of a young blonde woman. A flower arrangement surrounded by white candles adorned the base of the street lamp in memory, just like the one she'd seen at the entrance to the university.

Evelyn took another desperate breath, her heart feeling as if it could burst any moment. Then her wobbling legs gave way and she fell to the earth. Evelyn landed hard, tumbled under a bush.

She laid there face up in the dirt below the hedge and looked at the drifting clouds in a gloomy sky. Swaying pines towered around her like a protective wall. Soft branches scraped and creaked in the gentle ocean breeze and the violin could be heard from somewhere close. A familiar tune from a pastime she couldn't quite remember.

She felt cozy nestled in the privacy of the shrubbery and peacefulness of the community park. How long had it been since she'd last slept? Two, maybe three days now? She wasn't sure, but she knew she couldn't go on. Her eyelids tugged heavy with sleep. Her last thought was of David in his Navy uniform, his arms around another woman.

Chapter 21

"We'll be together, don't know where. Don't know when. But I know we'll meet again some sunny day..."

Evelyn sat at the dinner table across from her David. Though he remained quiet and troubled for most of the evening, she'd never felt so happy to see him. All she wanted was to hear his voice but he refused to say more than a few grunts. Sure, things were great at first, and their relationship had gone rocky from time to time, just as relationships tended to do, but a rocky moment didn't mean she stopped loving him. They both had issues to work on, she knew, but having his love and support made her feel as if she could overcome any obstacle. A simple hike through the woods, or a stroll down the pier was the chisel to crumble the emotional wall she'd built from past heartache, but he always made an excuse for not going. "Why, what's the point? What would we talk about?" he would say. It didn't matter what they talked about or what they did, but surely they'd find a topic that interested them both. She wanted to hear about his experiences traveling from port to port and the exotic foods he'd seen, the trouble he'd gotten into, or something, *anything*, would do. How do you expect to get to know someone if you don't spend time with them?

"*Till the blue skies drive the dark clouds far away. . .*" The music drifted into her thoughts.

He said he wanted to be there for her, but he didn't seem to understand how important it was to at least make an attempt to time together.

Even now he sat across the table avoiding her gaze. Between them, a human-size doll sat in the dinning chair with an uncanny similarity to Ivy-Rose, with a head so large it was almost cartoonish with brushed waist-length black hair and a kimono. The Ivy Rose doll was slumped forward with chopsticks in her hand with one black glass eye the size of a dinner plate and the other, slightly smaller and hollow, she locked onto Evelyn in a cold stare.

She wanted to tell David that she had a problem, but his disinterest in her was making it difficult. She was sick and she needed his help. She never learned to trust anyone. She wanted to trust him more than anyone ever, but she had to know, did he love her enough to stay with her? How could she share something meaningful with him if he refused to even take a simple and quick walk along the beach? What would it take to get through to him?

No, she'd have to hide it again. Maybe he just needed her to cool it for a bit. She had come off too strong too soon, she feared.

The music was set to playback. It warbled slowly on the phonograph at first. Then it sped up, and slowed again to a long drawl before briefly returning to normal. "*…When the man comes around the hairs on your arm will stand up at the terror. . .*"

Nightmare Eve

"It's nice to have you back on shore leave," Evelyn said. "I miss you when you're not around."

David gently pitched forward over the dining table, but his blank eyes stared into space.

The damage had been done. He had emotionally removed himself from her. How could he let her go so easily when she was trying so hard? She gave him everything she knew how to give! Her mind silently screamed for release, stuck as a prisoner in her own life.

"Why did you leave me back there on the pier?" Evelyn asked.

He didn't answer. His shoulders slipped forward more.

The Ivy Rose doll stared at the bowl of soup in front of her, still clutching the chopsticks in her porcelain hands. Evelyn never saw her move at all, and she never said anything, but Evelyn occasionally found her tipped over on the couch in front of the television, and then a few minutes later, she'd be lying under the bed in a crumped heap. She was grateful to have Ivy joining her and David for dinner, grateful for her company, but she could feel the coldness between them. Evelyn was the only one fighting to keep this relationship alive.

"Please, David, why won't you just talk to me?"

"*I looked and behold, a pale horse, and its name it said on him was Death, and Hell followed with him.*"

Under the weight of gravity, David finally slid forward and the crunch of his dried skin and withering bones cracked against the table. Patches hair had already begun to show in his decaying scalp, the skin pulling tight like dried leather in the sun. His fingers, still holding the silverware were too rigid and curled to move and Evelyn sighed. She rubbed her nose and felt the mucus collecting on her lip. A sense of abandonment overwhelmed her. She wiped the snot away with her arm, something she hadn't done since she was a child.

She needed some sign from him, but instead he was as cold as death.

Evelyn quietly placed her fork on the table and reached for the bottle of Moscato. The words he didn't speak were the words she heard the loudest.

He had given up. It was over.

Tears burned her eyes as she finished her dinner in silence.

Chapter 22

"Wake up. It's just a nightmare, Eve."

She stirred at the familiar voice. She wasn't sure which came first, the pulsing ache in her head or the silhouette of David standing over her, stroking her head. She was groggy and could hardly move but she managed to wriggle the fingers on her left hand and raise them to the caress the smooth, but chilling texture of David's cheek and the damp residue that remained. She felt too weak to hold out her hand any longer and let it fall back to bed. She'd never felt more close to death; he was like an angel hovering over her. If she was going to die now, she could think of no better way to go than in his arms. He was her heaven.

And she closed her eyes, waiting for death.

But death still wouldn't come.

Please, no, she begged. Let this be it. How much longer will this last?

The pain grew intense as consciousness drifted back.

This isn't heaven, this is hell, Evelyn thought.

Voices strayed from somewhere close. A heated argument between a man and a woman. He spat his words at her with the bitter hiss of a rejected lover. A tone Evelyn was too familiar with. Even lying beneath the warmth of the comforter and malleable padding of the luxurious mattress she still felt the nightmare closing in. Hell, disguised as a town of suspicious characters, untold crimes and broken hearts.

"What am I supposed to do with all these things?" The woman spoke with calm, rationality but lingering with a lack of patience.

That voice! It was so familiar. Sheriff Rhett, she realized.

He spoke with brash impatience, laden with frustration and annoyance. "Just leave all this there for a moment, would you?" Evelyn overheard Sheriff Rhett say to the young woman.

She replied in a softer, more submissive tone, too faint for Evelyn to hear.

"Uh-huh," Sheriff Rhett grumbled with skepticism. "And what else do you want?"

Floorboards creaked. Someone was moving through the room beside Evelyn.

"I want to be your friend," she said meekly. Evelyn knew the sincerity in her soft voice. She'd only met a few people during her horrendous stay in Amherst, but there was only one female voice she'd encountered that wasn't completely ripe with despair. The girl arguing with Sheriff Rhett was Carly from Pan's Art Gallery.

Evelyn squeezed her eyes shut and the ache in her head grew. Damn Doxepin. Rhett must've found her and given her a dose. She still couldn't remember how she ended up at the Shady Nook under Ms. Smith's care, but at least she could remember the lodge and how many days had passed. She still remembered the woman in the bar, before her black out and then waking up and everything until she fell asleep under the hedge in the park.

She fought through the grogginess and listened in on their conversation.

"You didn't see her the way I did!" Sheriff Rhett screamed. Evelyn felt the floorboards shake under heavy boots. She imagined him hovering over the poor, frightened girl, his face red and beaded with angry sweat. "She knew! She was dying in Jack's hospital bed with her last thoughts of you and me rolling around on the floor fucking like the end of days!"

"But it's normal for people to act out. When you are losing someone close there is no way to predict how you or anyone would respond." The woman's voice was still meek and submissive but pleading.

"Really? Is that why you went to Ms. Smith's that night?"

The woman's reply was too quiet for Evelyn to hear but Sheriff Rhett's voice was deep and strong that carried into her room.

"You wanted to make love—for it to be something special, but it's not anymore. It's just fucking. You and I have been over for months!" he shouted.

"I loved you *first*!" The woman shouted and Evelyn heard her voice clearly. It was Carly from Pan's Art Gallery.

"What did you use? Hemlock? Aconite?" He accused.

"I didn't do *anything*!" She screamed back. "The only crime I'm guilty of is loving you too much! You were supposed to be soul mate."

The young woman sobbed. Evelyn listened for Sheriff Rhett's heavy footfalls as he walked across the room.

After hearing the door slam shut, Evelyn waited until the house was still when she could be sure she was alone.

As close and intimate Ms. Smith had been with Dr. Dullahan that night he was murdered, Evelyn was sure that Ms.

Smith, as well as Sheriff Rhett, and possibly even Mr. Morgan had always known the truth behind Evelyn's past as well as her black outs and the prescription of Doxepin. Even if they hadn't known everything, they sure seemed to be trying awfully hard to keep *something* from her. In any case, peace of mind was enough justification for her to leave this house as soon as possible.

Feeling well rested, but uneasy and desperate to get some answers, Evelyn rose from the bed and crept down the narrow hall.

Evelyn moved into a short and narrow hall. Photographs, framed and mounted on the eggshell-white walls depicted Dr. Jack Dullahan among many other smiling faces, none of whom Evelyn recognized. Groups of small children beneath a painted white banner huddled around the smiling doctor at the same park where Evelyn had passed out. She presumed she was in the doctor's home when she saw another row of photos of Jack with several other locals and a stack of unopened mail addressed to him on the cluttered dining table. She moved with long, swift strides, ducking low like a criminal fleeing from a crime scene, taking note of the boxes stacked all around the room. Books and more photographs were organized into piles, clothes were draped over the couch, and some had fallen to the carpet. Carly, Evelyn gathered, was a close friend to the doctor and from the sounds of it, was in charge of clearing out his belongings.

Evelyn contemplated this as she pulled open the front door and stepped onto the porch and descended to path that lead her through the woods, past the mound were the doctor was found by hikers.

She'd never seen a place so lush and green. The forest floor was impossible with ferns and rampant growth beyond the pine needle-littered paths that curved around sheer cliff edges above and waterfalls that fell above the lingering fog. Tendrils of mist swirled at her feet as she kicked up soggy twigs. The trail

Nightmare Eve

led her around a moss-covered boulder to a small bridge made of wood, stretching across a gentle creek. The fragrant pine-scented freshness of heavy, moist air was almost dizzying and the cool spray of water from the falls dampened her hair and face in zestful exuberance.

She braced herself on the rough side of a damp boulder and admired the landscape, appreciating the unspoiled terrain in a fleeting moment of awe. The feeling was short lived. A man was murdered out here, Evelyn told herself and pushed away from the rock. She stepped along the last switchback and the trees parted at the edge of another neighborhood. She stepped out of the woods and into a parking lot, where she could see a tower stretching over the row of poplar trees, no more than a half mile or so away and scraping the clouds with its pointed roof.

She followed the path that brought her back to the University District and she recognized right away, the row of juniper and rosemary shrubs where she'd succumbed to sleep.

She had just gone in a circle. Exasperated, Evelyn felt like crying.

A faint noise, similar to the sound of a clicking pen, only louder, rose from the other side of the parking lot. Evelyn wiped her tears away. There was movement in the mist, footsteps on pavement, followed by the sound of pages rustling. The air was still; someone was near.

Sure enough, as Evelyn crossed the parking lot, she spotted Hunter. Her features grew hard and muscles tensed, angry with him for judging her and then locking her in that room with that horrible monster. She could've been killed if Mr. Morgan hadn't come in at the last second and sacrificed himself so Evelyn could live. In a way, she held Hunter partly responsible for Mr. Morgan's death.

Feeling her aggravation for Hunter growing, she felt inclined to turn back and find another way to the tower, but seeing as the few citizens remaining in Amherst had a tendency of ending up dead, like Dr. Jack Dullahan, the crying woman she'd first met in the bar, the woman in the church, Mrs. Lupez and her family at the train yard, Ms. Rosecrans, Mr. Norris and his entire family, two of the three punk kids, and now Mr. Morgan, Evelyn's options of company were slim. She didn't want to be next on the Executioner's list and, as irritating as Hunter could be, at least he was one of the few people still amongst the living who could possibly elucidate her about these strange events, or at least provide her with a direction to go.

When she approached, she saw the clicking sound had come from a staple gun in his right hand. His left hand carried various flyers—missing posters of families.

"It's not just the people anymore that are going missing now." Hunter spoke gravely. "The whole town is changing. I didn't see it before. I know how crazy this will sound, but at first it was just ordinary things going missing: wallets, cars, construction equipment. People thought it was just thieves, but it's more than that."

Hunter raised the next sheet of paper, a grey-scale photo of a missing middle-aged. In his other hand, he raised the staple-gun and used it to post the flyer. "People, buildings and even ships in the harbor. And do you see any traffic? Hear birds or crickets chirping? This place is like a ghost town. Something is wrong. I haven't seen anyone since—."

"—since you left me to die back there." Evelyn interrupted. Her eyes were narrowed into bitter slits. "I could've been killed! You just locked me in that room with that monster. You could've stayed and helped, then maybe we could've saved that boy and Mr. Morgan would still be alive."

"Wait, Evelyn slow down, I have no idea what you're talking about. I don't even know *who* you are talking about. Who are these people?"

Evelyn's face swelled red and tears filled her eyes. She was shook furiously. "They were people I met. They're dead now, just like the others." She felt hot tears fall from her cheeks

Nightmare Eve

and stared down at the pavement. "I just want David back. I'm so angry, I'm so hurt, but most of all I'm sorry. I'm so, so sorry."

Hunter bowed his head and spoke with gentle, but sincere concern. He placed his hand on her shoulder. "I'm sorry too. We'll figure this out. I've got a bit of good news. I found that song that was stuck in your head."

She didn't remember telling him anything about that song, had she?

He let go of her shoulder and together they walked past the next shop, it's windows dark and the building empty. Not another person in sight. Only Evelyn's lachrymose face glanced back from the reflection. Hunter shuffled through the stack of papers in his hand. He removed several crisp pages and handed them to Evelyn. It was the sheet music to *We'll Meet Again*.

It was such a strange and peculiar offering in such a nightmarish setting, but sweet still.

She looked up at Hunter with a genuine smile. Over his shoulder she noticed movement in the shop's dark window. Inches from the glass, a round boy sprang forward, brandishing a meat cleaver.

In one motion, Evelyn screamed, grabbed hunter by the shirt and forced them into a crouch. Her eyes darted over his hunched back and ignored the bewildered expression on his face—a mixture of fear and surprise. She scanned the doorway to see if he exited, but the shop's door remained closed, the windows still empty.

"Are you alright?" Hunter asked and rose to his feet, straightening his shirt and rubbing his neck.

"I saw a boy. I thought he—"

She stopped when she realized how crazy she sounded. Even if she knew what she'd seen: a boy with a meat cleaver, painted with blood and stringy shoulder length blonde hair matted with crimson to his round face, she couldn't risk Hunter thinking of excuses to leave her alone in this place.

Maybe she was crazy. The more she stayed in this place, the crazier she was starting to feel.

"I'm fine." she said.

"Are you sure you're feeling alright? We can get to to a bench to rest if you need."

"I don't want a bench! I just want David and Ivy back!" She sucked in a deep breath. "I want to be home."

Hunter nodded. "Things in this town have been always been weird, but lately it's reached a new level. I was thinking about the doctor and what you said. It just doesn't make any sense that he would die and Ms. Smith and her daughter become ill. One can only make conjecture with the information gathered from newspapers, but it seems obvious that Dr. Dullahan was poisoned."

Evelyn felt relieved.

"We need to tell someone." Hunter told her.

"But who do we tell?"

Evelyn and Hunter stared across the desert lots and empty streets. Fog and horrible creatures were its only inhabitants. The list of missing names had grown exponentially, the missing persons reports seemed pathetic and useless now. How can an entire town disappear in a matter of days without anyone knowing? Or what if they do?

What if whatever was going on in Amherst was happening everywhere else too? There wasn't a soul in sight.

Evelyn and Hunter stood alone.

"It's like living a nightmare," she said remembering the Ivy Rose doll at the dinner table. David's dried out corpse slumped in the chair, clad in his Navy uniform. Without him, life was a nightmare, and there was no escape—not even in her dreams. She wished she could remember everything and at the same time she wished she could forget. Perhaps Mr. Morgan was right. Her mysterious past was out there, clouded somewhere in the mist. But did she want to find it?

Nightmare Eve

"I'm no stranger to nightmares either," Hunter confessed. "The thing about nightmares is that no matter how recurring they are, it's an emotion you never get used to like reliving them each night as if it's the first. It may be a hard and difficult road in front of you, Eve, but it is one of the keys of releasing the past's hold over us."

Chapter 23

If Evelyn's body had grown hungry or tired, she was too conscious of the dangers around her to notice. She would inevitably need to stop for rest at some point and she couldn't remember the last time she'd eaten. It couldn't have been dinner with Dr. Dullahan and the Smith family at the Shady Nook, could it? That would've been several nights ago. She was so confused. She raised her eyes to the overcast sky. She couldn't tell how late in the day it, only that the sun would set again, just as it did every evening, and hated the idea of spending another night in this town.

Hunter moved with a confident a half-stride ahead of her. She'd been so frustrated by him the other evening, but since then he'd softened and she lacked the emotional strength to continue regarding him with glaring contempt. She admitted to herself that she'd much rather have him as company now, rather than no one at all.

They followed the road as it narrowed at an intersection. Each of the shops and houses were dark and even the traffic signals were out as if the power to the city had been cut.

There was a small Internet café next to a bookstore and in the window were several sheets of paper with a list of titles across from a class charts. No doubt it was the required material list for the University down the street. They were still in the University District, the clock tower looming many more blocks ahead, breaking above the tree line and piercing the low-hanging storm clouds. Across from the book store was a skateboard and surf shop and around the back where the dewy grass was beaten down into the mud was a stony trail of crushed seashell which lead to another sporting goods store with scuba gear displayed in the shadowy, hairline-cracked windows.

As she scanned the rain-drenched alleys and wobbly fences something caught her eye in the reflection of the bookstore. Movement of a figure drifting ghostlike among the misty alleyway.

She clenched onto Hunter and gasped. "Did you see that?"

His eyes were wide and lips drawn tight. Whatever it was, he'd seen it too.

"Quick, this way!" He gestured for her to follow, but he'd already taken a head start leaving her behind. He was much more athletic than she was and with speedy strides he followed the figure through the shadows and darted down a one-way street, leaving her struggling to keep up.

The one-way branched into a Y at another intersection with more winding paths of crushed seashells and round stepping stones between rows of cobblestone and wood buildings. She looked back over her shoulder. Maybe she'd taken a wrong turn somewhere? She faced forward again, straining for a hint of his location. She crept forward, uneasy.

Hunter poked his head around the corner of the sporting goods store, startling her. She grasped her chest and let out a sharp cry.

"I think, whoever it was, went inside one of these buildings. Maybe you could sneak around the front and I can cut them off from the back."

Evelyn was still breathing heavily when she agreed to his plan. It wasn't until she was standing in the musty doorway of the sporting good shop when she realized her mistake. She'd agreed to be left alone—again, hunting down god knows what.

Evelyn was still breathing heavily when she agreed to his plan. It wasn't until she was standing in the musty doorway of the sporting good shop when she realized her mistake. She'd agreed to be left alone—again, and was searching for. . .Well, she wasn't sure who. Or what.

She followed the path of seashells around another building separated from the other shops by a narrow strip of grass, sodden with mud and puddles of rainwater. When she emerged from around the corner, she saw Nora sitting on the wooden steps of the sporting goods store. She buried her face in the palms of her hands and whimpered with light, breathy squeaks.

"Nora, are you alright?"

The troubled young student raised her blood-shot eyes and shifted with uncomfortable edginess. She stuttered and pulled herself to her feet using the handrail for support.

"I forgot to replace the batteries." Her eyes dropped to her feet as she shook her head and trembled. "I'm sorry."

Evelyn reached out to console Nora but she jerked away. Her face crumpled in a mixture of hurt and rage and she screamed, "I'm sorry! *I'm sorry!*"

Her outburst startled Evelyn and she stumbled back.

Nora's chest rose and fell with deep, gasping sobs and her voice diminished. She looked around as if she'd forgotten where she was and then once again remembered Evelyn's presence.

Nora stared straight at Evelyn. "I'm sorry. I need to go."

"Wait, it's not safe out there!" In protest, Evelyn grabbed hold of Nora's arm but searing pain burnt her palms and fingertips. She pulled her hand away. Her palms were read where she'd grabbed Nora's arm. When she looked up, Nora had run off.

Was Nora one of them? Someone that would mutate into one of those creatures? She didn't even know what one of 'them' was. She needed answers still and she was growing impatient.

Then she had another thought. It was difficult enough for her to find information concerning her own past, but through her sleuthing she'd discovered numerous scandals among the townspeople. She knew that Mr. Norris, Dr. Brooke, and Dr. Dullahan had been involved with some malicious act involving The Mask of Flesh, The Wallet of Flesh and the other objects from the list.

There was the young girl, Charity Smith, who seemed surprised and downright upset that the company for dinner was Dr. Dullahan. Who'd she think was joining them? Then there was the strange way the doctor and the victualler, Ms. Smith had spoke over dinner, dancing around their words in Evelyn's company.

Then of course there was the woman in the bar who was utterly destroyed when her boyfriend left her. She'd loved him very much, Evelyn could tell, but she was a drunken mess and he couldn't handle her belligerent behavior when she was drunk.

Then there was Mr. Morgan who'd suffered from intense loneliness since his wife's passing.

And of course there was the weeping woman Evelyn had met in the café who had used her body to get what she wanted and then, in an instant, vaporized in a wooden box leaving puddles of her blood behind.

Nora and her erratic behavior had involved some kind of tragedy involving batteries, or maybe fire. Evelyn couldn't be sure.

And then there was that strange argument she'd overheard between Sheriff Rhett and Carly from Pan's Gallery involving some affair they'd been having.

Evelyn was aware that she might not have all the pieces just yet, she was making progress in unearthing the sordid past of the other townspeople. Still, not much about herself though. Maybe, through learning about the town, she could discover her own past. It was a stretch, but it was working so far, and she had Hunter's help.

Evelyn climbed the stairs to the sporting goods store and placed her tingling palms against the cold, watery surface of the wooden door, soothing her burns. She glanced up and down the alleys to see of Hunter had returned or if Nora had, for any reason, lingered nearby.

Nora had mentioned something about batteries like the one in Evelyn's pocket. There was only one reason Evelyn could think of. The girl had done something wrong and was burdened by guilt. And guilt, as Evelyn knew first hand, weighed heaviest on those who were most empathetic. And Nora seemed to be a very empathic girl.

Stepping into the shop, Evelyn's eyes landed on the uncoiled razor wire along the floor and a plethora of dark corners between wooden crates of heavy tools and hunting supplies.

Everything was in complete disarray, like a dusty junk-shop with random assortment of rusted tools, broken skateboards, fishing poles and spools of fishing line—stretched across the room with wet suits and coats on display. Evelyn coughed when she stepped deeper into the room; the air polluted with the fine haze of dust. Weak floorboards creaked with each attentive step as she maneuvered over the curls of razor wire. Electrical cords and other debris scattered the floor in a dangerous obstacle course. One snag of her shoelace on the razor wire or a trip of her toe under some hidden cables and she could fall and sever an artery. Compounding the danger was the fear of something lurking in the dark corners and hidden spaces between the crates. Paranoia manipulated her imagination.

Someone could be waiting behind the counter right now, watching her from the shadows, ready to snatch up the machete from the floor and hack her into bits. Then Hunter would come in and find her, nothing more than a quivering mass of chunks, scraped from the bone like piles of meat in a butcher shop.

She scolded herself for picturing such violent images. As long as she remained focused and on her guard she wouldn't be caught by surprise.

She cleared the jungle of wires and cords with scrupulous movements only to end up slipping on something wet. She caught herself on one of the wooden crates where the sharp point of a harpoon's blade came inches from her right eye. She muffled a short cry and a stifled gasp. An inch or two further and the harpoon would have popped her eye like a grape and embedded deep into her skull. She'd have to be more careful.

After her breath returned she peered down to see what she slipped on. At first she thought one of the cartons of oil stacked in the corner had leaked, but the fluid was almost black and much thicker. Coagulated blood. She followed the puddle to where it trailed between another tower of wooden crates along the sales counter and through a narrow hallway and finally past an empty office. Someone, or something, had lost a fatal amount of blood, right where she was standing, and then dragged out the back.

A horrific thought seized her body still. What if it was Hunter's blood? There were terrible monsters all around. Some, like the Executioner, were too massive and powerful to fight alone. Hunter wouldn't stand a chance. Evelyn had been lucky to escape when she did, but this bloody mess didn't look like the Executioner was responsible. The Executioner sliced people in half, but this looked like an animal attack.

Evelyn ran her fingers through her oily hair. In the back of the room, near the office, a gurgling noise surmounted the aching groans of the historical building. She took a step forward then stopped when the razor wire snagged the hem of her dirty cargo pants.

Across the room and against the wall stood a fat man, his shoulders slumped forward and the rotten malaise of death and seawater filled the room. His chest rose and fell with deep gurgling breaths due to the fleshy purple-green tubes protruding from his mouth and curving around his blubbery neckline into his chest. Evelyn took another cautious step. The floor creaked. The scuba-looking monster raised his head and she saw he wore a facemask. Behind the clouded mask, his swollen eyes protruded from their sockets. He gargled and choked on foul dark smelling liquid with the consistency of black sludge. Rotten seaweed ran down his several rows of corpuscular chins that shook like a jellyfish. He lunged at her with clumsy speed.

She darted right, straying into the catacomb of shelves and crates. The scuba man barreled toward her, unaffected by the razor wire tangling and slicing into his fat ankles. He groaned, spewing more black gunk from his face and sloshed his way around the crates, closing the distance between them. Evelyn's shin collided with an object obscured in the shadows. She winced and nearly crumbled to the floor, but forced herself to keep moving around the room while the scuba man swiped at her with pudgy black and purple fingers like a vicious animal or even—dare she say—a blood-thirsty zombie.

Nightmare Eve

She pivoted back around the room and hobbled over the wire stretching even further, trailing behind the scuba man. In a swift, graceful movement, she swiped the harpoon gun from the crate swung it around fired into the creature's bulbous head. The mask shattered inward and the long harpoon spike exploded out the back of his skull, splattering the wall with a murky purplish ooze. The copious monster fell back and landed in the mass of razor wire with a wet, *splat*!

She swallowed a deep, putrid gasp of sour air and remained still, blinking trying to sort out the events in her head. It all happened so quickly, but another stirring, this time from the front of the room, interrupted her moment of peace.

Movement caught her eye. More scuba men.

Time to run.

The fog swept through the back streets, but still Evelyn could see the swaggering pear-shaped figures bumbling towards her from beyond the moldering nooks and cluttered alleys. They appeared in the dark windows, pressing their oozing hands against the glass.

She sprinted from the alley into another lonely intersection, her eyes raced from street to street, her legs constantly shifting for her to flee but unsure of where to run. Go right, she told herself.

She'd only run for two blocks before her pace dwindled allowing her to catch her breath. Those monsters—those scuba men, may outweigh her by at least a hundred and fifty pounds, were impervious to pain, and outnumbered her, but Evelyn's advantage was speed. Their copious sizes, like swaggering blobs reminding Evelyn of graceless, clumsy sea lions. Easy to out run.

Evelyn assessed the environment. The houses were much nicer at this end of the University District with manicured lawns and signs that highlighted the historical significance. She paused at the curb of a single story brick office building where she spotted a wriggling body bag shoved beneath a juniper shrub. Frightening curiosity lingered in her mind. What could possibly still be living—or undead—trapped inside? Had the dead come back to life too?

She stepped past a row of young maple saplings to another display in the next yard. The skull of a corpse had been completely smashed in and spread across the cement walkway. The rest of his body sprawled across the path. Evelyn wasn't a forensics expert it would've been obvious to any amateur that the victim had been blitzed and brutally murdered by several crushing blows to the head. The gruesome scene lacked a murder weapon and she couldn't help but to wonder, were these creatures capable of using weapons? Why not? The Executioner demonstrated adept weapon skills.

In the greyness of fading light, ruins of a partially burnt four-story building stretched across the road as if it'd fallen randomly from the sky. The road, crumbling and broken, much like the rest of the town, continued right up to the face of the building then disappeared under the foundation. Winds soughed through the thick woods surrounding the dormitory like a barricade making any other way around, impossible. Behind the charred rooftop were the sharp towers of Westminster Concert Hall and the clock tower, which meant the library was near.

The ground sloped a little as Evelyn stepped up the rickety stairs. Many of the boards had rotted away and crumbled inwards, leaving a gaping hole where Evelyn could peer down inside and see churning ocean waters. She was close, the violin sounding just ahead.

Chapter 24

The door creaked open with ease and Evelyn stepped inside. Right away she sensed the sorrow weighing heavy in the austere foyer that was more like a reception office rather than the entrance to a dormitory. The layout reminded Evelyn of a hospital with a cork bulletin board mounted to the right wall, an emergency scape plan posted beside it and a long counter lined with burnt pages and a centimeter of ash. Somewhere, echoing down the smoky grey corridors, rose a faint crying from a young man. When she stepped further into the room, she could almost taste the bitter ash like a campfire smoldering in her mouth.

Any suspicions she had about Westminster once being a mental institution were reinforced when she continued down the claustrophobic blackened walls. The crying echoed all around her, faint, but somewhere unidentifiably close.

She hovered in the hallway beneath an archway listening to the man's sobs. She was getting closer. She stared up at the spiraling staircase and then down another set into the pool of darkness below. Another sob made her certain the man was in the basement. She bit her lip and called out.

She heard stirring, then shuffling from above. Evelyn took the first few weary steps before spotting the gaunt, young man with cheeks suffused of color. He had a black eye and thin line of blood ran down from his hairline to his chin. His nostrils bled and his bruised upper lip, split, had turned blue and purple. She reached out for him with genuine concern, but he shied away. He feared her.

"You need a hospital," she said. "This looks bad. You might have a concussion."

She lowered herself to his eye level, balanced on her left knee.

"It's no use. The doctor is dead and everyone else is missing. I can't leave this place, if I do, they'll find me again. They'll kill me."

Evelyn nodded. "John and his gang did this to you?" she said as more of a statement rather than a question.

The young man, no older than twenty, didn't respond.

He needed medical attention, but the only other doctor she'd seen was that sadistic surgeon removing Corey's organs in the front yard. If there was a hospital in town, Evelyn didn't want to see it.

"You probably shouldn't stay here too long, this place is dangerous. You're not safe."

"I was supposed to go out tonight," he said sadly. "Now look at me." He lifted his head and Evelyn could clearly see his bruises. His right eye, surrounded by purple and black welts, was nearly swollen shut. His other eye was blood shot and tears streaked his face mixing with blood. "I'm weak and pathetic. My clothes are ruined. These scars will never heal." He reached in his pocket and removed a folded paper. "Take my invitation.

Tell him I'm sorry and that no matter what happens, I will always love him."

Evelyn took the invitation from his hands. *Westminister Theatrical Society Admit One.*

Evelyn examined the ticket while the injured student climbed unsteadily to his feet and lumbered up the stairs. She called out for him to wait and asked for his name but he disappeared through the doorway leaving Evelyn alone in the stairwell clutching the recital invitation in her hand.

She rose from her kneeling position and placed the invitation in her left pocket where she kept the battery from the men's locker room and the small bowl carved from bone. In her other pocket, the mask and Wallet of Flesh and the folded sheet music bulged at her side.

Evelyn carried herself up the stairwell, noticing the smoky air becoming even more stuffy and suffocating. The scent of charred wood, like a smoldering campfire, was growing stronger and a haze of ash and soot clouded the darkness, lowering her visibility even more. She coughed from the dry, itchy tingling in her throat but the irritation went unrelieved.

Visibility worsened when she stepped into the second floor hallway, but the walls and ceiling all around her were with blackened and cracked with the texture of cooling lava. The floor bubbled with basketball-sized domes and Evelyn eased along the wall with caution, avoiding the weak floorboards and gaps that could send her plunging to the level below.

Ahead of her, the hazy shape of a young woman—the same woman photographed from the flowered shrines across campus—drifted with ghost-like strides away and vanished with a faint scream that lingered after she disappeared into the foggy sidewalks.

Evelyn flushed with adrenaline. She hated when they surprised her like that. She still wasn't sure what *they* were, but *they* seemed to be everywhere, appearing long enough to startle her and then vanish. Were they dead or were they alive or somewhere in-between? Evelyn clutched her chest and waited for her pulse to slow.

When she felt her heart rate and breath slow to a normal pace, her confidence returned. She continued forward in search of the library or the theatre. Whichever was closest.

As she neared the room at the end of the hall, the cracking sounds of fire made her to pause again, and she pivoted on her left foot while glancing over her shoulder to feel the heat against her face. A cloud of orange and red flickered through gray dust and the hallway behind her, consumed by unseen flames, glowed with heat. In seconds the air grew unbearably hot and Evelyn felt the breath being sucked out of her lungs. She doubled over gasping for fresh air. The glowing brightness moved closer and the temperature continued to rise, forcing her to run down the hallway and checked each door as she run. All were locked. It wasn't until she reached the final door at the end of the hall that she was able to escape the incipient fire danger.

She stood in a cramped dorm room with two other girls. Nora Brooke shuffled through her backpack while the other girl, the Charred Woman from the posters and again fading into the mist minutes ago, sat in her bed reading from a thick textbook and tapping the pages with a pen in her hand. They moved unaware of Evelyn's presence.

"There's a fire!" Evelyn blurted. They couldn't hear her. She was in their world now, and in their world, Evelyn was the ghost, unseen and unheard.

Everything appeared just as it did before the fire swept through. The warming, floral scent of vanilla and lavender danced through the room partitioned by two desks, similarly decorated with purple and yellow flowers in a beige vase and a stuffed teddy bare hugging a glass jar filled with rocks and bamboo. The styles between the two students meshed well— both organized and creative, with posters of silly yellow faces with wide grins next to anatomical images of the

Nightmare Eve

musculoskeletal system and a table of elements pinned to the narrow closet. Their room was an amalgam of entertainment and intellect. There was only one thing that appeared to stand out amongst the bright décor and organized layout. A grey scarf made of a fine, wiry material, much finer than horsehair but less coarse, lay crumpled in a heap near the corner of the very tidy room.

It seemed very strange that two young women with such exquisite taste in fashion would own such a hideous scarf.

It stood out much like the Mask and Wallet of Flesh and the Skull of Bone when she found them. As soon as she picked it up and felt the gritty texture in her hand, she knew right away it was made from human hair. The Scarf of Hair, another cryptic item to cross off her list.

Her lips curled downward, repulsed by the object. She felt the urge to vomit and wanted drop the hideous thing and wash her hands, but the object, she knew, was just as important as the others. To make matters worse, there was only enough space in her pockets for smaller objects, but not an entire scarf. She'd have to wear it around her neck. She cringed as the rough, brittle hairs slid around her neck.

She turned to Nora who dropped her backpack to the floor with a disgruntled sigh. "I left my homework in the labs. Dr. Dullahan is going to fail me if I don't get this project done by next week."

Nora Brooke's roommate shut her textbook. "The labs are open for another hour. It only takes a few minutes to walk. Just don't wake me up when you get back. I'm dead tired and I start finals tomorrow. I can't wait till the quarter is up. Then I can start taking more electives."

"I don't know how you do it, I can't even keep up with the pre-requisites I have now. I'm so absent minded these days, I'd forget my own head if it wasn't attached to my fabulously toned body."

Her roommate laughed and shut her textbook. "Well don't lose track of time, you still need your beauty sleep."

"I won't be long." Nora bobbed out of the room, leaving Evelyn alone with the roommate. The girl sighed, reached to her nightstand and flicked the switch of her lamp. The room would've been swallowed in darkness, but Evelyn noticed the lightweight curtains that were brushing against the long, narrow floor heater had singed edges and the heat rising from the heaters were causing the material to flutter.

Evelyn watched in horror as the roommate nodded off to sleep with headphones over her ears, unaware of the flammable material singed by the heaters and floating dangerously close to the lavender candle, which Nora had forgotten to blow out. Evelyn raised her eyes to the ceiling at the smoke detector and Nora's words flashed in her mind, "*I forgot to replace the batteries.*"

Evelyn finally understood. Smoke detectors beep when they run low on power. Distracted by the beeping, Nora removed the front of the smoke detector and removed the dead battery, intending to replace it at a more convenient time when she wasn't deep in her work. Then one night, during their study sessions, Nora rushed to retrieve her homework from Dr. Dullahan's classroom post haste, while her roommate took nap. With her eyes closed and headphones turned up, her roommate didn't sense the incipient fire.

It only took a few seconds before the highly combustible curtains to ignite. Wooden shelves stocked with books fueled the fire and before Nora's roommate had a chance to escape, the dorm became an inferno, burning her alive.

Survival instincts commandeered Evelyn's actions and she wrapped the scarf around her neck and reached for the door handle, burning hot in her hands. Just as the flames jumped from posters to the comforter where Nora's roommate slept, Evelyn jumped for the smoke detector.

A series of throaty coughs erupted with the crackling of the growing flames.

Evelyn pressed the back of her hands against the chair and maneuvered it underneath the smoke detector.

Nora's roommate stirred, tangled in her sheets, the synthetic fabric melting to her bubbling flesh as she shrieked. The fireball that was once Nora's roommate rolled onto the floor, spreading the flames further through the room.

Evelyn grasped the smoke detector and twisted off the cover revealing the empty space where a small battery should've been. Evelyn reached in her pocket for the battery from the locker room and inserted it into the smoke detector. The battery snapped into place and Evelyn placed the device back into its mount.

The dormitory became a blurry haze, the smoke so thick it stung her eyes. The ash clogged her nostrils and she choked as she fell to the floor, her body convulsing over hot embers and lungs filling with smoke. Her eyes stung with tears. She writhed with agony to the bleating wail of the revived smoke detector.

Chapter 25

"I'll always love you."

The feminine voice seemed close, yet so far. It took Evelyn a moment to realize the voice she heard was her own. She opened her eyes to the white haze cast over her. White snow flurried around, her eyes fluttering as the flakes brushed against her cheeks, settling around her. The memory of David faded, along with her words, as her surroundings took focus.

She lie face up, the grey afternoon sky coming into focus. What she thought were flakes of snow was actually ash from a fire falling from the blackened ceiling and crumbling walls. A sense of calmness inhabited the room. Evelyn pulled herself into a sitting position and blinked several times before rubbing her face. She felt the silky ash tickle her skin and she brought her hands away from her cheeks, she saw there were

Nightmare Eve

smeared with ash and soot. Above, the ceiling had burned away and sunlight from the bright blue sky poured through.

She rose to her feet and saw the rest of the room had been entirely consumed by the flame leaving a burnt, crusted shell. Everything was destroyed except for the smoke detector that flashed green from the new battery and appeared brand new, unscathed by the ravishing flames. Beside her, the poor young girls body lie on the floor, charred black and shriveled like dried fruit.

Evelyn managed to change the batteries, but the student wasn't spared. She doubted there was anything else she could've done to save the poor girl, Evelyn was merely a spectator to the past events. She couldn't change things entirely, but somehow replacing the batters had made her feel accomplished and her actions had affected Amherst with pleasant results. The spirits were gone and the air felt lighter, less suffocating than before. It felt right. Maybe these people, trapped by their misdoings, weren't meant to do her harm. Maybe they needed help. Each person she'd encountered had experienced some sort of tragedy. Sometimes they felt guilt, angry, scared or confused. It was like Hunter had said, it wasn't the town that was haunted, it was the people and they needed to find their peace through redemption—correcting the mistakes of their past and Evelyn was here to help them.

But then what about Evelyn? Why her?

Evelyn couldn't exist in this town without being part of something terrible and tragic, that's why it called to her. Something inside of her made her feel guilt with such intense passion that it brought her here, to a very dark place, and only she could remember what it was. Or she could if it weren't for the Doxepin. Whatever tragic event happened in her life, Evelyn was sorry for it and she'd do whatever it took to make up for it. If there was one thing Evelyn knew, it was that true love doesn't simply disappear. It's powerful and lasts beyond lifetimes. She vowed to live in Amherst and fight for those who are hurting, to uncover the truth of her past and to bear the consequences of her past actions by the hand of judgment, none other than the Executioner.

—

When Evelyn stepped out the back door of the dormitory, the air became stale again. From the roadway, she peered up at the ominous building looming over the park with burnt out windows like the black hollow eyes of a skull watching Evelyn as she took swift strides down the street.

Overturned in the gutter was a blood-splattered wheel chair. The wheel against the pavement appeared to have been crushed while the opposite wheel creaked as it spun. Evelyn moved on. Although unsettling, there were scarier things in Amherst than a wheelchair.

As soon as it was out of sight, the melodic keys of the familiar song reminded her of the folded sheet music stuffed in her pocket. She listened to the melody. It lasted only a few bars, just a few seconds at most, and then abruptly stopped, but just for a moment, and then started again from the beginning.

The music grew louder as she continued onward through the empty suburban homes and bloody driveways of sorority row. Every few steps the music would end, then start again, over and over. From what she remembered, according to the map the theatre was close.

She took a sharp left and the massive trees scattered through the yards parted revealing a scene so startling, her legs froze.

The townspeople, no more than grey, lifeless corpses now, were bound in straight jackets and hanged by ropes that reached endlessly into the abysmal sky. Hundreds of them in swayed from taught nooses that creaked and ached with every swivel, back and forth. Each of their faces had been covered by burlap sacks, just like the Executioner, but both eyeholes had been cut out to where Evelyn could see their penetrating stares. They were dead, yet they still watched her with unblinking eyes,

Nightmare Eve

shifting towards her and following her as she walked past. They swayed above her, dangling just high enough from the ground that their blue and purple rotting toes brushed against her shoulder.

She let out a whimper as the scraggly toes of a rotting old man slid across her face. With every step, his eyes followed her from above.

One to her left shuddered spasmodically. She cried out and stumbled back into another pair of legs, a young woman caked in dried blood. She glared at Evelyn, her left eye fluttering.

From the theatre, the song repeated.

Then she heard the snap of a rope finally breaking under the tension followed by the heavy thud of the body smacking against the pavement. Somewhere in the fog came a deep, mournful groan.

Just ahead, through wispy tendrils of white, Evelyn could see the outline of the hanged man spread out on the road, blood flowing from a traumatic head would seeping through the burlap sac. The rope stayed tied around his neck, but the break had left one long piece frayed at his waist.

The hanged man stirred and climbed to his feet letting out a guttural moan that sounded more animalistic than human. Its eyes wobbled in its head before spotting Evelyn and let out a snarled growl. The straightjacket, which had previously kept his arms bound to his sides, had come undone during the fall and scraped against the pavement as he shambled closer to her. Metal clanked on the road and when she saw the sharpened metal hooks in the lengthy white sleeves, she had her answer: they knew how to use weapons. Another snap echoed from somewhere around her. She raised her eyes to the dangling corpses, still watching her with hungry, vengeful eyes. She'd strolled right into a forest of predators: hundreds of hanged men, sadistic killers and haunted souls, each one dead and still capable of murder.

Evelyn brought her attention to the immediate threat shambling towards her, dragging the metal hooks along the road. Its head wobbled side to side and she opened her mouth—the startled cry of a doomed woman. It sounded weak, desperate and strangled.

It hadn't taken long for the hanged man to totter close enough for Evelyn to feint right. Luckily the monster was only slightly faster than the scuba men but still slow enough that Evelyn could walk past him The immediate danger only came when the hanged man reached close enough to where he could outstretch his elongated straightjacket arms and swing at her using the sharpened metal hooks He leaned back like a pitcher in a baseball game and flung his hooks toward her, missing her, and then clattered to the pavement. It took him a moment for him to withdraw the hooks, giving Evelyn a chance to maneuver passed, wishing she still had the harpoon or fire axe.

The hanged man let out a protesting moan as Evelyn evaded another metal claw attack by diving under his arm when he prepared to swing. As the monster shook, retracting his blade again, Evelyn fled down the street. Behind her in the soupy fog, Evelyn heard the snap of another failing rope.

Then another.

And another...

―

Evelyn planned to cut through the back alleys and hobble over shrubs and fences as much as possible; the main roads were too dangerous now. Hundreds of hanged men stalked the town now and all roads leading away had been washed out. If she could just make it to the theater, she'd be able to hunker down for the evening there—more preferably than sleeping under another rosemary bush. If she stayed in one spot for too long, the Executioner would surely find her and killer her.

A low moan permeated the sour fog. To her left, a park offered places to hide beneath a maze of tall and thick pines and vigorous bushes. Following the corner of the park with her eyes,

Nightmare Eve

she spotted the hanged man guarding the theatre entrance. His left eye shifted madly, stuck in a permanent spasm, the other bloodshot eye locked on her.

The path to Evelyn's left was clear. She leapt over the low shrubs lining the stone wall, and was nearly struck the hook of a hanged woman. The blade clanked off the wall and bounced into the bush. The monster snarled. Evelyn climbed over the chain and sprinted forward. Low branches snagged her scarf, but she didn't care. She stopped when the path curved right and collided with a hanged man, knocking him down. Behind the toppled monster, two scuba men trailed behind. These *things* were everywhere!

The other two hanged men moved in syncopated steps in an undead march while the scuba men lumbered forward, choking on the tar-like black fluids from their bloated wormy lips.

She heard the scrape behind her and realized she'd forgotten about the hanged woman she'd just escaped from, now dangerously close. With a ferocious cry, she threw herself into the shrubs, snapping the branches and stems as she tumbled. Lesions stung her cheeks and she burst out from the bushes face down in the grass. She was covered in pine needles and dirt, bruises on her face and arm and twigs sticking out of her frizzy hair. Fifty yards ahead, the theatre offered her escape. Behind her, the horde of nightmare creatures tore open a rift in the shrubs and barreled towards her.

She pushed herself off the ground just as another hook clawed into the disturbed soil where she'd fallen seconds before—a narrow escape. She sprinted to the theatre.

The damage from the storm hadn't been near as bad here as it had been in other places like the front of the university that had practically crumbled to ruins or the eastern roads that slid off the mountain. The massive stone theatre showed only minor signs of wear along the red roof accents. The stone steps up to the front door crumbled a bit around the edges that led to a beautiful wide patio with garden furniture and beautiful potted plants. In front was a sign that read: *by invitation only*.

She made her way up the steps, clutching the invitation that the young man had given to her.

"Are you alright?"

Evelyn stopped and turned to see Hunter emerge from the lavish patio to the top of the steps. She glanced back expecting the monsters to swarm them, but what she saw was a monster-free park.

"Hunter, what are you doing here?" Evelyn choked.

He sheepishly ran his fingers through his hear. "I you that I was stood up. It was supposed to be a date, but since all this has happened, I thought maybe. . ."

"There'd be others here? We're not the only ones left alive in this town."

"There's music coming from inside. I thought if other people heard it too, then maybe the survivors would head this way. But I guess it's just you and me so far."

The fact that he didn't appear as terrified as her made Evelyn feel even more worried. "Lets go check things out."

He bowed. "After you."

The doors creaked open and Evelyn stepped inside followed by Hunter.

The three-story theatre was just as musty as the other buildings and a light haze lingered in the still air and cobwebs adorned the crimson and black seats. Evelyn could see the thick layers of dust coating the railings and the matching crimson carpets appeared dingy with stains, dirty and light water damage.

The stage lights illuminated the violinist on stage, a strange mechanical puppet slanted on one leg shorter than the other. Its limbs were made of wood, but metal gears cranked in its open chest cavity while its head was a mesh of cranks and twin rusted pipes that gave the appearance of eyes.

Nightmare Eve

The bow slid forward and back, strumming on the violin while a young girl in white pirouetted across the stage. Chocolate brown curls bobbed at her cheeks as she bobbed and twirled until the strange automaton played a flat note that made both Evelyn and Hunter cringe. The young dancer on stage stumbled and ell to her hands and knees and burst into tears before dissipating into a cloud of vapor. Evelyn crept toward the stage and watched in awe as the music began from the beginning again, and the young girl re-materialized in her first position at the other end of the stage. She performed another pirouette until the automaton struck the flat key again, and again she fell.

Hunter took a seat in the front-center row. He watched unaware of the ghostly performance stuck on repeat.

In her pocket, Evelyn remembered the sheet music.

With the sheet music in hand, she walked down the aisle and climbed the stairs to the stage. Under the lights, the seats in the audience weren't visible, but she knew Hunter there.

At stage left, the mechanical statue, at least a head taller than Evelyn, repeated the melody. Rusted metal gears clicked inside, growing louder as she approached. In its chest cavity, along with the gears, was a device that looked like a rolling pin with notches made for a music scroll. She unfolded the pages in her hand and wedged them inside the automaton's chest so that the sheets lined with the notches in the cylindrical device. Once in place, she backed off stage. When returned to the orchestral seating, the house lights dimmed and the dancer reappeared in first position. She twisted and twirled to the music and pirouetted across the stage. Soon after, the music ended, the girl curtseyed, holding the corners of her white lace dress out, and the theatre filled with the disembodied applause of two hundred spectators. Hunter clapped with them. When the applause subsided, he rose to his feet.

"Aren't you staying?"

Evelyn shook her head. "I need to find out what happened to my fiancé."

Though Hunter appeared dubious, he nodded and said: "Are you sure you want to follow through with this? Sometimes it's better that we let go of our past and move on. Let sleeping corpses lie."

Evelyn shuddered. "I need to know. I love him."

Hunter looked at her thoughtfully. "You should check the library. It's at the other end of the park. The town's officials keep all the historical records in the basement. I'm sure you can find the answers your looking for there."

Evelyn thanked him.

"Just be careful." he added.

"You're not coming with me?"

Hunter shook his head. "No. I'm going to stay for the final act."

Chapter 26

On the way to Westminster Library, Evelyn heard the sad chorus of tormented hanged men and women. She ditched the invitation in a park trashcan and followed the stone pathway through the trees. Alongside the path she came across a construction site where workers had dug up the ground to replace a cracked water pipe. Just below the caution tape, several chunks of broken cement and a stack of metal pipes lie strewn about. A pipe wasn't a gun, but it would still serve as a better weapon than nothing. It weighed heavy in her hands, her swing would be slow, but cause considerable damage. She looked across the park and then to the canopy of trees above. The clock tower stretched into the sky. The path would take her there.

  A scuba man was stuck in the bushes ahead. It swiveled side to side, it's massive chest rising and falling. The scuba man's skin was still moist as if it'd just crawled from the murky depths below the harbor. Evelyn grasped the pipe and scuttled forward, pushing her body into the swing like a game of baseball. The pipe smashed through the creature, sending bone fragments and splatters of a fetid oily substance along the path. The scuba men fell to the ground, still.

Continuing through the park, Evelyn dispatched a second scuba man barreling from ahead and a hanged man, hunched over and snarling. Two strikes each leveled them, but Evelyn didn't stick around long enough to see if they returned to their feet.

A sinister looking edifice with large stone pillars and pointed archways peered from a copse of evergreens and alders. Evelyn walked toward the side ramp and spotted a police car with flashing lights in the parking lot out front. Sheriff Rhett stood with Ms. Smith and her daughter Charity immersed in a heated conversation. Ms. Smith wore a frazzled expression and gestured in a flustered way. Charity bowed her head. Sheriff Rhett appeared disappointed, with his eyes shifting away from her as he withdrew handcuffs and moved forward.

"You've left me no other choice." Sheriff Rhett said and placed the handcuffs on Ms. Smith.

"It wasn't supposed to be this way!" Ms. Smith declared. Sheriff Rhett recited her Miranda rights. "You don't understand! I didn't do it!"

Ms. Smith continued to mutter protesting remarks while allowing the sheriff to guide her to the back of the car.

Charity watched, pale and sick-looking as Evelyn approached. "He's arresting my mom for murder!"

Sheriff Rhett looked up in surprise. Ms. Smith stopped muttering when she saw her. Cherry begged for Evelyn to do something.

"Miss Harris, where have you been, we've been searching everywhere for you! You took off the Shady Nook and didn't come back. Watch your fingers, Barbara." said Rhett as he shut the car door.

"Listen, I'm not going anywhere until I get some answers."

The sheriff's face remained soft and thoughtful. Not the reaction she had expected. "Alright, but seeing as how it's getting late and I've got a curfew to enforce, why don't you come with me and the Smith's here back to the station. Then in the morning we can sort things out." The sheriff flashed a smile, but Evelyn wasn't buying it.

"I think I've managed well so far," she said and gave the pipe in her hand a twirl.

Sheriff Rhett shot her an angry glance. "Just stay inside the library. You'll be a lot safer there and I'll be back as soon as I can."

Evelyn gave an impatient nod while Charity climbed into the backseat, the sheriff in the driver's seat, and watched them pull away. When they were gone and a deathly breath of air rustled the park leaves, Evelyn grabbed the door handles and entered the Westminster Library.

Low orange lights, musty air and elegant crimson and gold décor reminded her of the theatre's foyer but massive with a maze of bookshelves and long, sturdy rectangular tables dominating the center of the impressive library. A pale haze that reminded her of cigar smoke in an old study wafted through the room. To her right, a wide cherry wood staircase with flowing red carpets led above and below the main floor. The second and third stories were as equally luxurious as the main floor with tall, narrow windows adorned with thick, velvety drapes the color of black cherries. Around the stairs, Evelyn spotted the librarian's desk.

Evelyn relaxed, pleasantly surprised by the library's immaculate preservation. She had half expected it to be more like the flooding university or the collapsed buildings downtown and occupied by monsters. Instead, it was an untouched sanctuary. When she moved around the first row of towering bookshelves, she saw the man at the desk, steeped in books and paperwork. He pushed a set of wire-rimmed glasses up the narrow bridge of his long nose. He gave his attention to an opened notebook on the desk then removed a page from the stack of files. He was a tall gangly man, handsome with golden brown hair parted down the center and caramel-colored eyes that seemed to emit golden light. His white shirt was unbuttoned at the top and perspiration dampened his neck.

"Excuse me." Evelyn placed her left hand on the desk.

He raised his head and used his forefinger to push his glasses up again. "We're closed."

Evelyn passed the pipe from her right hand to her left. "Sheriff Rhett told me to wait here. He said he'd be back as soon as he could."

The librarian glanced down at the source of his exasperation—more pages scattered across his desk. He raised his eyes to her again and replied by using only a swift and abrupt nod.

Evelyn muttered a thank you, but he took no notice as his eyes were already scanning the documents with meticulous scrutiny. She backed away from the desk and perused the maze of books.

In the dim lighting many of the titles were hard to read, but stopped when she came across a space where a book had been removed leaving a gap just over an inch wide. This would've been nothing unusual if it were in a normal library, but here, Evelyn noticed, there seemed to be no missing books anywhere else on this shelf. Every book, every volume was presently in its proper place, except for the one that belonged in this gap.

Hoping to get close enough to read the titles on either side of it, she lowered herself to eye level and saw the saw a pair of glass eyes from a porcelain doll starring back at her. The right eye, charcoal-colored and glossy, was much larger—

almost twice the size of the ruby-colored left eye. It reminded her of the Ivy Rose doll haunting her dreams. Its black hair was braided in tight pigtails and she was dressed in a matching red and black kimono. It was a child's porcelain doll, but everything about it from the misshapen eyes to the pale skin tone was more like something from a child's nightmare.

She rose to her feet and continued to browse the other shelves contemplating if she should go back and take the doll with her. She couldn't very well fit it in her pocket, as the doll was nearly a foot tall, so if she did take it with her, she'd have to carry it. One hand for the doll, the other for the pipe, but she preferred to have both hands to swing. She decided to come back for it later.

In the next room, a projection room, was a square shaped room only big enough for a set of chairs, a projector and a white screen six feet in diameter. Evelyn didn't know anything about projectors, but it looked very old and unkempt with a thick layer of dust that made her nose and eyes tingle and itch. The film real clicked as it spun and Evelyn figured whoever used it last had accidentally left it running.

Like the other items she had picked up along the way, the projector seemed set up in such an obvious way that Evelyn couldn't help noticing. These objects, like the battery, were placed there for Evelyn to find. They were items from the tormented citizens' pasts that were leading her to reveal the truth about her own. Evelyn stared at the blank projection screen, flickering ghostly pale like the creeping fog outside. These clues were showing her the way. What was it in her past that she wasn't seeing? And what was the film about to show her?

Chapter 27

Beads of sweat collected on the laborer's faces and dampened their shirts clinging against their skin. Some of the immigrant workers were hunched over a sluice—a long series of water-filled wooden boxes isolating gold from gravel. Others gripped the handles of farm tools and stabbed them into the fertile soils. The piercing, breathy whistle of a steamboat hailing into the harbor offered a welcoming hint of the approaching mid-day break where they would snack on fresh salmon from the local river and hearty portions of sticky rice. The work was strenuous and never-ending, but they smiled, grateful that they had jobs that provided well for their families. The year had offered them good health and lush soils for planting and rivers plentiful with fish. It had been a prosperous year, just like the year before. And many years before then.

Nightmare Eve

It was the end of the 1850's and the long dispute between the northern and southern states had escalated. The strip of southern states along New Mexico and Arizona was of many controversial racial debates as were the early qualities of women's rights. California, Minnesota and Kansas had recently been officially signed into the United States and wouldn't be longer until West Virginia and Nevada signed in as well.

Life in the United States was changing. Not just for the citizens of Amherst, but for the entire country. Every year it seemed there was a new flag, new states and new presidents. Life was quick. Movements and industrial ideas promised an increase of revenue and output for the financially inclined, a wealth of opportunities for anyone who wanted them. Life across the United States was tumbling ahead faster than anyone could've foreseen. Life in Amherst, tucked away in a nest of forests and sky-scraping peaks of the West Coast, remained an undiscovered treasure. The whole world changed from days to weeks and from months to years.

Technology was ever-changing, but the ethos of ancient traditions were as strong today in the immigrant workers as they were thousands of years ago.

The railroads were a time of escape for the Chinese workers. Some of them were forced to leave their homes and become slaves to the railroad while others sought this opportunity as a chance to start a new life, to save their families from whatever political horrors they'd come between. There was a myriad of reasons why people had to run—and why they hid, but for the majority of the deserters, the road had brought them to the Amherst community.

It seemed like the perfect escape. Picturesque trees and vibrant green mountainsides of spring water ponds beneath waterfalls cascading from mountain peaks shielded the humble town like impassible barricades. Hardly any roads confronted the dangerous passes and trains submitted to the treacherous landscapes. It was the ideal escape from politics, war, famine and even time itself.

Amherst-by-the-Sea was founded originally as an escape-town from Chinese immigrants who'd run from the deathly conditions of railway despots and villainous tyrants of their own country. They'd survived in the hillsides for generations preserving the ancient traditions passed down from generations including their religious beliefs as well as their political beliefs.

There came a time when a Priest was chosen by a select group of citizens known as The Dragon Order to rule the small American community into a time of great prosperity. He sat at his throne in a temple built high in the mountains where he could look upon the happiness of the township. One day while he sat looking over the prospering villagers, he noticed a young woman wandering the shore. She was the most beautiful woman he'd ever seen. They were married early that spring and their love flowed through the village like the bountiful rivers. On their wedding day, the High Priest placed a gong in a shrine overlooking the community. As long as their love remained strong, The Dragon Order blessed their new Priest and Priestess and promised the survival and secrecy of their village every year in a village-wide ritual. The community would gather coifed in scarlet-colored robes bearing candles and a uttering a secret prayer of love and peace while hiking up the mountainside which had isolated their village for so long. Every year, the head Priest would ring the gong washing the impurities of earth and guilty souls of the spiritual realms away from their community ensuring that their kingdom would survive in timeless happiness.

But there was a young woman who envied the Priestess and secretly desired the head priest all to herself. She knew he could never love her, for he was already married to a wife who promised a son so she devised a plan.

Nightmare Eve

On Eve of the Dragon, the darkest of nights where where dreams are manifested into reality and the community was granted another year of prosperity, she posed as the High Priestess and climbed to the top of the mountain where the sacred gong kept watch over the community. She struck the sacred gong and her passion, fueled by jealousy, anger and fear had broken the Dragon Order's ritual and plummeted the village into chaos, luring tormented souls to the town of everlasting darkness. And every year, on that same night, the lost souls of the lonely and despairing gather in the town square to pilgrimage up the mountainside in a ritual now known as the Eve of Nightmares.

The reel reached the end of the strip, which flicked and clattered as the spools continued to turn. She flipped off the switch and the raucous of the projector died. The room darkened. She stood in front of the blank silk screen and furrowed her brows in passing thoughts.

She turned away from the projector and felt her heart jump when she saw Sheriff Rhett standing in the back of the room. She hadn't heard him come in. It was strange he hadn't bothered to say anything to her.

He looked exhausted with a cadaverous face, heavy eye bags and pale skin that sagged off his prominent cheekbones. In his hands he carried a thin, pocket-sized book bound in aged dark leather. Sheriff Rhett caught her eyeing the book with suspicion.

"Is this yours?" He held the book tight in his left hand. His face was rigid and tone, aggressive. "Chemicals, herbs and poisons?"

"No, I—." Evelyn had never seen the book before in her life, but she knew what it was. The leather binding the material was unmistakable—the same as the wallet and the mask. It was human leather. A book bound by the flesh of a serial killer.

Nightmare Eve

"It was you, wasn't it? It was you all along. You did this. You told Ms. Smith about everything." Sheriff Rhett's brash tone and bitter eyes scowled an accusatory glare. He trembled and Evelyn felt incipient danger growing.

"I don't know what you're talking about." Evelyn took a step back, but the sheriff burst forward, his right arm outstretched as if to strike her.

"It was you who was spying on Dr. Dullahan that night he was murdered. You were spotted standing at your bedroom window watching him leave."

Evelyn's brain whirled with the memories of the exotic clerk spying on the doctor outside of Shady Nook. Evelyn had been standing by the window but not because she was spying on the doctor, but because she had inadvertently spotted Carly from Pan's Art Gallery hiding behind a grassy hill watching the doctor. To somebody coming up the path on the opposite side of the Shady Nook wouldn't have been able to see Carly hidden behind the boulders. He or she would've only been able to see Evelyn watching the doctor.

"I don't know what's going on here. All I want to do is find David and Ivy and get as far away from this place as possible."

Sheriff Rhett clutched the book, his features hard. His voice sounded stern, but spoke quieter. "No one is getting out of here tonight. Curfew is about to start and no one goes out after dark. Check the harbor tomorrow. It seems everyone who comes to Amherst can't help but to check out our beautiful beaches." Sheriff Rhett backed away, his face dripping with sweat, eyes black and skin pale as if he'd been suffering from a severe flu. In his hands he still clutched the Book of Flesh and shot her a glossy, bitter glare as he exited the projection room and entered the main room.

What had gotten into the sheriff? He acted so calm and well mannered before, even reassuring and confident. Now is half-dead stare and erratic behavior, the confused tone in his

224

voice, was terribly out of character for him and disturbed her. With or without knowing it, Sheriff Rhett had even admitted that the doctor had, in fact, been murdered when he had insisted so many times before that it was merely an accident.

Evelyn brushed her fingers through the knotted strands of muddy blonde hair tangled at her shoulders. She took once last glance at the projector before heading toward the door.

She reached for the handle when a sudden click from the project her made her stop and turn around. Impossible as it was, another image flickered on the screen.

A new reel had replaced the previous documentary. Now on the screen appeared a poor, run down country home and storage shed somewhere in the woods. Then a shot of an axe stuck in a log appeared. The film continued to cut in and out of various rooms, including the storage shed where a row of tools such as handsaws, hammers, machetes and several yards of orange twine lie scattered. Hooks and scythes hung from chains mounted from cross beams above bails of hay. Evelyn noticed in the background, on a bench full of tools, the outline of a missing meat cleaver. Then the screen faded into a long, narrow hallway with a wooden door at the far end. The door creaked open and a young boy looked down at the floor. Evelyn recognized him from the window of the abandoned shop earlier where Hunter had apologized for abandoning her. In the boy's hand was the missing meat cleaver, dark with what Evelyn assumed was blood. The child stood directly in the frame and raised his head. Over his face he wore a white paper mask that covered his nose and mouth and wore thick blood-splattered goggles around his head.

"*I see you, Evelyn.*" He raised the cleaver over his head and brought it down across the camera. The screen went dark, but Evelyn still heard his voice. "*I'm coming.*"

Fear rippled through her. Even though it was just a video, he had seen her. He had been looking right at her. He knew her fucking name. She had to get out of here.

She went for the door and returned to the main hall.

Sheriff Rhett had disappeared somewhere along the towers of books and Evelyn skimmed the enormous room wondering if there was a safe place to rest for a few minutes.

"You'll find more selections in the basement."

Evelyn looked at the librarian. His stack of paperwork had shrunk to a few pages, his notebook nearly full.

"Thanks." Evelyn forced an unconvincing smile. She turned away and made her way toward the exit hoping to bump into the sheriff, but a bookshelf blocked her path. She must've gotten turned around somehow. She crossed the hallway and stepped past several more rows of bookshelves and rounded the corner to the left and faced another dead end. All these books looked the same. There had to be an exit around here somewhere. Maybe if she made her way back to the librarian he could tell her where the sheriff had run off.

Excuse me, how do I get out of here?" She strode toward him.

He pointed with his right hand toward the Grand Staircase in the center of the library. "You'll find more selections in the basement."

Evelyn frowned and her eyes narrowed in frustration.

"I'm just looking for the way out." She repeated feeling her impatience growing.

"The basement." The librarian insisted again.

Evelyn backed away from him. His eyes locked on to hers and that's when she realized how *wrong* everything felt. Something had changed after she saw the filmstrip of the boy painted in blood. The towers of books that changed around her, always blocking the exit and the way the librarian stared. The closest she came was a bookshelf now standing where the exit should've been. There was a space on the shelf where a section of books had been removed. In their place was a curled strip of brown leather. Curious, Evelyn picked it up and saw it was a dog collar. It was another cryptic object, one more puzzle to solve in this nightmare city. Her pockets were nearly full but when she rolled the leather strip she could just barely squeeze it in the same pocket as the bowl made of bone, then turning away she was blocked by another bookshelf.

Now she was sure there wasn't one there before. She turned, headed right and then left and collided with another bookshelf. The more she searched, aisle after aisle, the more she became disoriented. It wasn't until she stopped searching for the exit and started searching for the stairs that she found herself out of the maze. The supernatural force wouldn't allow her to turn back, forcing her to explore the librarian's instructions, though the basement didn't sound like a place she wanted to be right now.

She walked to the staircase, her footsteps tapping on the lavish wood floors. A plush Chinese stair runner with brilliant gold designs intricately woven into a blue and red background cushioned her steps. She took one last glance, feeling her fear and apprehension growing. Everything in her instincts told her to turn back. She took a final glance at the librarian who stared at her with a penetrating gaze. She tilted her head low and descended into the abyss.

Chapter 28

Darkness swallowed Evelyn.

She moved blindly down the stairs, testing the height of each step before planting her foot on the carpet and clinging the handrail for dear life. The room was too dark to even make out the walls around her. She clutched the pipe and took each step with caution. The acrid odor of decayed soggy wood grew stronger in her descent. When she reached the final step, the tap of her shoes echoing on the hard surface, a soft glow lit up a small space behind a bookshelf. The lamp provided just enough light for Evelyn's eyes to catch a glimpse into the nightmare around her. But this time, she wasn't alone in this alternate world. Other voices echoed through the room.

She listened closer and took a step, feeling her way through the blackness. It felt as if she'd just walked into an old, dusty garage after decades of neglect. She heard the sound of trickling water and it was hard for her to breath, nearly suffocating. Bookshelves, spaced yards apart, were scarce of books. The ones that remained were brown with water damage, the shelves too. The ceilings were impossibly high. She looked to the nearest wall, rising infinitely into the darkness above. The floor had changed too, once lavish was now cracked and squished under her feet, some drooping under her weight. She slid her body along, using the bookshelves to feel her way along until she was close enough to eavesdrop on the conversation. Right away she recognized Sheriff Rhett and Carly again.

Between the bookshelves, Evelyn saw the sheriff standing at the edge of a table with Carly facing him. Another man slumped back in his chair, his face careening upwards with a book spread open on the table in front of him. It took her a moment to realize he was dead, yet Carly and Rhett continued, as they hadn't noticed, though clearly they had.

"You only see what you want to!" Sheriff Rhett slammed the Book of Flesh on the table. The force of the book jolted the table causing the body of the young man to topple forward slightly and hit the table with a wet thud. Sheriff Rhett continued. "You murdered my wife because you couldn't have me and then you poisoned the Smith family. You were jealous because you thought I was in love with Nora and believed she was the one meeting the Smith's for dinner instead of Jack. You wanted to poison her and blame it on the Smith's, but you didn't know Jack would be there instead and you ended up murdering him by mistake."

Carly recoiled. Her forehead wrinkled in anger.

"What are you saying? You think I killed the doctor? What about the others? You think I killed them too?"

Sheriff Rhett said nothing. His eyes were fixed on her.

The surprise in Carly's face crumpled into a bitter sneer. "You would've liked that, wouldn't you? You and your wife were both constantly fighting with each other. She was having an affair for three years before she died and when you found out, you couldn't handle it. Nothing was ever good enough for her, especially not you, and it drove you insane. You sit there and point your finger at me, say that I'm guilty and tell me that I only see what I want, but I can say the same for you. You could never have her the way you wanted, so you killed her. You murdered your own wife and now you're looking to place the guilt on someone else."

Sheriff Rhett looked like he would burst. Even from here, she could see his body shake in fury.

"You loved me, don't try to deny that." Carly's voice grew calm and sultry.

She swayed her hips as she took a soft step closer to the irate Sheriff.

"Love?" He spat. "I may have loved you once a long time ago, but I've already moved on. What we did, we were just fucking like animals and my wife was dead. It had nothing to do with loving you or my wife's death. If it weren't for Jack's efforts, she would've died long before. It was just bad timing. You—you are nothing to me."

Carly's hand shot out and slapped him hard across his face. His cheeks swelled back, eyes lit with hatred. He then pitched forward and struck her back. She fell to the floor and writhed in pain. Sheriff Rhett turned and exited through the darkness.

At the same moment, the familiar sharp noise of grinding metal echoed somewhere near. Evelyn felt the muscles in her face twist and the adrenaline course through her body. She knew the sounds of the blade and chains being dragged across the floor. The Executioner was approaching.

Carly stirred, groggy until she heard the screech of metal on metal. Her face crossed with fear and survival as she sprung to her feet and painfully limped into Sheriff Rhett's direction.

Evelyn dipped low in the shadows. Less than a second had passed when the source of the grinding emerged and into the dim orange light.

At first she was confused by what she saw: a waist-high metal frame on creaky wheels slowly coming closer. Once it rolled into the light, Evelyn realized it was a pushcart that librarians used to transport books from the return bin to the shelves, except this cart wasn't stocked with books. Instead, the severed limbs of the Executioner's victims were piled high leaving a trail of thick, sticky blood. A leg and foot wobbled like gelatin beneath several arms and leg segments. Evelyn felt bile rise in her stomach when she saw the meaty thigh with shredded flesh caked with dry flaking blood. There was no foot attached or torso, severed at the hip and kneecap. It was a strong, thick leg that had probably once belonged to a football player or weight lifter. Pushing the cart was the Executioner, bigger than Evelyn remembered. He lumbered toward the crawl space where Evelyn hid.

In the murky shadows of the basement, a single flickering light cast the room in hard shadows. She pressed herself against the wall, her heart hammering in her chest. The clink of chains and swaying blades came in a chorus of flat, dull notes, warning her of the approaching killer. One blow was all it would take and then she'd end up just like the others. Mrs. Rosecrans had been one of the lucky ones, a clean sweep.

Evelyn held her breath, the dust pricking her throat and lungs. She fought the urge to cough, but the itching intensified, burning her throat and bringing her eyes to tears. She pressed her palm against her mouth and squeezed her eyes shut, concentrating on subduing her trembling body.

The Executioner nearly passed her, but then lingered in the doorway. She heard his guttural moan as he trudged around, turning until he faced her. She'd been spotted!

This couldn't be happening. She couldn't run anymore, her limbs still weak, her body deprived of food and sleep.

Nightmare Eve

The monster raised the blade over his head, the glint of steel catching Evelyn's eye. She thought of Mrs. Rosecrans again, lying in the middle of the parking lot split in two. How horrible it'd been to see the contents of her torso spilling onto the asphalt like a ruptured bag of spaghetti and how pitiful it'd been to watch her scoop her eviscerated organs into her arms, desperate to feint imminent death. Now it was Evelyn's turn.

It's just a nightmare, Eve. She tried to convince herself but her efforts were in vain.

This wasn't a nightmare. Her lungs and throat burnt with irritation, the acrid aroma of rotten wood and moldy books invaded her nose and her heart, ready to burst. The stench was real and so was the pain. The adrenaline forced her to scramble out from the crawl space and the splinters dug into the soft flesh of her palms. No, this wasn't a nightmare—it was real. And so was the blade slicing down on her

Chapter 29

Evelyn heard the monster grunt as it heaved its massive body into the swing—a powerful blow that splintered the desk into thousands of air-born shards. She had to get out before it lunged at her again. The desk next to her snapped as if it were made from balsa wood.

Before Evelyn could duck low, sharp debris burst all around her as if she was a soldier scurrying through wartime trenches. The pipe fell from her hands. Evelyn felt the pain, instant and intense all over her body, her cheeks, her forehead, down through her back and legs. Her cashmere sweater, dyed red with blood, was punctured and torn where slivers of wood penetrated her skin like dozens of needles.

The corpse of the young man who'd been studying at the desk thudded to the floor in front of Evelyn, and still fleeing on her hands and knees, crawled over him. She avoided looking into his face as she inched from his spongy chest to his slanted jaw, to his dried, hollow eyes.

In a single powerful motion, the Executioner snagged the body with one of his hooked blades and yanked it to the side. He used his gigantic arms and grabbed the body like a plush toy and plopped it on top of the pile of severed limbs filling the pushcart.

In a dead stare, the Executioner watched Evelyn crawl to a pile of broken boards and a shattered table leg where the Book of Flesh poked out from underneath. One more object for her growing collection.

As she pulled the book from the under the shattered desk, the solid monster plodded forward, a horrendous growl bursting from his lungs. The Executioner raised his fist again; chains coiled up his mighty arm and lunged.

She rolled across the floor and evaded another attack from his violent swing. The curved blade stuck in the wooden floor and the chains clinked and shook as he struggled to dislodge it. The wood groaned under the stress but it provided Evelyn barely enough opportunity to stumble to her feet and run into the darkness and away from the flickering table lamp, in the direction where she was almost sure Rhett and Carly had run off.

She was alone in the dark, but hidden in the shadows hadn't made her feel any safer. At least in the light she could see him coming, but now she was blind in the total blackness and had to rely on her other senses. He was still there—his heavy footsteps clomping along the boarded floors, the sharp blade dragging across the grates then thudding on the wood. Chains clamored with every gigantic stride. He seemed to have lost her.

This was her chance to escape. She listened for his movements very closely. She didn't want to get turned around and lose track of him only to end up colliding with him face-to-face. She took a deep, silent breath and snuck forward making sure each step was inaudible. Her eyes played tricks on her in what little light there was and ignored the surmounting vertigo. In a heel-to-toe fashion, she headed in a straight line, leaving the Executioner pacing somewhere in the abysmal library.

Evelyn moved through the dark unable to see anything other than an overturned lamp on the wood floors, as it cast a beam of light on a shelf, void of books except for one, tipped on its side. The leather bound book appeared the same texture as the wallet made from human skin. She mentally crossed another item off her list. Now that she possessed the scarf, the wallet, the book and the bowl, all she needed was the mask.

She passed through the beam of light; her shadow rippled along the bookshelf, and she emerged into the nightmare version of the library. Infinitely high wood walls ascended upwards encompassing a desolate room with rusted sheet metal floors and a few busted shelves. Spiders made tattered cobwebs dotted with humidity, floating ghostly in a phantom wind.

She eased further into the room and stopped the librarian at his desk with blood down his white button-down shirt and tawny slacks. He stood in perfect posture and his milky white eyes followed Evelyn with every step. His ashen face, devoid of blood, made him appear emaciated, exposing his sharp, angular jaw. His lips parted slightly, as if too weak to speak, closed and then parted again.

Evelyn braced herself for a hand-to-hand fight, but the librarian remained still, except for his eyes. Her muscles relaxed as she crept forward, rapidly glancing back to make sure he hadn't snuck up on her. She passed between two more busted shelves and for a split second she lost sight of him.

Then she heard the rapid tapping, like footsteps sprinting toward her, but the sound was too light and the steps too rapid to be from an adult. She peaked between the busted out spaces in the shelf and confirmed that the librarian was still behind the desk and hadn't once taken his eyes off her. Not even a blink.

She heard the noise again. To her right this time, pattering down what was left of the crumbled aisle beside her. She felt her body twitch, her pulse throb, when it leapt for her. She spun around but saw nothing but a child's footprint in the dust. The light smudge at the heel was indication that the child had been running and then vanished. She glanced up at the librarian and then studied the footsteps, following them between the shelves and around the corner where the trail began. It too started in mid-stride in the center of the aisle.

Evelyn felt queasy.

There was no wall in front of her, only a dark void and as she continued forward, away from the phantasmal steps, the walls spread further apart. Wires embedded in the wood crisscrossed so that when there was no more wood, the wires became a fence and her path resembled an alley.

Somewhere behind her, the haunting echo of a little girl's laughter, high pitched and scratchy, echoed and then faded into the ether.

Ahead, the entire city made of wood rose up down the length of a massive city-sized pier, identical to the city in her dreams. Above the swaths of creeping mist, a menacing squall line drew across the horizon. Evelyn heard the rumble in the distance.

She emerged from the alley. All around her sodden buildings crumbled, their windows cracked, some entirely busted out. The road, just rows of dark brown planks creaked beneath her heedful steps. The sound of water crashed below. She resisted survival instincts, which told her to retreat and moved forward.

She studied the hidden corners of alleys and scanned the interiors of the old wooden shops and log-cabin homes expecting to see shadowy silhouettes like the ones in her dream. With the night upon them and the storm approaching, the monsters would become more aggressive. Like spiders, nightmare creatures were nocturnal hunters. Before she ventured to far, she needed a weapon.

Another distant rumble broke the silence. Overcast skies above; boiling clouds in the distance. She gazed into the simple square toy shop to her left. She stepped up to the busted out window and the sound of broken glass came from under her shoes. The shop smelled of decayed organic material. On the floor, the remainder of a wrecked toy train display reminded Evelyn of Mrs. Lupez and how she suffered from a tragic derailment and how guilty she felt as the only survivor. It was the same toy train from her dream except now it was in pieces on the floor.

Evelyn picked up the toy train and removed the debris that clung to it. She placed it on the windowsill.

There wasn't much else inside: a few blank sheets of soggy typing paper, mounds of soggy plaster and a couple bent steel rods that had fallen out from the collapsing walls. One of the rods was a little shorter than the pipe she'd lost and a lot thinner. She gave a few practice swings. It was easier to wield for its light weight, but it wouldn't do much damage like the heavy pipe. The helix edges were rusted too, so it scratched like sandpaper in her already sore hands.

A playful giggle broke through the silence.

She spun around to see who'd come into the room, but she stood alone again. She scanned the dark corners of the room and noticed the doll with black pigtails tied with red bows and one larger than the other, clad in a red and black kimono with a matching parasol. The same one from the library. Had the doll always been there and she had just overlooked it?

The doll's left eye blinked.

Evelyn jerked her hand out in a protective stance. More snickering. She glanced around her and then back to the doll which had risen to its feet. It stood nearly two feet tall with a permanent cheerful smile and the glint of dull light reflecting from its only eye. Through the other gaping eye socket Evelyn could see into the empty porcelain skull. It playfully sauntered toward Evelyn aiming the tip of the parasol at her lower abdomen. The bladed tip glinted like the doll's oversized eye.

The strike came quickly, Evelyn barely had time move. The blade grazed her upper thigh and she let out a stifled yelp. The doll's permanent grin remained solid, but her titter echoed through the toyshop.

Evelyn had to defend herself faster against the speedy doll than she had with the other shambling creatures. The doll recovered from her miss quickly, ready to strike a second later. Evelyn swung the rebar. It connected to the doll's shoulder. It tipped over, tumbled along the floor and landed face down where it twitched and started to climb to its feet.

Evelyn charged and plunged the rebar straight through the back of its head. Shards of porcelain scattered the floor. Outside rose the groans of restless creatures. With the only door barricaded by the sagging roof, the large window was the only escape—and entrance. If any of those things climbed through the window, or gathered outside, she'd be trapped. She couldn't sleep here and time was running out.

Evelyn climbed over the windowsill back onto the boardwalk. She was greeted with the sound of thunder closing in and a woeful groan from somewhere even closer.

Chapter 30

The murky fog parted as Evelyn approached the woodsy farmhouse.

Sheriff Rhett had told her to continue her search down by the water. Chary with specifics, she hated to trust him, but Evelyn had searched nearly everywhere else. It just didn't feel right that David would've taken Ivy there. They all have had enough of water since their last vacation, especially David who'd spent most of his life on naval ships. But instead of finding the marina, harbor, or even a shore—any shore, she only found the edge of the boardwalk into endless ocean. There was no shore anywhere that she could see. Instead of finding the marina, she happened upon this farmhouse surrounded by aspens and Yew trees among other various pines.

Nearing the front steps Evelyn heard the incoherent shouts of a man overlapping a woman's muffled cries. A dog barked madly and Evelyn suddenly remembered the dog collar she picked up from the library was still stuffed in her pocket.

Standing at the bottom of the front porch now, the house appeared vacant, but the shouting had intensified. She tiptoed across the wooden street to the overgrown yard spotted with dew. A fence encompassed the yard from the side of the house to the back. The first thing she saw was a scraggly white Labrador retriever tugging at the end of a leash, nothing more than a scratchy weathered rope. The dog, scratching to get to the front door, curled its lips back in a protective snarl. In the house came a woman's terrified scream followed by something crashing against the wall.

"*Shut that fucking dog up or I will shut it up for you!*" Shouted the irate man.

The back door slid open and a boy, approximately eleven years old stepped onto the back porch. The dog ceased and his tail wagged playfully, his tongue greedily lapping at the child's face. He giggled through his sniffles and pulled away with a sad little smile.

The woman inside screamed something back to the man. It was hard to hear what the fighting was all about, but it didn't matter.

From afar, she looked at the young boy's pudgy face as he stroked the dust-covered dog. Another crash from inside and the dog let out another series of barks. The young boy tried to hush his dog when the back door slid open with a bang and the father, carrying a half-empty bottle of Jack, came roaring at them, snatching a rifle leaning against the rail.

Evelyn climbed to her feet and screamed, "That's *enough!*" but was drowned out by gunfire.

The shot narrowly missed his son who tumbled back in the dirt, but the dog's head had split open to the neck. The boy trembled in shock, his eyes opened as wide as they could get and a light spackle of blood angled down his face and shirt.

Nightmare Eve

Evelyn saw something in the boy's pupils dissipate, a last glimmer of hope in an otherwise bleak world. It was if he'd gone catatonic, except that he rose to his feet with quaking legs, his expression entire blank, his eyes glossed over, moving hypnotically. Taking short, rigid steps he didn't seem to hear is father screaming at him or his mother cursing from the porch. Everything moved in slow motion, all sounds far away.

The boy took another step closer. Then another, and another until he stood in front of his father. The father, at eye level to the boy, screamed in slow motion loud enough to bristle the hairs across the boys forehead. The boy didn't blink, didn't move.

And then all of the sudden time sped up. The boy lunged forward and sank his teeth into his fathers cheek, ripping away a chunk of flesh that exposed two rows of bloody teeth. Caught off guard, the father grabbed his face and screeched as he collapsed to his knees.

The boy approached again, but the father cracked the butt of the gun against the side of his son's face, sending him sprawling to the porch.

The dad's eyes rolled around and up into his head while he clutched the wound erupted with blood like a fire hydrant. He crawled for the patio door, leaving streaks of bloody handprints as he slid back down.

The boy had returned to his feet, the gun in hand. Still, without expression, the boy pointed the barrel at his father and fired, killing him instantly.

Out of shots, the boy let the gun fall to the porch and strode across the yard to the tool shed. His mother scrambled her husband's side emitting a constant, high-pitched scream between heaves. She lowered her head when vomit passed through her mouth. She never saw her son standing above her with the meat cleaver.

The strike to the back of her head didn't kill her. It made the sound like a carving knife being stabbed into a

241

pumpkin, and made a sucking sound as blood pulsed from her skull to the patio. She was on her knees, gawking into her reflection with the meat cleaver sticking out of the back of her head, her son standing behind her trying to dislodge the blade from her brain.

Agonizing screams turned into gargled spasms. Her limbs flopped like a fish on dry land and her eyelids blinked erratically. He yanked again and she emitted another groan. When he succeeded, she pitched forward, her head colliding with the patio door. The side of her face smeared the glass as she slid down. Her body continued to twitch until the blade came down a final time severing her spinal cord at the back of the neck.

The son, painted in red, removed the meat cleaver and entered the house.

Then came another scream. His sister, Evelyn realized.

Evelyn tore her eyes away from the house and the three bodies and then backed away from the fence, too tall to hoist herself over. The only other way was to go directly through the house where she was sure the painted son would be waiting.

Chapter 31

The house belonged to the Flynn's. A couple of tattered family photos hung over a stone mantle littered with cigarette butts, soda cans, and about an inch of dust. Duct tape had been used to patch up the broken, dusty couches covered in hair and mysterious stains.

On the dinning room table, a mound of miscellaneous stuff like Styrofoam cups, crumpled papers, magazine cut outs, empty rolls of tobacco and a myriad of other items, offered clues about the family who lived here.

She found math homework with the name Bobby Flynn scribbled at the top of the page next to a perfect grade.

Ah, yes. Bobby Flynn. Now she remembered. It was national news twenty years ago. Harold Flynn became a heavy drinker after he was let go from a local hearth workshop eight months earlier. His wife, once beautiful, had lost her pretty complexion over years of chain smoking, heavy drinking and pill addiction. She had been known to have psychological disorders, angered easy and often and verbally abusive to her husband and children and as the father, he was just as abusive and unfaithful.

As for their son, Bobby Flynn, the news reports exposed a long record of negative anti-social behavior, a disregard for rules, but a gifted craftsman. One day he snapped. Bobby's semen had been found inside his teenage sister, *after* he removed her head and, because their bodies were too heavy for him to carry, he disposed of them piece-by-piece over the course of a weekend.

This was his house.

A photo of Bobby hung on the wall to her left. Next to it, on the mantle, was a high school picture of his sister, Audra. It looked relatively new as it was the only thing in the room that wasn't covered in ashes or dust. She was a pretty teenage girl with long brunette hair, amber eyes and a mean smile.

A stirring drew her attention to the hall. On the wall outside the bedroom, Bobby and his sister's shadowy silhouettes played out the murder scene.

Evelyn crept toward the sliding patio door. The floor beneath her feet creaked. When she looked up, Bobby appeared in the hall, meat cleaver in hand and a pair of goggles around his head.

He marched toward her; she raised her rebar and swung. The blow rocketed him into the wall. He was down for only a split second before he stood up again and swung the cleaver. She slipped just out of range and the cleaver bounced off the corner of the wall, throwing him off balance.

She sucked in a deep breath and burst to the dining room. He was already on his feet and coming toward her. He was a bit slower than the Ivy Doll, but not by much. The force of his swings, however, was powerful. She backed away and he swung again, and again. And *again*, then tilted dizzy, side-to-side.

Nightmare Eve

He took a moment to recover giving her just long enough to dark across the room to the glass door. She yanked hard and the door slid wide. Evelyn lurched onto the porch, slipping on the blood with Bobby Flynn bounding toward her. He was already through the doorway when she leapt from the porch and landed at the bottom of the steps beside the dog. She didn't feel the pain shoot through her leg right away, but she knew she'd be feeling it later.

Just as Bobby raised the cleaver high over her head, she withdrew the dog collar in her pocket and tossed it to the ground at Bobby's feet.

She shut her eyes and waited for the fatal blow to rip her from this endless nightmare, but death never came. She opened her eyes to see the meat cleaver fall from Bobby's hand. He bent over and reached the leather strip with his pudgy blood stained fingers. Then, with his head hunched low, he let out a devastated sob and turned away from Evelyn and faded into the fog.

The yard fell silent.

Evelyn sucked in a deep breath, trying to calm her rapid heart beats. Once she regained her composure she rose to her feet and her eyes immediately fell to the toolshed where a gate had appeared in the fence. When she stepped through, the streets had returned to its normal gloomy state of overcast morning skies, the boardwalk replaced by paved roads and green yards. The town's lack of population and an occasional blood smear across the sidewalk indicated things hadn't completely returned to normal.

A few blocks to her left, at the entrance to the marina, a wooden sign labeled *Amherst Aquarium* hung above a statue of an octopus and a bench made of a carved-out log and a three-inch thick rope. Just beyond the aquarium Evelyn spotted a boat launch and the slight decline of a sandy beach into the bay. A pier expanded over gentle waves and at the end, a male figure gazed into the grey marine layer.

Her heart did a backflip in her chest. David! She found him at last! She took a large step forward, but the road ended at the water's edge. She spotted Ivy sitting on a bench swinging her legs and playing with a doll in her lap.

Evelyn felt her face crumble as she exploded with joyful sobs. She could already feel the weight of his arms around her. They had finally reached the end, surrounded by water. There was no other place for them to go. Not this time. The only thing that separated them now was the dock access through the aquarium.

Chapter 32

Stepping into the aquarium was like stepping into a sauna. The humid air dampened her skin and she had to loosen the scarf around her neck to keep from overheating. She moved through a narrow hallway lined with posters of sharks and flyers for various oceanography benefit programs, maps of the building, and an ad for the United States Navy. A serious-faced man stared at her from the cover. Her heart jumped in her throat, the man resembled David, the same plump red lips and vibrant, sparkling eyes and prominent, narrow brows. Her muscles tensed but she kept moving.

The hall opened to vast room lined with anatomy posters of various sea-creatures. Above her, mounted by dozens of sturdy cables was a life-size prosthetic shark—a Great White, with rows of triangular jagged teeth. The entire model, according to the chart on the wall, was six and a quarter meters in length. It was enormous. In the center of the room was a cylindrical fish tank. Evelyn could see shadows swimming around the decorative rocks and in between the forest of plants swaying in the water. A vibrant blue light made a humming sound, flickering at first as she stepped past. She rolled up the blood-caked sleeves of her sweater and pulled the collar down. Condensation from the humid room and beads of sweat collected on her forehead and along her collarbone. Her breaths slowed, but deepened and she could feel her muscles begin to relax.

Near the back of the room was a gift shop where plush turtles and a wide-eyed dolphin with a cartoonish grin were tossed in a bin with other children's toys. A long, narrow and clear tank no more than two feet tall spanned the entire length of the wall across the room. A slosh of water pulsed forward. She followed the wave as it propelled to the other end of the tank where a miniature village was spread out over fake sand. The wave, once it reached the shallow water surrounding the model village, swelled into a mini-tsunami and overwhelmed the little town. More sounds of water sloshing as the water receded.

Once the water returned to its normal level, the sloshing sounds continued, but not from in front of her—from behind. She spun around in time to see another shadow move behind the fish tank. Behind the greenish-brown seaweed the shadow of a large fish swam in circles around the tank, when something strange caught her eye. One of the shadows had ceased to move. Then she realized why: she was starring into a face, looking back at her from the other side of the fish tank.

Evelyn let out a startled cry and stumbled back. The shadow darted right.

Evelyn prepared to swing at the creature and waited for it to emerge, but it never did. She peered around the cylindrical tank and saw just an empty space between her and the wall. Some kind of strange saltwater fish bobbed at eye level puckering its lips. She felt like that fish, wondering if that creature she'd seen was looking at her too.

She turned toward the back of the room between the long Tsunami tank and anatomy posters and squinted into the heavy shadows, searching for the scuba man. She didn't see him but there was a strange door beneath the flickering exit sign. In the center of the door was a flat, circular object fashioned of rusted metal and wooden stakes. More bars extended from the metal plate across the door, braced in the frame. Along the outer rim were nine labels and eight bloodied handprints. Inspecting the door closer, she felt the warm damp metal, rough under her finger and noticed notches in door behind the plate. The wooden stakes and metal bars were locked in place, holding the door shut. Evelyn took a step back to view the door in its entirety and noted the contraption shared similar characteristics as a combination lock. Evelyn imagined David with Ivy on the other side of the pier enjoying the view.

She clenched her teeth. The only way to reach them was by solving the cryptic puzzle. Nine labels surrounded the round plates. They read:

The Solicitous Woman
The Painted Son
The Scarred Prince
The Weeping Man
The Charred Woman
The Twirling Debutante
The Despairing Mother
The Mercy Three
The Seeking Bride.

All labels, except for two; *The Scarred Prince* and *The Seeking Bride*, were smeared with crimson handprints. Nine names, eight bloody handprints, each one representing someone she'd met her in Amherst, eight of them dead. She considered their names carefully. Mr. Morgan was the Weeping Man for sure. Every time she'd seen him he was on the verge of tears. He was the first person she met of the bunch, but he wasn't killed until after the punk kid, Eddy and his buddy, Corey. There was still John to look out for too, which was probably why the Mercy Three wasn't crossed off yet, *Mercy*, the title the poem on the gym floor that was written in front of the torture device. The Mercy Three came right before the Weeping Man. Then after Mr. Morgan's death, where had she gone? Did she snatch the scarf from the Scarred Woman before it burnt up?

She read the list again trying. The Solicitous Woman's name stood out. Evelyn could practically hear her velvety voice. She hadn't met her first, but she was the first to "die." Beside her name the bloody handprint was a requiem. Evelyn cranked the plate until the notch pointed to her name.

The gears within the door groaned awake. Next came a click.

Alright, who came next? Evelyn remembered that after she left the church, she'd hiked up the road for a bit and met Hunter. Was it Mrs. Rosecrans?

Evelyn checked the list, but no pseudonyms reminded her of Mrs. Rosecrans. There was, however, the Despairing Mother and Mrs. Lupez seemed to fit that description perfectly. Her children and husband had died on that train while she had lived which caused her tremendous guilt.

Evelyn thought of Ivy. She may not have been her biological daughter, but every ounce of Evelyn loved her as if she was.

Evelyn turned the crank six names to the left until it landed on the Despairing Mother.

The gears within the door creaked again before emitting a second click.

The Mercy Three was the third name on the list. Those foolish teenagers and their repulsive behaviors caused angst all around town. There was the poor young man who'd been severely beaten, hiding away in the dormitories who'd given Evelyn his theatre admissions, and another man she'd discovered behind the dumpster upon their meeting.

Of the three of them, Eddy seemed the most impressionable, and the most apologetic. Before the brace twisted his bones and crushed his skull, Evelyn stared in his panicked eyes and knew that he'd been sorry for what he did. She wanted to forgive him, but to forgive a man capable of such horror, she couldn't bring herself to do it, and the chains and leather shredded him to pieces and crushed his skull. Below his chair, written in blood, was the poem, *Mercy*. His buddy, Corey, was victim of the mad doctor. Both were dead, but John was still out there. If their paths crossed again, she would demonstrate the meaning of mercy and forgiveness.

Evelyn turned the plat eight notches to the left until it pointed to the Mercy Three. The door clunked again and she noticed each time the plate turned a bit more smoothly. She was on the right track.

Next came Mr. Morgan who bravely sacrificed himself to the Executioner. His sacrifice had allowed her to escape. Such a sweet and gentle old man, but so very sad and lonely. His only relatives Evelyn could be sure of was her live-in assistant, Anna Morgan. Or soon-to-be former assistant if she didn't get back home soon. Evelyn had been gone for days and hadn't spoken with her assistant since she left. Anna must be worried sick.

Five clicks to the right for Mr. Morgan, the Weeping Man.

The plate cranked with ease as she reflected upon the other's lives. The grief and realization that these people whom she'd crossed paths with were ostracized for their crimes. Yes, they'd certainly made mistakes and murder, in any means, was inexcusable, but there was a kind of innocence in them. Evil is not born, it's made. They wouldn't live in here if they didn't feel regret for their mistakes. Amherst was for the guilty and the haunted.

The Charred Woman came after Mr. Morgan. Nora Brooke had removed the batteries from the chirping smoke detector late one night while they were studying for finals and had forgotten to replace them when her roommate informed her that her assignment was still in the labs. Unfortunately the lit candles burned the dorms down, killing her roommate who'd fallen asleep. Nora believed her roommate haunted her and was forced to live on with crippling guilt. It was such a tragic, innocent mistake. Eight cranks to the left.

Who's next?

After Evelyn escaped the burning building, she saw the hanged men for the first time. She found Hunter at the Westminster Performing Arts Theatre and gave the music to the automaton on stage. The child ballet dancer, the Twirling Debutante, finally completed her routine. Public humiliation, especially to a child, could damage him or her for life. It planted the seeds of fear that grows with the child into adulthood. One click to the right.

The only other name on the list with the bloodstained hand beside it belonged to the Painted Son: the sad tale of talented Bobby Flynn who'd finally snapped and butchered his family and defiled his sister's body. If it weren't for his parents, he could've grown up to become the worlds most admired artist. There was no place for him to go, nowhere to hide. In Bobby Flynn's case, murder was his only escape from the abuse. Though a monster, he lived in chains and died free.

At the final click, Evelyn felt the sting of empathetic tears. Society, family and fate had taught them to be ruthless and vile. They'd been pushed to their limits and burdened by tragedy, pain and guilt. A person should be responsible for their own actions, but to be human meant that one could only take so much shit before they snap, and through torment, a monster is created. They'd been pushed to their limits.

And so had Evelyn.

The bars retracted, the door creaked open and revealed her fiancé standing at the end of the misty pier. She resisted the urge to run to him. Maybe she didn't deserve him anymore.

She looked again at the names with bloodied handprints beside them and then to the ones without.

Eighteen months ago, she couldn't wait to get married to David. Twelve months ago, they were believed to have drowned. Four days ago, she had reason to believe they were still alive. She'd searched all over for David, nearly getting herself killed in the process. It'd been so long, so much death and a year of lonely nights and now finally it was over.

She pushed open the door and stepped onto the pier.

Chapter 33

The boards shook under Evelyn's feet as she ran toward David. The dock extended between boats of various sizes from small inflatable rafts to large luxury crafts. Ivy wore a grin as she splashed in the water at David's feet. He dipped his hand in the water and gave her a gentle splashed. She squealed and playfully protested and tried to splash him back.

Over his shoulder, David spotted Evelyn. He rose to his feet, a grim expression on his sleepless face. Dark bags tugged below his puffy, glassy eyes. He turned again, this time with his back shunning her.

"David?" Evelyn tried to approach, but he took a step forward and Evelyn thought he'd fall into the water, but still he stood at the end of the dock. "David? Where are you going?" She approached him, but he took another step without falling in the water.

The fog must be playing ticks on her eyes, or she had terrible depth perception because after two steps, he should've fallen into the harbor. There was nowhere else for him to go.

She looked down at Ivy who sat in her inflatable raft, her black hair covering her face. She hummed softly and wriggled her toes in the water.

"David, please, wait!"

Evelyn was exhausted, bruised, bleeding and starving. It'd been days since she'd eaten a whole meal and longer since she'd slept a whole night. On top of everything, this nightmare had deconstructed her until she was an emotional wreck. She couldn't stop the tears from streaming down her face and wanted nothing more than to touch him and feel him and know that he was really there.

"Every relationship has problems," Evelyn begged. "We could've worked things out."

He didn't move. Didn't blink. Didn't even appear to breathe. "We needed time to recover from one fight before getting into another."

Evelyn shook her head. She didn't understand.

"I don't love you," said David, "I never believed our marriage would last. You're not my soul mate."

"Stop it, David! Why are you saying these things?"

David was steady. His voice was matter-of-fact. "I've dated other women before you and they've pouted just like you are."

Evelyn was stung. She didn't know what else to say except, "I'm sorry."

"I've moved on, Evelyn. I moved on a long time ago."

"I'm *sorry!*" Evelyn screamed. She burst into sobs and fell to her knees. She cupped her face in her hands. "I'm so sorry."

He stared at her with hateful eyes sharp as needles. "Apology *not* accepted."

Nightmare Eve

The sky darkened and a strong offshore gale rose, churning the ocean waters. Violent rain shook the docks and melted away the marina like crayons in a fire pit. The black ocean waves beat against the sides of old wooden boats and spilled over the docks, now made of rotting planks and crisscrossing wires. Ivy Rose screamed from her raft as she was thrashed by the waves and pulled out to sea.

"Ivy!" David screamed for his daughter.

Evelyn tried to locate her in the water, but in the violent downpour and wind that ripped at her face, she was forced to shield her eyes. A ferocious gust brought her to her knees and when she raised her eyes, vision blurred, she saw that David was gone. When she called out to him, her frantic wail was carried into the night by the wind.

Ahead, a brilliant streak of lightning ripped through the sky, illuminating the whitecaps and spotted both Ivy and David being swallowed by the ocean.

Evelyn sucked in a deep breath and threw herself into the mercy of the tempest.

Chapter 34

Seagulls squealed in delight as merry plovers scuttled across the wet sand. The sun hovered above the horizon casting long purple shadows of soughing palms beneath a pastel sky of bubble-gum pink and lavender. The first early stars of the evening sparkled above the hazy moon and the gentle splash of waves collapsing across the sand sprayed a soothing, calm mist on Evelyn's face. She smiled at David with romantic, fluttering eyes and her lips curled into her most perfect smile. He was the man of her dreams, so handsome in a pastel blue suit and bare feet in the sand. He smiled proudly back at her, with blue eyes that rivaled the ocean.

"*We'll be together, don't know where, don't know when...*"

The young pianist clad in a sailor's uniform danced his hands along the keyboard, his body swayed by the strings connecting him to the sky. His head bobbed and rolled to the side as if his neck had been broken and the greenish hue of dead skin peopled away to expose chunks of his grey skull. The strings controlled his movements, a marionette manipulated by the clouds above. He wobbled again and then slumped forward. His body struck the keyboard in an unpleasant thump of flat chords. He grinned nefariously with cracking jaw bones and curled back lips.

Evelyn looked into the faces of those who attended her wedding. Mrs. Lupez and Mrs. Rosecrans sat beside each other. Mrs. Lupez's face had been mangled, her skin shredded like tissue paper and shrapnel lie embedded in her skull above her left eye. Mrs. Rosecrans, or at least half of her, was propped up against the back of the chair. Across from them, the insane doctor coiffed in his bloodstained white scrubs rested his hand around Corey's shoulder. His chest cavity was wide open so Evelyn could see the complex gears and pockets working symbiotically with his organs. Corey's eyes had been replaced with oversized glass eyes and a strained smile adorned his face. Behind the duo, Nora Brooke's roommate was easy to spot, her skin and clothes charred black and glowed with the heat of smoldering embers.

And coming down the aisle was the Executioner—his arms wielding the massive blade, already in mid swing. No time to react.

Evelyn screamed as the blade swooped upon her.

David grinned.

—

Evelyn chocked on the salty water. It purged from her mouth as she rolled to her side and heaved again. The stench, like dead fish, bad breath and vomit made her heave a third time.

"David?" Evelyn sat up confused.

"They're already gone."

Nightmare Eve

Evelyn careened her neck to the side and spotted Hunter sitting at the edge of a chair. He stared at her, flushed with concern.

Her eyes focused. She was sitting on the floor at Hunter's feet, wrapped in blankets. A pillow had been placed beneath her head. Around the room, dozens of photos of campers, boating enthusiasts and fishermen displayed their latest catch. A row of postcards was displayed on various stands with license plate key chains and silvery fish and other marine-related designs. The air was strong of fishing bait and something else, something edible, like barbeque. Her stomach growled.

Evelyn climbed to her feet, unsteady, but very much alive.

"Hold on, you should probably take it easy," said Hunter.

But Evelyn was obdurate. "I'm fine."

She ignored the spinning in head and the foul taste that plagued her mouth. The room appeared to be some kind of bait shop with touristy gifts, snack food like Gatorade and Cheetos, candy bars, chips and salsa, jerky, maritime maps, fishing poles and a couple of picnic tables outside. Behind her against the back wall, near the kitchen, was a couple of worn booths. On the one closest to them, Evelyn saw a backpack, a first aid kit, a couple of energy drinks and an uncorked bottle of wine.

"Is this yours?"

Hunter nodded.

She snatched up the bottle and took several deep gulps. A red wine. Cheap, but it got the job done. The foul taste in her mouth was replaced by the acidic cabernet sauvignon.

"I've also got coffee brewing in the back. Thought you could use something warm."

"After what I've been through, I could use something stronger than that."

Hunter frowned. As he moved behind the counter of the abandoned bait shop he explained how he'd found her just as she dove into the water. She was fortunate to survive after nearly being pummeled by massive waves or nearly crushed between the large boats and the dock. H went on to explain how he managed to fish her out by tying a rope around one of the handles on the dock and diving in after her. While he explained the miraculous rescue, Evelyn browsed the cloths hanging off the rack. She needed something with a lot of pockets to carry the items she'd collected along her trip and finally settled with another pair of cargo pants and a long sleeved black shirt with a fishing vest with ample storage room. She changed quickly unashamed of Hunter's presence.

"What were you doing out there anyway?" Hunter asked suspiciously.

"I saw them drown." Evelyn took another swig of cheap wine. With an empty stomach, she could already feel the light buzz. "It seemed so real."

"The fog has a way of playing tricks on the mind. Perhaps this time it helped you remember something you'd forgotten." He approached her. "You do remember, don't you, Evelyn?"

Evelyn's gaze was lost into the wine bottle. Her foggy memory was now as clear as it's ever been.

"It was a very grey day you watched your fiancé and his daughter drown, wasn't it?" Hunter bowed his head forward, fishing the truth from her.

Evelyn kept her eyes locked on the wine bottle. She took another swig then placed it on the table between them. She couldn't meet his gaze, her eyes drifting to the floor.

"He never liked the beach. He spent many yeas in the Navy and lived a very lonely sea life. He grew to hate the water. David and I—we had a lot of things in common. More than he wanted to admit. He was such a pessimist about everything, always choosing to see what separated us rather than kept us

Nightmare Eve

together. One of our differences was the ocean. But life on the ocean is still different than life on the beach. We didn't realize how suddenly the tides could change. Storms had the potential to appear within a matter of minutes."

Evelyn took a small sip of wine. Hunter continued to listen from the kitchen doorway as he retrieved their food.

Evelyn continued. I loved him so much. I would've done anything for him. But through all the drinking and the bars exacerbated the stupid fights we'd get into, over stupid little things that didn't even matter. I don't even remember what most of them were about. He began to resent me. He blamed me for everything that was wrong in his life. If his phone stopped working, he'd capitulate to the idea that I had destroyed it on purpose somehow. He demonized me that way. Granted, I wasn't the best person I could be either. When I realized where the relationship was headed, I wanted to do something to fix it. I worked very hard on myself to change, but it was too late. He had already moved on. I guess it was my final attempt to save our relationship by suggesting we took a vacation up the coast.

Hunter returned with two baskets of grilled hamburger with fried potato wedges and a large bottle of water for them to share. She took another sip of wine followed by a mouthful of hamburger. Her shivering had subsided and her muscles began to relax.

"David was so stubborn," Evelyn continued, "nobody's perfect, but he didn't believe in second changes or that anybody could change. He shot me down before I even had a chance and I couldn't handle it. There was shouting and I just couldn't stop crying. I must've looked so pathetic to him. He took Ivy down to the beach to swim and when I heard the thunder and the wind, I thought I'd better check on them. They were still out in the water together. The storm had come up so sudden." Tears swelled in her eyes. "I tried to save them, but the currents pulled me under too. It was my fault."

Hunter looked at her dead in the eyes. "You can't control the weather, Evelyn. It wasn't your fault. It was an accident and there was nothing you could do."

"But that's just it, Hunter. I could've. I think part of me was so angry by how he treated me that I wanted to see him suffer. I wanted him to see Ivy drown. I wanted her out so he'd spend some time with me. I'm a monster."

Hunter was calm. "That may have been how you felt, but you did try to save him. You were just angry at him, that's all. You ran to the edge of the dock and dove in. You nearly got yourself killed doing it."

Evelyn took another drink of wine and then from the water bottle. "I was lucky to have washed up on shore."

"It wasn't luck," said Hunter. "I was there in the harbor that afternoon. Just by the way you jumped into the water I could tell you weren't a strong swimmer. There was no way you'd make it. I pulled you out then like I did just now. I went to the hospital to make sure you were okay, but Dr. Dullahan said you were stable enough to return home, but not alone. Ms. Smith offered to look after you until you were well enough. You were out for days and once you woke up, you didn't seem to remember. You wandered like a lost soul down to the pier without any memory of who or where you were. You'd be spotted by some of the locals and Sheriff Rhett would come get you and bring you back to the Shady Nook Lodge."

"I've done this before?" Evelyn felt like she was ready for a second bottle of wine.

"Not like this. We tried to tell you what happened before and you'd go into shock and forget everything the next day. This time you got away from Sheriff Rhett and started putting the puzzles together on your own. You started to get your memory back, so we let you continue."

"It all seemed so real though, those *monsters*, the Executioner, was that all a nightmare too?" Evelyn looked down at her pile of wet clothes on the floor with the scarf made of

Nightmare Eve

hair on top, her cargo pants still bulging with the other objects. They were real as empty bottle of wine between her and Hunter.

Hunter adjusted uncomfortably. "The coffee should be ready by now. How are you feeling?"

Evelyn didn't know where to begin. She hunched over, fluster. "No, I feel worse. What am I supposed to do now? What about these objects I found, what about Amherst? Is the legend about the Gong real or did I just imagine that too?"

Hunter forced an awkward laugh. "I'm no historian, but according the town's legend, but only a male priest of the Dragon Order is allowed to ring the gong. That's just ancient folklore passed down from Chinese immigrants back when Amherst was originally founded. I wouldn't take it too seriously if I were you."

Hunter must've noticed the look of contemplation on her face because he stood up and moved to the counter with a gun in his hand.

"They say anyone from the outside who rings the gong is guaranteed the answers the seek, but with terrible consequences. It'll plunge the town into a realm of eternal darkness. But like I said, it's just folklore. This however,"—hands Evelyn the gun—"is real. And I suggest that if you insist on continuing to wander all over town on your own, you should take this to defend yourself."

"If it wasn't real, then what am I defending myself from?" Evelyn accepted the gun.

He shrugged. "Let's hope you don't have to find out."

Chapter 35

Evelyn ran alongside the handrail recalling her memory for the city's layout. The curving cement paths weaving between the restaurants at the marina should let out in the parking lot. Just beyond, Seaview Drive which would take her to the Nordic Trail, a two-mile hike up the steep mountain. She would have to move fast and remain vigilant. In her vest, she carried only three clips and hoped that didn't need any more.

As she reached the parking lot, she slowed her brisk pace and scanned the north entrance. The soupy fog obscured her view beyond the first two empty rows. She stepped off the curb and paused, swinging around in the direction of the south entrance. She knew it was there somewhere in the thick haze. Right or left? If the Marina faced west then south would take her downtown and eventually back toward Shady Nook Lodge, so she needed to travel south—left. She couldn't see much but as she jogged past a lamppost she heard the sloshing footsteps of an approaching scuba man.

She raised her gun, but the fog obscured her view. She could only hear the rapid squishing as the monster bounded toward her.

She checked over her left shoulder and then to the right. Her visibility reached a few yards which didn't give her much time to aim and fire.

From the left, the creature came toward her, too close to aim, and the scuba man plowed into her. One bloated hand latched on to her shoulder and the other formed a meaty fist coming at her.

Evelyn raised her left arm and caught the creature in the neck with her elbow. Black gunge spilled from it's gnawing mouth. She brought the gun up and fired a single shot directly into its skull. The bullet exploded out of the back of the scuba man's head along with more black gunk. It staggered to the side and hit the pavement.

She clutched the gun close to her shoulder, her finger resting beneath the trigger. Her brisk strides were light as she hurried across the parking lot, scanning Seaview Drive for other signs of movement.

More scuffling from behind her, but she didn't stop. More scuba men trickled out from the alleys and banged on the windows from inside shops. She didn't want to waste her bullets on them, there were other creatures more dangerous than them. The hanged people had a treacherous range.

Evelyn had finally understood what Hunter had meant when he said, "It's not the town that's haunted, it's the people." He'd been right all along. Her biggest fear was losing David and Ivy. She couldn't move on with these demons haunting her and now her guilt had trapped her in this place somewhere between reality and a nightmare.

There were four scuba men behind her now, their black and purple bare feet slapping against the pavement, flailing with their chubby arms. She outran them, leaving them behind in the fog.

She'd been so preoccupied with evading the monsters that she almost ran past the turnoff to the Nordic Trails. They seemed familiar too her, remembering how she had invited David to join her, hoping to reconnect with him during the long stroll, but even on this spontaneous trip, he shot her down.

"What would we talk about?" He would ask without taking his eyes off the television in their room.

Whatever comes up. You know, have a conversation like we used to. Do we have to plan what we talk about or can't it just happen?"

He didn't reply. It was the same every time. She was trying to make an effort but he didn't see it. And if he did he'd been purposely deflecting.

"It's such a long drive, I just feel like staying in. There's lots of good movies on tonight, but don't let me stop you from doing what you want to do."

Evelyn let out a disgruntled sigh. There was a time when he looked forward to going out with her, but his lackluster attitude worried her. As she walked out the door she gave him one final glance and said, "Are you sure you don't want to join me?"

He never did.

Evelyn had only gone partway up the mountain when another wave of hopelessness swelled within her. Net even the beautiful view from the Carver Cliff vista point could assuage her worries. The view wasn't as pleasant without him. She had decided to turn back. She wanted to spend time with him, even if it meant staying in for the night, only when she returned to the town, she happened to pass by a bar and spotted him singing into a karaoke machine with a microphone in one hand and a drink in the other. Had he purposely blown her off? She didn't say anything to him and instead purchased a bottle of wine and returned to the lodge alone.

Nightmare Eve

David was trashed by the time he returned and Evelyn too. She accused him of purposely neglecting her with the intentions of making her upset. He denied it, of course, but continued to avoid her, which drove her mad, the alcohol exacerbating her emotions.

The alcohol impaired her memory and she didn't remember the brutal details of their argument, only that they both had said awful things to each other and left the room, slamming the door behind her and didn't return for hours. That was the last time she spoke to them. Their first date was on the pier—where their relationship began and now, on another pier, their relationship had ended.

And now she hiked the Nordic Trail alone hunting for the gong that would bring them back. She gazed at the stormy horizon from midway up Carver Cliff and instead of despair and sadness there was renewed determination.

She ducked low under a cypress tree in order to maneuver through a clump of bushes dividing the road from a beach trail. She figured cutting along the beach paths would save her a few extra minutes—reaching the top of Carver Cliff before midnight.

Just a few steps from the dune, she spotted a red-cloaked figure moving trance-like along the beach. A hood kept her from seeing the figure's face and she leaned forward for a better look and saw another clocked figure following about a yard behind. Then another, each with their heads bowed low and hooded red cloaks shadowing their faces. One after another they moved toward the cliff.

She steadied herself by palming the rough edge of a stone, only slightly bigger than a tennis ball. She watched as another figure marched passed when she felt the gentle tap of a finger on her shoulder. When she looked up, Sheriff Rhett hovered over her, a contemptuous look on his face.

267

Chapter 36

"Just come with me back to the station We'll figure it all out when we get there," said Rhett. It wasn't a suggestion.

She contemplated running, but he was much stronger and faster. It wouldn't be far before he caught up with her again. He eyed the gun in her hand. The feelings of mistrust between them was mutual.

She surrendered and allowed him to guide her back seat of the police car.

"You shouldn't even have a gun, especially one that doesn't belong to you. Where'd you get it?"

She remained silent and diverted her gaze out the window.

"Are you hurt?" he asked. "Do you need to go to the hospital?"

"I'm fine." Evelyn replied coldly.

Nightmare Eve

Sheriff Rhett said something again, but she was lost among her own thoughts. He cranked his neck so he could look over his shoulder. Must've been waiting for her to reply, but she had nothing to say to him.

For the remainder of the short drive, they sat in silence. It wasn't until they stepped inside the station that Evelyn could see that things there were just as bleak as the world outside. The room was stale and colorless and the surface of Sheriff Rhett's desk was clear of papers.

"Can I get you anything? Water, coffee or hot chocolate?" Sheriff Rhett hovered over Evelyn. His sleepless eyes studied her, his face dour.

Water and coffee both sounded excellent, but she didn't want to eat or drink anything that had been prepared by him.

I'd rather just get going. You know, curfew and all."

"Please, have a seat." He gestured toward the chair pushed neatly in its place opposite of his side of the desk.

Evelyn was disaffected with him. She breathed in a deep, impatient breath before complying. She pulled the chair away from the desk then sat, upright and rigid.

The Sheriff moved around to his side of the desk then sat down across from her. For a moment they said nothing. He leaned back in his chair and folded his arms across his chest. He watched her for a moment, studying her edgy countenance. "The curfew hasn't seemed to keep you from running off. Tell me, did you find him?"

She stared at him, puzzled.

"You're fiancé. Did you find him?"

Evelyn was unsure of how to respond. Hunter had told her that Sheriff Rhett was there when David and Ivy drowned. If she said yes, she had found them, then he would know she was lying and then surely he'd start asking more questions. More questions than she cared for. If he knew what she was up to, there's no telling what he'd do to her.

"No, I didn't find him." She broke her gaze and forced her body to relax in the chair, trying to appear as casual as possible. The tone in her voice was relaxed and nonchalant. "I'm tired of looking for him. He can't be that great of a guy if he's just going to walk out on me like that, right? I don't know what I was thinking, investing so much of myself into him."

She shook her head and forced a smile. His stare remained hard. Was he buying it?

She couldn't be sure. But then he nodded his head and his expression softened. "You're a brave woman, Evelyn Harris."

"No use dwelling in the past. What good would that do? It is what it is." She remembered the phrase that David had said so often to frustrate her. She held her armrest to keep from trembling. "I see no reason why I should stay in Amherst any longer. After all, I still have article deadlines to keep up with."

Sheriff Rhett's drooping eyes narrowed with concern. "So you're vacation here is over?"

Evelyn shrugged fretfully. "It's been pleasant."

"You're not leaving tonight though, right? It's already so late and I wouldn't be a very good sheriff if I let you go out after curfew, especially after I caught you hiding in the bushes with a gun." He pulled his chair to the side and braced his hands on the desk so he could lean towards her. "I've got a place for you to stay tonight." His eyes challenged hers. He wasn't buying it.

Evelyn sprang to her feet, the chair clattering to the floor. Rhett was closing in when she flung herself through the doorway. Halfway down the hall he caught up to her and tackled her to the floor. Her elbow cracked against his cheekbone stunning him long enough for her to scramble to her hands and knees. She felt his sold grip latch to her ankle. She kicked with her free leg connecting with the top of his head and he yelped, but didn't let go.

Nightmare Eve

"You're making this harder on yourself, Evelyn!" The Sheriff reached for her with his other hand. She shook her legs but he clamped down harder. "Love makes us sick, Evelyn. You should know, look where it brought you!"

She dug her fingers into the carpet attempting to drag herself away, but he secured her in place. He crawled up her and once in range, she flung her fist just below his left eye. The force of the punch rocked him back and she broke free. She climbed to her knees when he lunged at her again, this time the force brought her down and he braced his elbow against her neck in tactical police style.

Evelyn whimpered as pain shot through her. She struggled, but his grip held her in place. She wasn't going anywhere. Not this time.

"It destroys our days and it turns the sunny skies into endless storms," the sheriff continued, "there's no one else to blame when the world is bright yet all you see is rain. Love is a disease and it can be cured by death."

Her voice quivered. "You killed your wife." She remembered when they'd met, he mentioned that he lost his wife before he came to Amherst. She could still picture the expression on his face, so sad, so guilty.

"It was an accident, not that it's any of your fucking business." He yanked her to her feet. She yelped as sharp pain shot through her right shoulder. "I loved her more than anything else in the world. She cheated. She broke my fucking heart like I was nothing to her. I tried to win her back, but she wasn't interested. We fought. Neither of us was thinking clearly. She was at the edge of the staircase when I tried to take her luggage from her. She fell." He shoved her forward. "Let's move."

She obeyed his brusque orders and allowed herself to be led to a dark hall with rows of jail cells.

Sheriff Rhett pinned her against the bars as he shuffled in his pockets for the keys. The pressure of the cold, irons bars against her face caused severe pain in her cheekbones and her left eye blurred. "If you haven't figured it out yet, you're under arrest."

"For what?" Evelyn argued.

"Breaking curfew, suspicion of murder, and being a fucking nuisance."

The jail cell door slid open with a loud clank and he gave Evelyn a violent shove inside. She stumbled inward then jerked around as the cell door slammed closed. The sheriff stared at her from the dimly lit hallway, hard shadows darkening his sinister face like a child telling ghost stories around a campfire. "Over time you'll realize Amherst is a final destination. There is nowhere else to go, except the cemetery."

Evelyn sighed as she watched Sheriff Rhett exit the cellblock. Before he disappeared through the doorway, Evelyn muttered, "Worst vacation *ever*."

Chapter 37

Evelyn couldn't see the man who stirred in the dark cell across from her, but his voice was gruff and sibilant, the voice of a depressed man who'd spent the better part of his life drowning in well whiskey and chain smoking.

"Life here is a prison," he said, "we're detained here, barred by our search for truth and when we learn it, we choose to stay trapped in the nightmare we've created." The man let out a long wheezing sigh. "People like us belong here."

Evelyn's eyes fell on the stark interior of her cell. Nothing out of the ordinary, a basic jail furnished with the bare essentials: a soiled mattress and a grungy toilette. The walls were solid stone.

She pushed against each bar hoping at least one of them would budge, working her way to the right of the jail cell. Then she faced the corner and ran her palms against the cinderblock wall and tapping occasionally. She swept the entire surface as high as she could reach before encountering the sink. Gripping the porcelain rim she pressed herself against it, wondering if it would budge enough to reveal a hidden passage. But it was an ordinary sink. She turned to the toilet and hesitated.

I don't think so, thought Evelyn.

"You won't find a way out." The man said despairingly. "Not without forgiveness. Forgiveness is the key."

Evelyn's face flushed with frustration. "Forgiveness won't bring my family back," she snapped.

"I am going to find a way. There is a man out there that I love and I'm not going to give up. I will get him back."

"Love, huh?" The man huffed. "That's what does us all in. That's why I'm here too. I had it bad. She was beautiful but I lost her. I was desperate to get her back so I came up with a plan. I got swindled. Got taken advantage of. Called me a liar and a thief. I never would've done those things but she chose to believe them over me. Prosecuted for things I never did. I wasn't thinking clearly because I was in love. And now I'm here."

"In Jail?" Evelyn popped her head up from under the bed. There was nothing below. Maybe under the mattress?

"No." He responded bitterly. "In the storm. In the fog. The rain. In *Amherst*."

The mattress was thin, easy to lift. The rusted bed frame creaked. And between them were two small squares of folded paper; a note from the previous occupant:

June 6th.

There is something seriously wrong with the people here and it's not just the sheriff. It's only my first day and even though the forest surrounding Carver Cliff is public property, I was arrested for trespassing.

There is something up there. I know it. Something they don't want me to see.

I read about a strange ritual that takes place in the mountains. According to the books I found in the library, the ritual ensures the survival of the town but with terrible consequences.

As soon as I find a way to get out of this cell, I'm going back up there.

June ?

I'm scared.

I think Sheriff Rhett forgot I was in here. I had to sleep in my cell last night and he still hasn't returned.

I had nightmares of a man all night. He looked like my brother but I couldn't be sure. When I woke up everything had changed. I can see outside now and it's still dark. How long was I asleep? How many days had passed? How long have I been trapped in this cell?

There was no name on the letter. Evelyn folded the scraps and placed them in her pocket. They probably wouldn't serve a major purpose unlike the other key objects she'd come across, but still she didn't want to take any chances. She may have to refer back to them in the future. Important or otherwise, the note wasn't going to break her out of jail. She read the note again, more carefully this time. Whoever had written this had also experienced some strange phenomena. Like Evelyn, he was determined to hike the Nordic Trail to the ritual site above Carver Cliff. There was a lighthouse somewhere up there. First thing first, she had to break out of the jail cell.

She read the last paragraph again. The author mentioned he'd gone to sleep on the bed, had a nightmare, and when he woke up everything had changed. He could see outside again.

Had he seen the city of wood too?

Evelyn looked down at the lumpy bed. It felt damp and smelled of mold. She thought about taking her chances with the floor, but if the jail was going to transition, she somehow felt safer knowing she was in a bed rather than exposed to whatever monsters may be lurking nearby. The bed springs squeaked when she sat. It was horribly uncomfortable and although she felt dirty just for laying on it, she reminded herself of the morbid objects made from human flesh and bone and even the scarf of hair still draped around her neck. This is hell, she thought. Evelyn hated sleeping anyways and now that the Doxepin was out of her system, it would allow the nightmares to return, granting her escape from jail.

If sleep would grant her that freedom—to be free of that guilt and sorrow, then she would've chosen to sleep forever. She squeezed her eyes shut, just for a moment, long enough to clear her mind of all thoughts except for David's smiling face. She imagined his beautiful eyes gazing down at her, the warmth of his body and the scent of his skin against hers as he pulled her deeper into his arms. Nestled against him was her favorite place to sleep. She sighed deeply feeling her body give in to him, giving into the darkness.

When she opened her eyes, she was still in her cell.

Chapter 38

The moment she opened her eyes, she saw the same cracks in the ceiling and chipped cinderblock walls. Nothing had changed like the letter suggested.

The cellblock, still lit by the flickering low-wattage bulbs, remained locked. The stench of the soiled mattress still lingered in her nose. She lay there wondering if she'd even fallen asleep.

Her body felt rested even though her mind was emotionally exhausted. She stared into the shadowed jail cell across from her, listening for the man's heavy breathing or any kind of sign that he was still there. She doubted Sheriff Rhett would've let him out and if he had, Evelyn surely would've woken up from the clanking of the doors sliding open. The only sound in the cellblock was the humming from the lights. When she heard no other sounds, a strange feeling crept over her. The

Nightmare Eve

hairs on her neck and arms pricked until they stood upright and the muscles in her chest grew tight. Something had changed, but what?

Evelyn rose to her feet and took another glance around the room. Everything remained how it was before, but Evelyn was certain something was different. She could feel it all around her.

Evelyn rose to her feet; her eyes deadlocked on the cell across from her. A clatter from the end of the hall startled her. The lights fizzled and then died.

She gasped and backed away from the bars. Another clatter, softer this time. A buzz came from the lamp above. Sparks shot out with a burst of light followed by a clap and a hiss. There was someone in the opposite cell after all. She continued to step back until she stood in the center of the cell, her eyes darting all around as they adjusted to the darkness.

In the brief moment sputtering light, Evelyn saw the body on the floor of the jail cell across from her. She wanted to call out to him, but her voice was tight with fear. Blood pooled around him, he wasn't moving, but something else around him was. There was something else moving along the cellblock. She held her breath and listened.

Thump... Squish, squish.

It was right in front of her jail cell now. A clank on the bars made her muscles tighten.

The light flickered on—but only for a split-second. Long enough for Evelyn to identify the bulbous head crushed between the bars of her own cell. He'd been a stocky man with thinning hair, but she couldn't tell—his head was squeezed like a water-balloon about to burst and his wide eyes were bulging from their bloody sockets.

He grinned at her as if he'd played some sick joke. Behind the severed head a trail of blood lead from within his cell and somewhere to the right. When the lights flickered out a half-second later, she could still see his eyes starring at her through the darkness. She took a step back and stumbled when her heal slipped on something on the floor. She looked down after catching herself.

The porcelain sink had fallen to the floor and shattered. There was other debris too, chunks of cinderblock, chipped porcelain and crumbles of rock. There was the sound of water leaking from the broken pipes and even in the suffocating darkness, Evelyn could see part of the back wall had fallen out. The pipes rising from the floor to the ceiling were spaced out far enough that if Evelyn turned to the side she could just barely slip through.

It was a tight fit, struggling just a bit and sucking in to allow for the extra bulk of the vest, but still she succeeded with only a few minor snags.

Darkness swirled all around her and gravel crunched under foot like she was in some kind of otherworldly tunnel. She moved forward, each step growing more confident. Although she was blind in the tunnel, the floor felt solid and it seemed to be heading in a direct line. Whispers in the void echoed from the shaft ahead of her and, as her pace quickened, the voices grew louder, as if they spoke to her at once.

She shut her eyes and allowed her other senses to take over and trying to shut out the voices. She was scared to touch the walls, imagining they were crawling with biting insects or rigged with dangerous spikes. Between the incoherent whispering and the black void, she was down two senses and was forced to slow her pace.

Darkness is a very lonely place, Eve. Perhaps you should share it with someone.

She felt a drop on her cheek. She reached up to touch it then brought her hand to her face, an inadvertent motion— useless in the pitch-black room. She took another blind step forward. The black world turned to night with every step until she emerged from the tunnel. Back outside, the fog drifted through Amherst's wide streets.

Nightmare Eve

Through the nighttime marine layer settling over the beaches, she could barely make out the silhouette of the trailhead at the base of the mountain. Leaning against the sign post was a rusted, hand-sized axe. Perhaps left behind by some unfortunate campers. And somewhere, in those mountains, above the marine layer and beneath the starry, moonlit sky was her freedom. Her salvation.

And unimaginable horrors.

Chapter 39

Thanks to several downed trees that had collapsed across the main trail, Evelyn's mount hike had taken a short detour along the water front.

Although the water lapped against the tree-line shore, a the ocean surface was smooth and unmoving like a placid lake. The night was still and the silence was ruptured by a creaking dock from somewhere beyond the bend. Whispering voices faded into the soughing canopy of Douglas-firs.

A pine needle-laden hiking trail snaking through the dense woods and around mossy granite boulders the size of SUVs, then wraped back to shore before a steep incline rose nearly straight up the mountain. Her despair worsened when she saw the scuba man shambling from the woods and bounding down the trail towards her, it's arm flopping and mouth gurgling with the intentions of assault.

There was no time to wallow in despair, she had to remain vigilant and hopeful.

At the side of the path, Evelyn reached for a sold rock that fit well in her hand. The scuba man came closer and she raised the rock and bashed it against his skull.

She nimbly dodged another swipe from a second scuba man close behind and darted up the path. Other creatures stirred in the bushes, the paths too narrow for them to follow. Far ahead, in the dirt, Evelyn came across another journal entry near a small shrub. The stationary was the same as the one she found in the jail cell.

June 4th

First day. Got a room for the weekend at a local bed and breakfast. Shady Nook Lodge. Hospitable. Get an interview and photograph innkeeper, Barbara Smith.
Tonight: Rest.
Tomorrow: The Library and the Trails.
Day 2: Interview with Dean Charles Greyson,
    Photograph items of Flesh @ museum.
Final Day: Investigate Dr. Theodore Brooke's basement followed by dinner with Jack and Barbara.

She barely had time for her thoughts to catch up when she heard the clank of metal, the terrifyingly familiar sound of blades dragging against the earth and a low, drawn out grunt. Her eyes scanned the path behind her where it twisted through the trees and saw the Executioner stomping towards her. Time to move!

She raced stealthily along the path, ducking under low branches and checking over her shoulder to see if he was still following her. Even though she couldn't see him through the forest, she could still hear his footsteps shuffling up the path.

Nightmare Eve

She glanced up the mountain breaking above the marine layer. There was still a long way to go.

As the trail rounded another boulder, she spotted a dock bobbing on the smooth ocean surface. Movement behind the boathouse arrested her attention and so she paused long enough to identify the man inside. John, the surviving member of those juvenile delinquents she'd met hanging out behind the general store. She could see his mouth moving, speaking to someone else inside. Who would he be speaking to if all his cronies were dead? Was he working with Sheriff Rhett?

The path dipped low then opened up to a small clearing leading to the boathouse. A broken wire fence blocked the path but the posts were tilted and crumbling enough that Evelyn could barely squeeze through. Bits of debris, dead leaves, scraps of paper and other litter collected on the fence's perimeter and as she grew closer, she recognized the familiar handwriting. It was another note. Somehow the documents and whatever papers he had been carrying had gotten away, littering the trails. Did the writer purposely leave them behind like SOS messages? Or was it to prove his innocence over whatever crime he had been accused of? Or maybe they served as a guide for other lost souls like Evelyn. She wasn't sure, but the one thing she could be sure of was that the letter had helped her escape from the cell and thus far trusted the messages more than she trusted anyone else in this town.

Evelyn plucked the letter from the barbed wire and read.

I've been wandering through the town for what seems like days. I can't tell anymore. The sun never rises. The streets are empty and the buildings abandoned. The few people still around have either gone mad or turned into monsters. And my brother. . .

Nightmare Eve

I keep searching for him on the mountain trails. I wasn't dreaming but I know it couldn't have been him. My brother is dead.

I have to find him.

Whoever wrote these letters had been in danger too. The first memo she found explained that that he, or she, had been arrested after learning something he, or she wasn't supposed to. When he woke up, the jail cell had changed providing a means of escape. Before the arrest was made though, the author had booked a room at the Shady Nook Lodge where Evelyn had also been staying. It seemed safe to assume too that the writer of these letters also had some knowledge of the items made from flesh and hair. Information that led him to Dr. Theodore Brooke's basement. Nora had known something too, perhaps the same thing that the author had known judging by her frantic expression. These items were all connected somehow to Sheriff Rhett, Theodore Brooke, Dr. Charles Greyson and Dr. Jack Dullahan.

After she finished the letter, she crumpled it up and shoved it in the right breast pocket along with the others.

She peered again through the window. John glared at someone else and gestured with his knife. He took an furious step forward and brandished the knife again, shouting, his face bright red.

Evelyn followed the building around and spotted a shovel, rake and pitchfork leaning against the side of the building. She reached for the shovel and hovered in the side door, tilting her head so that between the cracked door and the large window she could see the entire shop and what she saw both angered and frightened her.

The young man she'd met outside the dorm rooms who'd been savagely beaten—the Scarred Prince—had been bound to a log. His head was bowed low and blood spilled from fresh wounds. His cheek had been sliced open and his left eye was swollen shut, the color of eggplants, but he was alive. His chest rose and fell and he struggled to lift his head.

In the back of the shop, across from John, Hunter stood with his hands raised over his head in defense, tears streaming down his cheeks. He locked eyes with the Scarred Prince and it was then Evelyn realized how deeply they cared for each other. He was the one who had stood up Hunter at the Westminster Theatre. He didn't mean to, Evelyn saw the bloody and broken condition John put the young man in.

Evelyn looked horrified at John, now merrily twirling the knife, and then scanned the room for a stealthy way to interlope. A blitz attack while his back was turned would've been ideal, but he stood against the wall and the only other door was on the dock-side of the boathouse which would put her right next to Hunter, in front of their attacker. Not a very stealthy move, but maybe a distraction could help.

The look on John's face twisted into a sneer. He lunged forward with the knife and slid it deeply across the Scarred Prince's throat.

Hunter bellowed and rushed the knife-wielding maniac and screamed loud enough that half the forest heard.

The Scarred Prince's head dropped low and blood flowed like a waterfall onto the dirt floor. Hunter wailed, an inhuman guttural sound and plowed into John, falling out the door, close to the battered dock.

Evelyn burst into their view with the shovel raised high, but both Hunter and John were frozen, looking at each other with matching expressions. Evelyn stopped too when she realized one of them had been stabbed.

They both titled their heads down, looking at their own abdomen. When they revealed their hands, only Hunter's was covered in blood.

"No!" Evelyn gasped.

Nightmare Eve

Their attacker grinned triumphantly. Hunter fell to his knees. He looked at Evelyn before he toppled off the dock and disappeared into the ocean's black surface.

The young man, still smiling wide, turned to Evelyn and gently waved the knife in front of her face.

He sprang first, catching her in the ribs. She fell back to the dirt. Pain shot through her elbow and into her neck. She kicked up the dirt as she struggled back to her feet, but he pushed her back down and raised the knife over his head.

Then the room exploded like thunder, splintered wood and snapped branches raining over them. At first Evelyn was confused. Had he stabbed her? But in the explosion, she saw that the man had been shoved to the side, his knife skidding across the dock. And then she saw through settling dust, the Executioner standing over him. The juggernaut reached for the nearest object—which happened to be Evelyn's attacker, and snatched him by his right leg and dangled him upside down while obliterating the remaining wall with his other massive fist.

Evelyn ducked as more boards flew past her head and then climbed to her feet. She hurled herself down the path and away from the boathouse. As she ran, she glanced over her shoulder and watched the Executioner, grasp the young man's right leg with one hand and his left arm with the other, and then pulled. He shrieked as his limbs tore at the joints.

Evelyn looked away. She didn't want to see the gruesome scene. She continued to run leaving his shrieks behind her and didn't stop until she reached the trail's midpoint.

—

It's true. He's gone. I should've helped him the first time he came to me. I knew he was in trouble but I didn't know they'd kill him. I could've stopped them. I could've saved his life. The guilt is driving me insane. I can't keep living like this, knowing that I was responsible.

Nightmare Eve

But there might be a way I can bring him back. There is legend of a gong located at the center of a ritual site located at the top of Carver Cliff. If I can reach it I can bring him back and fix the mistakes I've made.

It will be dangerous. The townspeople are trying to stop me and there are other creatures stalking me in these woods. If I'm careful and I stay low, I know I can make it.

Everything will be okay.

Evelyn found the note on the ranger's desk among the disorganized clutter of ranger files.

The fetid air in the cabin reeked of fading cologne, soot and moldering ranger uniforms and something else too—like rotten snails or bad breath. It was no surprise to Evelyn that she found a small paper plate of rotten food under some maps and the sleeve of a dark jacket—home to moths, maggots and other insects. The food, whatever it was, was unidentifiable and now looked like some microscopic alien colony from the Twilight Zone.

Another strange thing she noticed was the lingering shadow of another person near a coffee table between a pair of wooden chairs. The frozen shadow reminded Evelyn of photos she'd seen of Japanese shadows burned into cement after the bombing of Hiroshima. She shivered despite the tepid air and raised her eyes to the human skeleton on display near the back door, locked by some unknown mechanism.

The skeleton's eyes, although hollow, seemed to sense her presence in the room and when she brushed her fingers against the smooth surface she came to the realization that this figure wasn't a replica—it was an *actual* human skeleton.

Another strange thing she noticed was the lingering shadow of another person near a coffee table between a pair of wooden chairs. The frozen shadow reminded Evelyn of photos she'd seen of Japanese shadows burned into cement after the bombing of Hiroshima. She shivered despite the tepid air and raised her eyes to the human skeleton on display near the back door, locked by some unknown mechanism.

The skeleton's eyes, although hollow, seemed to sense her presence in the room and when she brushed her fingers against the smooth surface she came to the realization that this figure wasn't a replica—it was an *actual* human skeleton.

She dropped her gaze to the plaque mounted to the wall between the door and the skeleton.

There are approximately 206 bones in the human body. Sixty are in the hands and arms alone...

The plaque went on to describe in further detail about the various types of bones, cartilage and ligaments but Evelyn didn't find it relative at the moment. Something else had gotten her attention on the counter beside a small mini-fridge with a door handle smeared red. A formal-looking envelope, crisp and white stood out among the other soiled and stained letters. The handwriting was the same as the other notes and was dated two days before Sheriff Rhett arrested the author. She read the name across the front: Declan Meyers.

Obviously there's no one around anymore so what harm could it do if she helped herself? She tore open the envelope and read the letter.

June 2rd

Attention: Declan Meyers

I've made arrangements to leave tomorrow and should arrive in Amherst the following evening. I'll send you written coverage detailing the locations and provide you with photographs to enlighten your perspective of your endorsements of this project. Your support is most appreciated. Please contact me regarding any concerns.

Matthew Lumley

Introduction:
What is it about cities that attract certain energies? The Bermuda Triangle, Asbury Park in New Jersey, the eccentric personalities of Brisbane, Arizona and San Zhi, Taiwan all epitomize the diverse culture and mysteries around the world. But today we are going to show you mysteries in your own back yard by taking you to the charming yet shadowy oceanfront community of Amherst-by-the-Sea.

Evelyn returned the letter to the envelope, which she folded and kept in the opposite breast pocket as the others. So the author has a name after all. Michael Lumley, whom Evelyn presumed was some kind of journalist, location scout or maybe even a documentary filmmaker, had received funding from a Mr. Declan Meyers.

Mathew Lumley had arrived in Amherst expecting to start a new job and instead found something more upsetting—the ghost of his dead brother. Matthew, like so many others in Amherst, had experienced a tragic loss and had traveled the same path as Evelyn in search of his loved ones and redemption, vouchsafed by the town's legend, a gong located high in the mountains in a sacred place that would deliver them from their guilt and suffering and allow them to live in preservation.

Evelyn turned to the refrigerator. Dried blood on the handle had turned brown. A bloodied refrigerator was nothing compared to the horrors she'd seen these last few days. She had grown to be more aggressive and brave. She knew how to fight and how to problem solve. She'd come so far since the meek woman who arrived in Amherst. She learned to be a fighter and a survivor. With that in mind, she yanked open the mini-fridge door. Inside was a bunch of plastic internal organs—a couple of kidneys, a liver and a stomach were carelessly tossed inside. She looked over her shoulder and saw the skeleton watching her, grinning with a mouth full of teeth, then back to the plastic organs.

Another puzzle, simple this time.

The organs were hollow and light in her hands. She scooped them up, piling them in her arms and cradled them to the skeleton. She stared at him and wondered about Hunter and his partner, how they were still in the boathouse, their bodies slowly rotting until they'd eventually become skeletons just like this one. She hadn't even a moment to cry over his death, too busy running from the Executioner.

She tried to save them, but she failed, just like she failed all the others. Just like she failed David and Ivy.

But that was all going to change once she reached the gong.

Evelyn shoved each one of the organs in the appropriate location within skeletons body, but there was still something missing.

Evelyn removed each letter quickly scanning the words across each page. It only took her a second to see Mathew had mentioned the items of flesh, the same she still had in her possession. Dr. Dullahan, Theodore Brooke. Dr. Charles Greyson. Sheriff Rhett.

The skeleton grinned. She figured it out and the answer made her feel sick.

She braced herself against the counter feeling the nauseous wave of realization. They had done something horrible. Unimaginable even. The skeleton had in fact belonged to somebody. Somebody she knew very well, a vicious psycho killer with blades who had been stalking the town at night. The Executioner.

That's why Dr. Dullahan had been frightened the night he was murdered and why the sheriff kept lying to everyone, and why Nora Brooke had been so upset. The Executioner, from what Evelyn recalled in those unusual visions, had been a serial killer being transported by boat. The boat sank just off the coast of Amherst, but he escaped and continued his rampage through the town. In order to protect the citizens, the sheriff had initiated the curfew. Eventually the man was captured, but instead of sentencing him they brought him to Theodore Brooke's basement—a professor of chemistry who had been working at the university.

It was written in Matthew's note that one of his investigations would take place in the basement—an unusual place to highlight in a documentary. That must've been where they tortured the killer, then skinned him turning pieces of him into seemingly ordinary items.

Evelyn had collected them all and the Executioner wanted them back.

After they were finished, they thought the murders would stop. But he'd been a malevolent, unstoppable force. Even after they separated the items, the murders continued. After curfew, he set out to seek revenge on the ones who did this to him. The citizens believed he was evil, but they allowed themselves to be corrupted, driven by anger, hate and selfishness. Evelyn felt the items in her pocket and the scarf of hair around her neck. She had to return the items to the Executioner with unpredictable consequences.

She reached in her pocket and retrieved the Wallet of Flesh. She unfolded it and placed it on the Executioner's chest. She did the same for each item, placing the book bound by his flesh and ink made from his blood in the palm of his overturned hand. The book stayed without any adjustments, like he was holding on even though is palms were spread open.

Nightmare Eve

Then the bowl of bone completing his skull. She unwound the scarf made from his hair and placed it on the very top of his head.

And then the final piece: the mask that had been made from the skin stripped from his face.

Using her right hand, she slowly, carefully brought the mask to his skull so that the eyeholes lined with the sockets. A perfect fit.

The Executioner was complete.

There was an echoing click from the door and a warm breeze brushed through the ranger station. She looked around the room. All the windows and doors were still shut tight.

A second later, footsteps thudded through the room as if an invisible person had run out the back door. When she took a step closer, the shadow on the floor was gone. Evelyn turned back to the door. The Executioner stood guard. Her skin crawled when she stood beside him and reached for the door handle. His face seemed so realistic that right before she stepped into the night, she could've swore she saw him take a breath.

Chapter 40

Evelyn felt less determined when her eyes fell upon the blooded man slumped outside the ranger station's back door.

He was a Asian man in his mid-thirties with shaggy dark hair and olive skin. Blood had masked much of his face and a deep cut across is forehead continued to ooze. She rushed to the man's side. His skin was warm to her touch, but he had no pulse. He hadn't been dead for long. More blood seeped from a hidden wound beneath his dressy button-up shirt, probably the most likely cause of his death rather than his head wound. She let go of his wrist and noticed a crumpled slip of paper in his other hand. His fingers clenched it tight enough that she struggled to free the note without tearing it.

Nightmare Eve

It was a mistake to come here.

I was selfish. I must deal with my guilt alone or the consequences will destroy everything. It's a malign force that preys on the guilty and the sorrowful, turnings us into horrible creatures. I don't want to become one of them.

There's something else out there, too. Like those monsters only bigger and carrying blades. I can hear them scraping along the trail now. He's searching for me but I can't hide forever.

Maybe there's another way. . .

So this was Matthew Lumley. Guess he never found his other way.
  Was it true what Sheriff Rhett had told her in the jail cell? Was death the only escape from this place? She tried to think about all the people she'd met since the day she arrived in Amherst. There'd been so many stories. So many faces and names. And death had followed almost each of them. And now that Hunter and his partner was gone, all she had was the Executioner, Sheriff Rhett and Ms. Smith who'd been wrongfully arrested for Jack Dullahan's murder. And what of her daughter, Charity and the other two girls she met—Carly and Nora? Were they gone too? Had they met their fate somewhere else without Evelyn knowing? She tried to remain hopeful and optimistic but the numbers didn't like. The odds of survival were not in her favor.
  She remembered Matthew's previous letter. He, too, had ended his letter with 'everything will be okay'. And look how far that got him.

Evelyn rose to her feet and dusted her hands off on her shirt. They were still tender and sore from the abuse but she'd been so preoccupied she hadn't really thought of them.

A rustle in the trees behind her made her look up from his body. There was movement nearby. Then she heard the blades dragging along the dirt path.

The Executioner had returned.

Evelyn ran through the darkness, bounded through the trees and leaped over toppled logs, ferns and thorny vines. She ascended the mountain even higher above the marine layer and for the first time was able to see each star in the crystal clear night sky. Up here the air was fresh too, a comfortable temperature. She took this as a good sign but still continued to run until the trail appeared to end when it reached the base of a pile of rocks. On closer inspection, and after clearing away the draping vines, Evelyn saw it was a cave—the entrance, wider than she thought. The inside was even wider, cavernous even. The caves, although tall, weren't very long. She could still see the glittering stars on the other side. Below the stars, not too much further, was the lighthouse peaking between the massive pines.

She put her right foot into the cave first, making sure the ground was solid and once confirmed, she lowered her other foot and hoisted herself inside. The cave floors were surprisingly smooth and Evelyn wondered if somebody had purposely smoothed it out, making it safer for hikers. It seemed safe enough, not at all rocky or damp like she would've thought. Even when she moved deeper, and the entrance faded behind her, enough starlight reflected off the glittering mica allowing her to see well enough to stay on a straight path without bumping into the walls.

To her left were rows of metal bars, she figured to help stabilize the mountainside, but as she continued to move deeper she noticed the bars resembled a jail cell.

Her heart beat loud in her chest and she shook her head with a slight gasp and muttered, "No, this is impossible."

The deeper she ran, cells began to appear in the rocks. Inside one of them, a man stepped into the dim, cavernous light. His features were cold and hard and the shadows casting over his face made him appear sinister, like a demon rising from fire. She felt her heart jump when she recognized him as a distorted, angry version of David. He watched her with a hard, bitter, accusing stare.

It's just a trick, she told herself. It's not really him.

She burst from the other side of the cave and landed in a soft patch of moss and loose soil.

Don't worry, David. I'm coming for you. And Ivy too.

When she raised her eyes from the forest floor, she saw the lighthouse in front of her. Her long journey was over. It stood ahead, a glowing obelisk, a beacon of hope in an otherwise gloomy night. Below, moving through the darkness, people had gathered coifed in dark red robes—the same she'd witnessed from the beach. Twelve of them filed one at a time through the doorway at the base and then ascended the stairs.

She watched intently until a pair of strong hands grabbed her from behind.

"Hunter!" She breathed. "What are you doing? I thought you were dead!"

Hunter ducked low behind a low branch, partially obscured by another massive rock. He leaned toward Evelyn and she could see he'd been crying. His face was pale and grief-stricken and spoke in a quiet, melancholy tone.

"I know what you're going through. When you lose the one you love, the feelings are devastating. They become part of your soul and without them, you're incomplete. You don't feel alive anymore, like there's a void inside that eats away at you until day-to-day life becomes impossible and you become lost in a fog. Nothing will ever be the same for you, Evelyn."

Nightmare Eve

"But I know a way to fix things," declared Evelyn. "I can make everything right. I can change it and make things better again."

Hunter sadly shook his head. His face remained somber, verging on tears. "I don't think that's a very good idea."

Evelyn stared at him, a curious expression growing on her tired face. "How—how did you survive? I saw John stab you."

Hunter reached down to the hem of his shirt and lifted it up so Evelyn could see the heavy bandages wrapped over the wound, not as deep as Evelyn had first thought.

She pulled her eyes away from the wound and looked back at Hunter's face.

"They helped me." Hunter pointed over Evelyn's shoulder.

She turned and saw some of the robbed people had stopped filing in, turned and stared directly at her from under the shadows of their hoods.

"They helped me." Hunter repeated. "They pulled me out of the water and bandaged me up real nice. Shouldn't be a long recovery."

Evelyn's face crumbled from concern to realization and then shock when Hunter pulled out a knife.

"I'm sorry it's got to come to this, Evelyn. But I know what you're trying to do, and I can't let you do it. I can't let you ring that gong."

And then he raised the knife high and plunged it down over Evelyn's chest.

Chapter 41

Evelyn tumbled left as the knife came down. It whizzed through the air where she stood a second ago. She pleaded for him to stop.

His advanced on her with powerful, leaping strides.

She scooted backward, her hand landing on a piece of broken tree branch. "Please, it doesn't have to be this way," Evelyn begged.

His sad eyes, locked on her, glared with vengeance. "It's your fault the nightmares are here. You know what your problem is? You are always looking on the dark side of things. You had sunny days but all you wanted to see was rain. You had a good job, and fiancé who loved you, but it never was good enough! You took them for granted and now that they're gone you're willing to unleash this darkness on the town forever. If you ring that gong you'll bring them back, but everything we will all live an eternity in this nightmare."

Nightmare Eve

She lunged forward and swung the broken limb at his head. Evelyn hadn't come this far to give up. She lost David already and she wasn't about to lose him again.

The branch connected with the side of his skull. A thin gash appeared on his cheek and he toppled back.

While Hunter was recovering, Evelyn spun on the balls of her feet and charged at the robed figures. Hands shot out from beneath the heavy red material, grabbing her and trying to hold her down. She swung the branch and felt it connect broadside against someone's shoulder. She felt a set of hands release her. She swung again.

They lumbered after her. Another figure grabbed her shoulder but she slipped away and ascended the stairs.

Nearing the top, a burly middle-aged man wrapped his arms around her torso, but an elbow shiv to his gut caused him to release her before they tumbled down the stairs.

There was a sudden crash below. The stairwell rocked violently and Evelyn thought for sure she was about to plummet to her death. She held tightly to the handrail. Down below in the settling dust was the Executioner. He ripped through the walls and up the stairs. Each step crumbled behind him as he bombarded closer, violently flailing in a final, desperate attempt to reach Evelyn.

The stairwell shifted again and another loud crash blasted through the wall almost beside her and she could feel the floor give way beneath her feet, but not before she lunged ahead.

When she burst through the door at the top of the lighthouse, she paused at the sight of the wide room at least fifty feet in diameter, impossibly large for the tip of a lighthouse. The cylindrical room contained no solid walls, but instead was lined with glass for a full 360-degree landscape view. In the center of the room stood a gong as tall as her. As she approached, the hooded figures slid peacefully around the circumference of the glass room, each with red cloaks with hoods shrouding their face.

None of them moved, but together they chanted in soft words she didn't recognize. A beam of light spun steadily around the landscape causing Evelyn to feel disoriented momentarily. The floor trembled as the Executioner approached.

The gong! She needed to move fast.

She saw the long wooden handle and the solid, yet rubbery tip bound by sturdy rope to the dark-stained wooden beams that supported the metal disk.

She burst forward with the energy of a track star and snatched the handle just as the Executioner broke through the beautiful blue and gold floorboards with an angry snarl.

She narrowed her eyes triumphantly. All she needed to do now was swing. "My name is Eve," she said, "and this is *my* nightmare now."

She swung as hard as she could, just as the Executioner did.

The mallet clamored against the gong in a deep brassy noise that echoed from the lighthouse, across the town and reverberated between the mountains. And at the same moment, Evelyn was struck by the broad side of the Executioner's blade.

Evelyn felt no pain as the world around her exploded. Or when the blow shot her body through the air and exploded through the glass wall. She soared, almost endlessly in slow-motion through the starry, moonlit night, high above the marine layer like clouds. For a moment she felt like she would soar higher and forever above the heavens, hundreds of feet above Carver Cliff. And then slowly she rolled over in the air and made her rapid descent toward earth, falling through the beam just as the light whipped around, blinding her. Everything went white.

—

"Wake up. It's just a nightmare, Eve."

Nightmare Eve

Evelyn woke to find herself leaning against a tombstone. A thick white fog blanketed earth. Charity crouched beside her tugging at the overgrown threads of grass.

"The world out there isn't much better than the one in here," Charity said, "I'm sorry for the things I've done too. Your fiancé seems great, though. If he loves you like he said he did, then he'll forgive you. Mom said everybody makes mistakes so I really hope you get to be with him again some day."

Evelyn looked down at the sympathetic teenager. She tried to smile, but she couldn't muster the emotion. It was strange to feel nothing. She couldn't even remember what love felt like, even though she had it once before. In a way, she'd gotten what she wanted. "No, I only had one chance with him. No second chances."

"He must be perfect to not know what it feels like to make a mistake."

In a way, Charity was much more grown-up than her. Sometimes she even forgot how young Charity actually was.

"If my despicable behavior—my barbaric treatment towards David, the man I was madly in love with, was punishable by law, then I should be imprisoned for the things I've said and done. I cannot undo the hurt I've caused him, and for that I've suffered more regret and guilt than I ever have before."

Evelyn felt coldness on her cheek. A feeling she hadn't experienced in a long time. She looked at Charity and then gazed beyond the cemetery gates. It would only be a matter of time before Amherst received more visitors. God help them.

She felt a chill and looked up at the sky. Would there be fog tonight?

OASIS Creative

Keep up on the latest new releases, author appearances, chats, news, and more on Facebook and Twitter.

Facebook: www.facebook.com/logan.scott.9889

Twitter: @LKScott1

OASIS CREATIVE
PROUDLY PRESENTS

Coming Soon...

SHE TRIED THE WINDOW
By
L.K. SCOTT

Available Soon in Hardcover
Paperback and eBook formats
From

Oasis Creative

Printed in Great Britain
by Amazon.co.uk, Ltd.,
Marston Gate.